"The plot is smooth and exciting, the polemics are subtle but smart, and the characters are heartfelt."

—TIPHANIE YANIQUE,
author of *Land of Love and Drowning*

"*The Lesson* isn't just a serious, important book—it's also a fun and rewarding one."

—ANALOG SCIENCE FICTION AND FACT

"[A] bold and provocative debut...On the island of St. Thomas, a family collides with intergalactic meddlers, stranding two lovers with souls in distant worlds. A forbidding panoply of colonial mischief."

—KRIS LACKEY,
USA Today bestselling author of *Nail's Crossing*

"[A] rich debut novel about family, love, and loyalty in turbulent times...Turnbull uses a beautifully drawn cast of black characters to convey the complexity of ordinary hardship in extraordinary times."

—PUBLISHERS WEEKLY (starred review)

"A compelling and layered narrative that explores colonialism and our messy human flaws through a diverse and painfully real cast of characters. *The Lesson* is smart, full of dry wit and creeping dread—a unique and artful debut."

—M. K. ENGLAND,
author of *The Disasters*

"Three families wind up in a horrific cycle of violence in a book about family in turbulent times in a debut that has been spoken of in the same breath as last year's standout *Rosewater*."

—B&N SCI-FI & FANTASY BLOG

"*The Lesson* is a story that should not be missed by readers who embraced such books as Emily St. John Mandel's *Station Eleven* or even Arthur C. Clarke's *Childhood's End*...Truly gripping and shocking."

—SFF180

THE
LESSON

THE LESSON

A NOVEL

CADWELL TURNBULL

BLACK STONE
PUBLISHING

Printed in the United States of America

First edition: 2019
ISBN 978-1-5385-8464-4
Fiction / Science Fiction / General

1 3 5 7 9 10 8 6 4 2

CIP data for this book is available
from the Library of Congress

Blackstone Publishing
31 Mistletoe Rd.
Ashland, OR 97520

www.BlackstonePublishing.com

To Mom, Sis, and Nanay

WATER ISLAND

Fifteen days before

After school, Patrice and Derrick rushed to beat midafternoon traffic. They got out of Charlotte Amalie gate fast enough, but it still took thirty minutes to pick up Derrick's little sister, Lee, from Ulla F. Muller Elementary School and climb the steep hill to home.

They both lived at the same residence, an attractive two-story maroon-and-white house. Patrice's family owned the house and lived on the top floor, while Derrick and his family rented out the bottom floor. Derrick's family had been living there several years, since before Derrick's father died. Now he lived there with his grandmother, Ms. Reed, and his little sister, Lee.

As soon as they parked, Lee ran downstairs. By the time Derrick and Patrice made it down into the house, she was already telling her grandmother about the day.

"And then the teacher gave him six lashes, Grandma!" Lee made emphatic gestures with her hands as she talked, mimicking the scene for her grandmother. "He cried and cried."

Grandma Reed chuckled. "Sounds like he deserve it, though."

"It not funny, Grandma."

"You two hungry?" Ms. Reed asked, addressing Patrice and Derrick. They were standing near the doorway, not wanting to interrupt the conversation.

"Afternoon, Grams."

"Afternoon, Ms. Reed."

"Well, you hungry, or what?" Ms. Reed asked again.

"A little," said Derrick.

"Got some food on the stove. Fix your sister and Patrice a plate."

Derrick nodded and moved to the kitchen. Patrice followed. Lee kept talking to Ms. Reed, whose larger-than-life laughter echoed through the house.

The kitchen wasn't big, but they had managed to cram a dining room table into it. Derrick rinsed plates and shared out food. Light from the window over the sink emptied into the room, contrasting with the relative darkness of the rest of the kitchen. As Derrick stood in front of the window, Patrice watched him from behind, observing the way the light caught around his body like a halo.

Derrick brought all the plates to the table. Stew chicken, rice and beans, and fried plantain steamed on well-used china. He called Lee for food, and she came running in and sat in the chair next to Patrice, as she always did. Derrick and Patrice ate quietly and listened as Lee talked about her day at school, recounting to them all the things she had said to her grandmother in the other room. Then, when they were done, Derrick put the empty dishes in the sink, sent Lee back into the living room to watch cartoons with her grandmother, and took Patrice down the hall to his room, to begin studying for Ms. Robin's biology test.

"Aren't you going to close the door?" Patrice asked.

"Grams said I can't close the door if I have a girl in my room."

"We grew up together."

"That's the problem. You grown now. Can't have you up in my room with the door shut."

Patrice glared at him, communicating all she could.

"Her words," Derrick said.

"Boy, don't you close that door!" Grandma Reed yelled from the living room.

"I know, Grams."

"Come here for a second!"

"Be right back," Derrick said. He grabbed some home clothes as he left to change out of his school uniform.

Patrice sat on Derrick's bed. She dusted off her pleated navy-blue skirt and watched the green trees through the window as they swayed with the wind.

The heavy breathing of Derrick's old desktop computer made the room seem alive. His walls were filled with posters, some drawn, some bought. Spaceships of different kinds. *Star Trek*'s *Enterprise. Star Wars*' *Death Star.* A hand painting of *Firefly*'s *Serenity. Battlestar Galactica. Stargate*'s *Prometheus, Daedalus*, and *Destiny.* Drawings of strange creatures with several heads; multiple eyes; and long, hanging limbs ending in large hands, talons, three-toe feet. On the desk next to his computer were stacks of comic books and *National Geographic* and *Discovery* magazines.

It seemed as though every time Patrice came over, Derrick had more posters and more books.

He had a bookshelf on his far wall. On it, the worn spines of paperbacks stood pressed tight together, their uneven sides forming a bar graph of color and book titles. The Foundation trilogy. *1984*. *The Left Hand of Darkness*. The Earthsea series. *Native Tongue*. *The Dispossessed*. *Green Mars*. On the edge of the bookshelf, smashed between *The Silmarillion* and dark wood was a pristine hardcover Student Bible. Patrice pulled it out.

The book creaked as she opened it, the white pages flowing by as she thumbed through, making the sound of pigeon wings. She found a passage and started reading. Genesis, chapter 3. The hum of the desktop disappeared from Patrice's awareness. She skipped to the end of the Bible. The Four Horsemen of the Apocalypse. The beasts of Earth rising up to kill men.

"Yeah, Grams gave it to me," Derrick said. He was standing behind her.

Patrice turned to face him.

Derrick wore an old and torn blue shirt, his wiry, thin arms ending in the pockets of his white-and-blue sweatpants. He still had the awkward look of a preteen adjusting to the various changes to his body, but good looks were starting to peek out from his acne-ridden face.

"You use it?" she asked.

"Come on, Trice," he answered. "You know me." His eyes lit up as if he had remembered something. "I got something to show you." Derrick went to his bed, stooped down, and started rummaging under it. He slid out a crate filled with books, magazines, and old comics and started pulling out all the contents. "Remember that Greek mythology book we had to read for Ms. Parks?"

"Yeah," Patrice answered.

He stopped taking out books. "Take a look at these."

Patrice looked down into the crate. She read the titles of the books on top of the remaining pile. *Oriental Mythology. Egyptian Mythology. Central African Myth. The Life of the Buddha. Tao Te Ching.* "What are these?"

"Can't say Ms. Parks didn't inspire *something* in me. Been learning a whole lot."

"About what?"

"World religions. Philosophy. Myth. Things beyond the little rock we live on."

Patrice sat on the bed and picked up *Oriental Mythology*. She read the name of the writer: Joseph Campbell. She knew nothing about Oriental mythology and couldn't imagine a version of herself that would even care about it. "Okay. Cool."

"I know you's a little church girl."

"We go to the same church, Derrick."

"You never think about it?"

"Think about what?"

"That we might be wrong. That there's a whole world out there that think different than we do. How we know we right about any of it?" He sat down next to her on the bed, staring at her without blinking.

Patrice sighed. "You got your head in the clouds again, Derrick." She quickly put the book back down into the crate.

"Do me a favor, no?"

"What?"

"Just take one of them home. See what I talking about."

"Don't want to, Derrick. Don't have time for no foolishness."

"Come on, Trice. Trust me on this one."

Derrick had a way of looking at her when he really wanted something, his eyes getting all puppylike so she couldn't say no. Her stomach was in knots. What was that about? She looked back down at the books, each laid out for her. She picked up *Oriental Mythology* again.

"I'll take this one."

"Tell me what you think, okay?"

"Yeah." She put it in her school bag. "So we going to get started on this homework, or what?"

"Yeah," Derrick said, but he didn't move to take anything out of his bag. Instead, he inched closer to Patrice. He put his hand on the folds of her pleated school skirt. The gesture alarmed both of them. "It would mean a lot if you read it. I don't get to talk about this with anyone."

She nodded.

The room got really quiet. Patrice could hear the hum of Derrick's desktop computer again, this time right in her ears. He leaned in a little more.

"Promise me."

She nodded again.

"Boy, come wash up these dishes!" yelled Grandma Reed, shocking them both out of the moment.

"Grams, we about to do some homework."

"Did I ask you something, or did I tell you to come wash these dishes?"

"Be right back," Derrick said.

Patrice laughed.

"She always harassing me." Derrick left the room.

Patrice went into her bag to pull out her books for class. There was still that feeling in her stomach, like something rolling around in there. She could feel her heartbeat. Her eyes fell on the book again. This was her fourth time now studying the title—its magenta letters and serif font.

On the cover, a pale Asian woman with dark hair lay enclosed in a circle. She leaned on a stack of what looked like paper, her eyes closed as if asleep. Below her was another group of words: "The Masks of God." Patrice repeated the words over and over in her mind, trying to understand their meaning. Then she opened the book and looked inside.

• • •

Fourteen days before

It was early Saturday afternoon. Jackson read a book out on the porch, swatting away mosquitoes.

The sun lit the green coconut trees in front of their house, giving the leaves a whitish shine. They rustled in the gentle breeze. In the shade of a big genip tree, a brown iguana lay dormant on a branch, its unmoving body the color of bark. A silver-purple hummingbird hovered at a bush of bright red hibiscus flowers, its wings fluttering in a loud blur, long tongue stretching to reach the sweet nectar within. The blue sky and the sunlight reflecting off all the vibrant green plant surfaces were almost too much to look at, but Jackson lifted his gaze periodically from his book to admire the view.

Beyond the line of trees, down the sloped green hills, he could see Charlotte Amalie Harbor. Past the pink-roofed buildings of Harbor View, cruise ships lined Havensight Dock, their pearly white sides eclipsing the buildings in their shadow, puffs of gray smoke rising from their funnels. Disney Cruise Line. Carnival.

Royal Caribbean. They stretched almost past the peninsula of Frenchman's Reef, their multiple decks rising almost to the height of the hills behind them.

In the middle of the harbor were Hassel Island, with its small wood-and-concrete dock and old stone castle, and the larger Water Island, with its big, elegant homes and villas. A little channel stretched between the two islets, its deep blue water sparkling in the sun.

Jackson could hear his wife, Aubrey, cooking inside, his daughter, Patrice, talking, and the TV blaring some silly commercial.

His phone buzzed in his pocket. It was a text.

Hey Mr. Paige!

He texted back.

Who is this?

Lisa.

Jackson stared at the phone for a moment, confused. Lisa had been one of his best students ten years ago. And she loved to write stories. More importantly, she loved giving them to Jackson for feedback, and had been doing so on and off since she'd graduated. He didn't mind. He enjoyed helping, the feeling of being needed.

You need me to read one of your stories? Just email it to me.

No messages came for another thirty minutes. Jackson continued reading.

His phone buzzed again.

No. Still working on the story.

What do you need, then?

Was just wondering about you.

Jackson stared at the cell phone again for a long time. It crossed his mind to tell her that he didn't think she should do that: wonder about him. But he decided to just not respond. He closed his eyes and listened to the sound of the trees. Their rustling sounded to him like a wave that came in but never left, forever crashing. He lay there in thought for a while, and then when the phone didn't vibrate again for a time, he returned to his book.

Later that evening, another text came through.

I'm sorry Mr. P. Just needed
someone to talk to.

It's fine. You okay?

No more text messages came that day. Jackson thought he would feel relieved. He thought maybe she had realized on her own how inappropriate it was, and that he wouldn't have to bother breaking it to her. But as the weekend dragged on, he found himself compulsively checking his phone.

• • •

Thirteen days before

Jackson's phone rattled on the nightstand, waking him up. Angry, he grabbed the phone and squinted at the text message.

I can't sleep.

Lisa again.

He went into the bathroom, closed the door, and sat on the toilet.

What's wrong?

Just thinking. What you doing?

I was sleeping. You really shouldn't be texting me this late.

I know. I'm sorry Mr. P. Hey, you have a first name?

Jackson.

That's a last name. You got two last names?

My mother's doing.

LOL. I like it though. People call
you Jack?

Some people.

A few minutes passed before she texted again. Jackson sat on the toilet seat, staring at the cell phone in his hand. He rubbed his knee where he had overworked it jogging around the high school track. He was fifty-four. His habitual jog was becoming increasingly harder. Lately, he had fought this difficulty by pushing a little too hard.

The phone buzzed. The touch screen lit up the dark bathroom.

You married Jack?

Yes. Why?

Another few minutes.

That's a shame.

Why you say that?

Five minutes.

No reason.

???

Lisa must have known he was married. How couldn't she?

Jackson sat on the toilet seat and stared at the wall, waiting. No response came. In his mind, he traced a line through the spaces between the tiles as if following a maze. He didn't know why he was doing it. The phone on his lap felt unusually heavy. A few times, it almost seemed to vibrate. He didn't know how much time passed while he sat there. But the phone just got heavier and heavier as he traced the lines of grout in the dark.

• • •

Twelve days before

Aubrey got up on her tiptoes to stir the dog food as she always did. Her small but powerful slender body angled, her arm moving in quick natural circles as she worked the yellow scooper into a blur. The dog-food pellets made the sound of disturbed gravel as they rolled around in the hollow container.

Aubrey let her muscle memory take over as she drifted along in daydreams. She thought of the softness of her bed. The day at the animal shelter had just begun, and she already felt tired. She wondered why it was so hard to be happy with what she was doing. Why did she always want to be somewhere else?

While she was lost in thought, Alice knocked on the door. Aubrey turned. Alice had her hands folded over her green veterinary scrubs. She leaned on the door frame.

Alice was not a native islander. She had come fresh out of college to work at the St. Thomas Humane Society as a veterinarian and had stayed for over a decade. She seemed white to Aubrey, but apparently, her father was a light-skinned Brazilian man. Alice had a broad, pretty smile that took up most of her face, tanned skin, dark freckles on her cheeks, and thick, beautiful curly hair that fell to her shoulders.

"You mind helping me with something?" Alice asked.

"Of course not."

Aubrey followed Alice into the vet's room. The small room was painted light blue. Its fluorescent lights seemed too bright and hurt the eyes. She squinted a little to get used to it.

In the center of the room was a single brown cot, covered in a thin sheet of white paper. A cat sat in a cage atop the counter against the far wall, by the sink. The cat's eyes were half closed, its fur uneven and patchy, its face covered in scabs.

"I need you to help me keep her calm," Alice said.

Aubrey nodded and walked over to the table and opened the cat's cage. She made a little sucking sound with her teeth. "Come here, cat."

The cat jerked backward in the cage but then relaxed. Its shoulders lowered, and it moved slowly toward Aubrey's hands. She reached in and wrapped her hands around the cat's midsection, lifting it. She could feel the ribs under the thin layer of skin and patchy fur. The cat's limbs dangled as Aubrey moved it, its eyes thin slits. There was a musty, sickly odor.

Aubrey placed the cat on the cot. She petted it, and it opened its eyes just a little to see her. It purred and shut them again. *That easy to establish trust.*

"How did you get her?" she asked.

"She's just a stray. You know."

Aubrey nodded, petting the cat softly.

"She seems to like you." Alice went over to the counter. She opened a cabinet and took out some swabs, a small brown bottle, and a needle. "How's the husband?"

"He's good."

Alice smiled. She had been married to an older Dominican man, but it didn't last more than a year. She never said why. She placed the objects on a table next to the cot.

"He's retiring in a year," Aubrey continued. "He won't say it, but I think it is bothering him a little."

"You think he'll miss the students?"

"No, not that. I think he's worried about what he will be doing once he's done. He's been teaching for a long time."

The cat's purr got louder. Aubrey felt the vibrations under her hands. Little rumbles of pleasure.

Alice stuck the needle into the small metal cap of the bottle and extracted some bubble gum–colored liquid. "He'll be okay," Alice said. "I wish I could retire."

"No, you don't. You won't know what to do with yourself."

"Isn't that the point, though? Not knowing? Not needing to know?"

Alice stuck the needle into the cat's lower neck, right between the shoulder blades. Aubrey felt the purring stop, and a single tiny shudder of the cat's body under her hands. Its eyes opened; it stared up at Aubrey—thin needlelike pupils wrapped in baby-blue irises—and Aubrey made another little sucking sound.

"It's okay," she whispered.

"You ever think of what you'll do when you retire?" Alice asked.

"Sometimes. I think I'll travel. Go on a few cruises, maybe."

"That's so dull. What do you need a cruise for? You live on an island."

"People go on cruises for the experience of going on a cruise. Travel's just the bonus. Besides, I haven't been to too many islands. I think I should."

Aubrey felt a little tremor under her hands.

"Maybe we can go on one together," Alice said. She leaned over the table a little, smiling her big smile.

"Maybe."

"Maybe we can make it a little trip, just the two of us girls having fun. Why wait for retirement?"

Aubrey felt the cat's final little shiver. Then stillness, pure and complete. She had the feeling that she was petting carpet wrapped around stone.

"It would be great," Alice said. "And then—"

"Don't."

"What?"

"You need any help with this?" Aubrey motioned toward the dead cat with her eyes.

Alice shook her head and then looked away. "You can go back to making the food for the dogs if you want." She turned and moved back to the countertop, her actions obscured by her back and her hair. "I'll take care of it."

"See you at lunch," Aubrey said as she left.

"See you," Alice replied softly.

• • •

Ten days before

Patrice went to her usual spot on the stairs by the cafeteria and opened the book, reading as a steady stream of high schoolers passed her by. The constant music of percussive footsteps and giddy chatter melted away into background noise.

Patrice spent most of her lunchtime reading that damn book. She had read through half of it already and hated every word so far. She hated the dismissive tone that the author chose when he described Christianity as just the latest installment in a history of changing beliefs, talking about religion as if it were some ongoing narrative.

Patrice couldn't help being frustrated. She also couldn't help but keep reading, each page hitting her harder than the last, like some self-induced mental torture scenario where she pressed the button herself and then couldn't help pressing again and again.

She wanted to dismiss all of it, the whole thing, as something insignificant. She wanted to say, *They're just stories. They can't be true.* But every time she thought it, she heard Derrick's voice in her head asking, *Why not? Because you heard another story first?*

She was familiar with Derrick's particular form of blasphemy and would shut him up before he said anything too damaging to himself. But now all she had were blasphemous thoughts.

It wasn't just the book, either. The thoughts brought on by the book were just the latest in a series of personal changes.

Patrice was short and petite like her mother. She was an amalgam of small features: small, thin lips; a tiny, knobby nose; thin, muscled arms; and a long, slender neck. This didn't apply to her boobs, which had grown large for her size and got the unwelcome attention of boys. Many other girls her age would have welcomed this kind of attention. Some of her friends were particularly boy crazy. But Patrice hated it. She was painfully shy and bookish. She dressed the part: loose-fitting, blue button-up shirts and long pleated skirts. Overcompliant with her school uniform requirements, but this didn't stop the boys from staring at her breasts.

To add to this, Patrice had begun running track and played the flute in the marching band. This significantly strengthened her legs and thighs. Some of the boys from class, the same ones who made fun of her for being a teacher's pet, would come to track practices and sit in the stands. When she came out on the field in her shorts, they would yell, "Look at Trice's bana, me boy! And them breasts! You better cup those breasts or they'll fall off!" Red faced—visible even with her milky-brown complexion—she would run with her arms close to her chest, and her hands balled up like a boxer's.

This didn't do much for Patrice's opinion of boys. In fact, the attention had done more to extinguish any potential desires than to kindle them. Most days, Patrice found herself hating boys.

With the exception of one.

This was the biggest change.

She had grown up with Derrick. The longevity of their friendship placed him completely out of bounds. She couldn't. She wouldn't. But all the while, she found herself hopelessly drowning in new emotions.

• • •

Lisa came by Jackson's classroom during lunchtime. When he got up to greet her, she pulled him in for a hug. She had gone for the shoulders, so Jackson had no choice but to take the waist. The hug was tight and long. At first, it was her. But when she loosened up, Jackson found himself holding her tighter. He thought to let go a few times before he actually did. And when he did, they spent another few moments just standing close, Jackson's hand still on her waist.

Footsteps just outside the door made them separate. He sat at his desk. She pulled a chair and sat close to him.

"How are you?" Jackson asked.

"I'm good. Been having trouble sleeping." She was looking at her lap. He followed her eyes down and settled on her legs. She was wearing a short maroon dress.

"Are you okay?"

"Yes. I just have a lot on my mind." She looked up at him and the intensity of her gaze startled him a little.

"You worried about what you're going to do after grad school?"

"That's one of many things I'm worried about. Don't remind me."

"You're a kid. You have time to figure it out."

"I'm a woman." She smiled. "I was thinking of traveling maybe. Getting out of here for a while. I'm feeling claustrophobic."

"Sounds good."

"Have you ever traveled?"

"A little. Nothing out of the Caribbean and the States."

"Ever thought of going abroad?"

"Yes. But I don't think it's going to happen."

"Why not?"

"My wife's not a big fan."

"That's a shame."

"Yes."

"So your wife. What she like?"

Jackson cringed a little. He looked at Lisa, trying to decipher

her like a puzzle. "She's nice. A little bossy when she wants to be."

"How long have you been married?"

"Twenty-three years."

"How old is she?"

"A lot of questions, don't you think?"

"I'm sorry. You don't have to answer if you're uncomfortable."

"She's forty-three."

"A younger woman." She uncrossed and crossed her legs.

Jackson watched. He cleared his throat. "The other night, you—"

"So what did you think of the story?"

"It's good."

"Good enough that I could submit it somewhere?"

"Yes. Just needs a little work."

"I really appreciate this." She leaned toward him a little.

"It's no problem."

He pulled the story manuscript out of his bag. He had marked it up quite a bit, but he wasn't lying. The prose was beautiful. Like so many of her stories, it had a romantic theme. In places, it was a little too sentimental, but overall, it was exceptional. He gave her the pages and watched as she reviewed his comments and corrections. A few times, he noted the changes in her expression. At one point, she stopped and stared at the page for a long time.

"You think this is too sentimental?"

"Yes."

"Why?"

"Your character. To say that she could never find another man she could love but him is simplistic, naive. Love doesn't work that way. People fall into love. And more often than not, they fall out of it. She's known him for only three weeks and she already thinks she has a love that will last forever?"

Lisa adjusted in her chair and took a deep breath. She leaned forward, putting her elbows on her knees, holding the paper loosely. The dress was low-cut. Jackson could see the lacy outline of her bra.

"You don't believe love can happen that fast?"

"Attraction, yes. Love, no. And I think most people share my opinion."

She sat back up in her seat, her legs open slightly. "How long did you know your wife before you married her?"

"A year. And even then, I wasn't sure."

"So what made you sure?"

"I don't know if it happened like that for me. I don't think I made my decision on certainty."

"So what did you make it on?"

"Compatibility. We seemed to fit." He paused, looking at her. "And love, of course."

"Of course."

She started reading through Jackson's comments again. Every time she turned the page, she looked at him and waited for him to meet her eyes before reading again. Jackson didn't know what to make of the action, but he was finding it hard to sit still. He felt tense, sensitive, as though he could easily break.

A few weeks ago, as had become her custom over the years, Lisa had returned after a short hiatus with a sheaf of stories she wanted him to look over. And so he did. It was odd, he thought, after all those years, but he really did enjoy helping, and their conversations were always about the writing. The asking about his personal life, the texting his phone on the weekends and late at night—that was a new thing.

When Lisa was done, she put the paper back on his desk. "Jack. Why not go abroad on your own?"

"I don't know about that. I have a family."

"Your daughter. She's a junior isn't she?"

"Yes."

"You have any younger kids?"

"No."

"You should go, then. You could teach abroad for a year. It's something I'm thinking about. How long until you retire?"

"Lisa."

"Yes."

"I … maybe we shouldn't meet like this anymore."

"Why not?"

Jackson didn't say anything. The silence lingered uninterrupted. He could smell her, the sweet smell of whatever she was wearing. He tried not to pay attention to every breath she took, the way it looked in that tight dress. But he had to catch himself a few times. He felt hot all over.

Lisa's face slowly moved from concern to something else. Jackson didn't want to decipher the expression, but it made him feel guilty somehow. Then it changed again to recognition. She let out a sigh. She got up without a word and started toward the door, her steps slow, each click of her shoes painfully deliberate. He watched each step, the way her calf muscles flexed.

She stopped at the door and turned. "I'm sorry," she said. Her face was blank, indecipherable. "I didn't mean to make you uncomfortable. I just … well, thanks for your help." And then she was gone.

Jackson got another text later that night, before bed.

You ever wonder how all these
rules for human behavior came
to exist?

He stared at the message for a while and then decided to
answer.

Sometimes.

It's just exhausting. We run
around in circles trying to do
what's right. Trying to be good.
And in the end we're just tired.
Sometimes I wish the whole
world would just stop and say
let's start over. Let's make new
rules. Don't you think that
would be better? Don't you
think we would all be happier?

Maybe.

You ever get tired, Jack? You
ever think that there is more
and you're just missing it
because you are too busy trying
to do what's "right"?

Jackson didn't respond. He turned his phone off and went to bed, tossing and turning through the night.

• • •

Nine days before

Aubrey had moved most of the dogs into the play area. She kept the violent ones in their kennels; she would have to let them out separately. The good ones ran around and played, and she kept an eye on them as she washed out the open kennels with the high-powered hose. The radio was on, and Aubrey half-listened to the news report. A woman with a soft, youthful voice and an English accent talked excitedly. Apparently, an object would pass by Earth in a little over a week. There was a lot of speculation about what it might be. Aubrey could not pretend to care. She was more tired than usual; Jackson had kept her up all night with his crazy sleep. She felt as if she were weighed down by bricks.

As she worked and watched the dogs play, her mind drifted off to secret things.

It had happened a few years ago. Aubrey was drunk at the time. They were in a bathroom stall. Now she couldn't remember how she got there. It was an accident; that's what she had told herself. She didn't stop the hand from going under her dress. Their lips had touched, and she was surprised. She didn't expect it to feel good. She remembered the heat of it, all over her, between her thighs, the ringing in her ears. She grinded as the finger made circles inside her.

When the bathroom door opened and a group of women

entered talking excitedly, Aubrey came back to her senses. She stopped the whole thing, waited for the women to leave, and then left the stall, alone.

"Wait," Alice whispered.

Aubrey ignored her.

Nothing happened after that.

But Aubrey's world was shook. She didn't know what her feelings were. She had been married to a man all her adult life—a good man, she had thought. But what if …

Years passed, and it didn't matter. Life moved on, and it didn't matter. She pretended her world was as it always had been. And she found that it was easy for a while. Lately, though, it was getting harder to pretend that something wasn't wrong.

● ● ●

Six days before

After school, Derrick had to go to Max Mart, a small grocery store across the street, where he worked. That meant Patrice had to wait until her dad was done grading papers before they could leave school. As usual, Dad stopped at the grocery store to pick up some stuff that Mom needed for her baking projects. And as usual, Patrice stayed in the car. Thankfully, Dad had left the keys.

The parking lot of Pueblo Supermarket was crowded. Patrice watched as bag boys ran grocery carts to the cars of patrons, as kids stomped behind their indifferent parents, as an old man walked back and forth in the lot talking to himself, and as the mango lady next to the road talked and laughed loudly with her friends and customers.

Patrice sighed. The heat was sweltering, even with the windows down. She unbuttoned a few buttons of her uniform, rolled up the windows, and turned on the air conditioner. She turned the radio to 105 Jamz to drown out some of the sounds. It was reggae Thursday; Jamz was playing an old Buju song called "I Wanna Be Loved." Patrice sang along, her head bobbing to the easy offbeat of the drums and Buju's raspy voice, sweetly thick.

She reached into her bag, took out the book, and opened it. She picked a page and started reading. It was an old Hindu creation myth. First, there was man, and he was alone in the void. He created woman from himself because he was lonely. Then they took many forms, each time giving birth to new beings, until the world was populated with all the beasts, the fish, the birds. They were happy at their work.

Patrice read on.

A loud buzz distracted her from her reading. Patrice looked down and saw that Dad had left his phone on the center console of the car. She assumed Mom was texting Dad to pick up something she had forgotten to put on her list. Patrice rolled her eyes as she reached for the phone. Now she would have to run inside and tell him. She hated having to do that.

When she opened the text message, she was surprised to find that it was not her mother. It was a text from some woman named Lisa.

• • •

Five days before

Did you get my message?

Jackson texted back.

No.

He looked through his message history to find the last message he had gotten from Lisa before today. He had never seen a notification for a new message, yet there it was. Like it had already been read. And he had not been the one to read it.

**I'm sorry Jack. I was wondering
if I could see you one last time.
To talk. I need to be honest
about a few things. I think you
may need to be honest too.**

He thought for a moment. Then he texted her:

**I will think about it and get
back to you.**

It was nighttime. Jackson leaned back in his usual chair on the porch, looking up at the black sky, the gray clouds, the glimmering white stars. The mosquitoes were out, and so were the bats. He scratched his new bug bites absently as he watched the bats in their haphazard flight, turning in quick angles through the sky.

Jackson had always been afraid of getting old. That was

why he had kept himself in shape. It was something he prided himself on. But even with his regular visits to the gym, age was catching up to him. He found that he was achy more and more, deep down. There was popping in his joints, and his bones creaked and moaned like rusted gears. He had found himself spending more hours at the gym and eating less of the food he loved. He had a little pudgy midsection that wouldn't go away.

He was a cliché, and he knew it. He had thought that when this time came in his life, he would be content, happy, grateful for all the opportunities he'd been given, for the family and the job he had been blessed with. But all he could think of was all the things he hadn't done. His students didn't do much for him anymore. He found that he couldn't hold out for the few who wanted to be there. He had started phoning it in, half-assing.

And his wife. They had been married a long time. This Lisa thing was the biggest cliché of all.

He had once had other dreams: places he wanted to go, things he wanted to do, books he wanted to write. But he had trapped himself on this damned island, marooned himself in a stagnant existence. He had settled, and his life had passed him by.

He felt like an hourglass, giving to the bottom by taking from the top. He didn't have much else to give, and he found himself, in his worst moments, indulging in the most selfish thoughts: That he'd given enough. That a man should have the right to say he was done, with no hard feelings from the people he had devoted his life to.

But that was not the way the world worked. You couldn't go through life filling holes in yourself by digging them elsewhere. And wouldn't that be even worse? Imagine what Aubrey would have to endure—the snickers, the little whispering voices as she passed by. He couldn't do that to her. How could he ever forgive himself if he did? Still, he found himself thinking that there must be a middle ground, a way for him to have both.

• • •

Four days before

"What?" Aubrey was having a hard time accepting the words she was hearing. "What are we talking about here?"

"Aubrey. I need to do this. For *me*."

"It a little late for a midlife crisis, Jack," she said, her St. Thomian English getting thick with her frustration. "And we can't uproot our whole life here because you want teach in a foreign country."

"I'm not asking you to."

"What?"

"I want to do this on my own."

A part of her wanted to be more understanding somehow, more reasonable. But all she could hear herself saying was that this was crazy.

"This is crazy," she finally said aloud. Their room seemed smaller, as if the walls had closed in when she wasn't looking. They both were sitting on their bed. The room was dimly lit, and she could see only the part of his face closest to her, the other half eclipsed in shadow.

"I can wait a year until Pat is done with school. But then I'm going."

"Is this about these text messages you been getting late at night?"

Jackson moved to say something but didn't.

"You think I ain't notice? You'n marry no idiot, Jack."

"That's not what this is about. We can talk about that later."

"Later? You gon' even ask what *I* want? Or is that not a part of this marriage anymore?" She waited for him to answer, but he just stared at her in that stupid way he did when he felt backed into a corner. The thought of him feeling that way made Aubrey even angrier. She continued. "You not the only one that has been tempted, Jack. Most people get over it. They cheat or they don't. They don't pick up and go to a foreign country."

He glared at her. "Who is he?"

"There's no *he*. And you don't get to ask me anything. I'm not leaving you."

"I'm not saying the marriage is over. I just need to do this. You can wait if you want."

"*If I want?*" Aubrey scoffed.

"If you want. I can't make you."

"How long?"

"A year. Two, maybe."

"*Two years?* You can go fuck yourself while you at it."

Jackson tried to reach out and touch her, but she was way past being consoled. She felt sick at her stomach. She had prepared herself for this conversation. She had read the signs, but she wasn't sure now what else she would do, what she would say. She felt powerless. She felt betrayed.

"I don't want you going," she said.

"I need to. I feel boxed in. I need to stretch my legs."

"Then, take a vacation!"

"It's more than that. Living here doesn't feel like living anymore."

"Now, how that supposed to make me feel?"

Jackson cleared his throat. In the dim lighting, he almost seemed like a whole other person. She could see the age on them both. Their years together stretched back in her mind. She couldn't remember a time when he wasn't there. Even her memories before him seemed to be inhabited by him, like some hovering spirit. Yet, as she looked at him, he felt completely alien, as if he had never really been there at all.

"This really isn't about you," he said softly.

"No. It really isn't."

"What do you want to do?"

She looked up at him, anger flaring in her eyes. She wanted to burn her anger into him, somehow let him know, just with her eyes, how it felt to feel the way she was feeling now. "I don't know." She looked away, feeling something within her shift, deflate, and said again, "I don't know."

• • •

Three days before

Patrice was always afraid of the shadows, especially once her feet had kicked up enough sand to make the water surrounding her foggy. She moved unsteadily and uneasily as Derrick splashed around, completely at home. The sea breeze was light. Seagulls soared through the sky making their repetitive call, and they could hear the distant chatter of people a little way down Lindbergh Beach.

Patrice loved the beach because it didn't have a lot of seaweed. But lately, squirming little weeds were showing up, taking more and more space. She hated that more than any kicked-up sand. Worse, she couldn't figure out why it was happening. The seaweed wasn't there before. Ever. Not in her whole life.

It was global warming, perhaps. Or maybe things were just changing. She didn't like it, all this change.

"I read some of that book," she admitted to Derrick.

"What you think?" Derrick asked, slapping his hands against the surface until the water turned white and foamy.

"It's interesting."

"That it?"

"Made me think."

"Good. Thought it would."

"I don't know if it is." Patrice paused and gathered herself. "It's confusing. It's like he is trying to say we made the whole thing up."

"Yes," he agreed. It seemed for a moment, the way his face turned away from her, that he had decided to say nothing else. But then he said, "A story time makes true."

Patrice nodded.

"Well," he said, "you want another one?"

"No, thank you. I'm still working through this one."

Patrice thought she felt something brush up against her leg, and with a little squeal she jumped on Derrick, wrapping her legs around him. Usually, Derrick responded by taking her farther out, only making Patrice scream out more as he laughed. This time, he didn't move at all. He just let her cling to him, his arms down, lightly brushing against her bare legs. Patrice had mixed feelings about his light touch.

"You gon' be just fine."

"How you so calm?"

"Because me'n no punk like you."

"Yeah, okay. Whatever, boy." Patrice was beginning to feel her thighs inching lower and lower on Derrick's body. She wrapped her arms around his neck tight.

"You think you ready to get off?" Derrick said, sounding a little uncomfortable.

"Why? Something wrong?"

"No. You're just getting heavy."

"Please, boy. We practically on the moon."

Patrice smiled. She wrapped around him tighter, which seemed to be making him more uncomfortable, though he had stopped avoiding her gaze. She could feel every point of contact simultaneously. Her skin felt hot, her head light, and she leaned in closer to him, close enough to feel his breath on her wet skin. She took in heavy breaths. She felt the wild thumping of her heart.

Something in her stirred, and she felt suddenly distrustful of the moment, suddenly suspicious. She allowed herself to slide off him. As her body slid down his, she felt something solid rub against her. Surprised, she jerked backward.

Derrick didn't say anything.

Patrice decided not to comment on it, either. She recognized what it was from the few moments when boys had grinded up on her at parties. She never liked dancing with boys. They always put their hands in places they shouldn't, and she would have to push them off. But this wasn't a boy at a party. This was Derrick. She wondered how much of what she rubbed up against was meant for her. She had heard that sometimes these things happened by accident. And recently, she had had her trust in men shaken. She would never know unless she asked him. And she would never ask, so she would never know.

The sky was beginning to change colors from blue to pink. The water was darker, and now there was no hope of seeing the bottom. "We should go." Patrice moved to get out of the water.

"Okay. Give me a second."

Patrice got out, grabbed her towel that was hanging on a nearby tree, and yelled back to Derrick, "You know we should be getting back with your grandmother's car."

"Just let me swim a little, dread. I gon' be out in a minute."

Patrice couldn't help but laugh.

"What you laughing about?" asked Derrick, still splashing around in the water.

•   •   •

One day before

Aubrey was in the play area with one of the dogs, applying flea dip. Chewed-up toys and half-eaten mangoes that had fallen in from the neighbor's yard lay scattered about the play area. Small streams of dirty water converged to form a murky puddle by the stairs that led up to the dog kennels. The air smelled of wet dog, mango, and chemicals.

Aubrey let her thoughts drift as she scooped flea dip with a metal dog-food container and poured it on the unhappy dog. It was small, a mix of Yorkshire terrier and something else. Its long, unmanaged hair sagged and dripped with the white liquid. The dip gave off a scent almost like gasoline.

The dogs in their kennels suddenly went wild with desperate barking.

"How is everything back here?" Alice asked, appearing at the top of stairs, where the kennels and play area met. The dogs barked and jumped at the doors of their cages.

"Good. You need something?"

"No. No, I'm fine."

The dog Aubrey was cleaning barked at the other dogs. "*Shhh*," she commanded, and the dog obeyed.

Alice caught on and descended the stairs. The dogs slowly got quiet. Aubrey hardly ever saw Alice back here in the play area. Her scrubs glowed in the sunlight.

"This is the last one," Aubrey said, not knowing what else to say.

"Oh," Alice answered.

They both were quiet now, and in the lingering silence, Aubrey thought of all the things that had changed and all the things that would. She looked forward through time, and the oppressiveness of it made her burn inside.

"I was thinking," she started, not completely knowing how she would finish, "I want to go on a trip. Nothing as big as a cruise, but maybe an island hop. Somewhere I've never been before."

"Sounds like fun," Alice said. She wasn't looking at Aubrey. Just staring down at the dog as it panted and shivered.

"You want to join me?" Aubrey asked finally. "I think maybe we can make a weekend of it."

Alice looked up at her. She tilted her head just a little. Then a smile, not as large as her usual smiles, came to her face. She moved a stray curl of hair out of her eyesight. "When?"

• • •

The day

It was another Saturday afternoon, the sun high up in the sky, the trade winds blowing in. The arms of the coconut trees moved back and forth as if waving.

Jackson was leaning against the porch rail in his brown boots, white shirt, and khaki pants. A machete leaned against one of the porch columns, next to his feet, its blade freshly stained green from the yard work he had done. Unruly bush surrounded three sides of the house and had to be beaten back on occasion. Jackson inhaled the smell of cut grass, taking pride in the morning's work.

He was moving his phone from one hand to the other, fully aware of the smooth polymer in his hands, and the way it felt against his callused palms. His upper right arm throbbed deep within the muscle. His knee ached.

Jackson watched as a cat strolled into the yard. The cat regarded him with equal awareness, staring right up at him. It didn't move, its slender body tensed and ready, its fur slick black and shiny. Their porch was on the second floor, high above the yard; Jackson's presence was no real threat.

Still, they continued their stare-off. The cat was wild, had been wild its whole life, living off mice, lizards, garden snakes, young iguanas, and the occasional food scraps it could find. Jackson could tell all this just by looking at it. The cat had never been touched by human hands.

It took another few hyperalert steps and lost interest in Jackson. Its head bobbed upward in a quick jerk, spotting something in the grass, and it gave chase. Jackson went back to moving his phone between his hands, thinking.

The phone buzzed, and sure enough, it was Lisa.

So about seeing you? We really
should talk.

Jackson pressed REPLY on his touch screen and began typing.

• • •

Patrice left her room to look for her father. She had a lot of stuff on her mind. Heavy stuff. She found him on the porch, leaning against the rail, pressing buttons on his phone.

"What are you doing?"

When her father heard her, he pressed a button and put his phone away. "Just canceling an appointment with someone."

"Oh. Won't the person be disappointed?"

"Probably," her father answered distractedly, looking up from his hands.

When he looked up, he caught sight of something. He leaned forward, squinting at the thing in the distance. Patrice followed his eyes to a little dot in the sky, growing bigger as they watched.

"I'm confused," Patrice said, following the dot as it moved across the blue, cloudless sky.

"Oh?" Her father had a serious expression but was still paying attention to her. "About what?"

"I don't know," Patrice answered. "Everything."

There were cruise ships in the harbor. The Disney Cruise Line blared its signature seven-note call of arrival, taken from "When You Wish upon a Star." The sound of it pulled them momentarily away from the thing in the sky. But before long, they both were looking up again, following the object.

"You'll have to be more specific than that, Pat. What is that thing? Aubrey, come check this out!"

"I cooking," her mother yelled back.

"Take a break!"

No answer came from the house.

"What were you saying, lil' miss? What you confused about?"

"I don't know," Patrice said again. Usually, these conversations were easier to navigate, but so many things had changed in her head. She didn't know where or how to start. She knew what the words felt like but not what the words *were*. They drifted somewhere in the back of her mind, where she couldn't reach.

"It looks like it's coming here," she said. "A seaplane maybe?" There was a seaplane port in the harbor. Patrice liked to watch them land on the water, like massive metal birds.

"No," Jackson answered. "It doesn't look right."

In the coming months, Patrice would remember this day, wishing she were somehow more prepared for the further crumbling of her already fragile world. Wishing she had seen that little dot on the horizon and known it for what it was: the harbinger of so many things.

But she would come to realize that life didn't prepare you for the big things. They didn't announce themselves or watch their feet, mindful of their intrusion.

All big things were rude strangers.

"Maybe it's a drone or something," her father said to no one in particular. "These young people and their toys."

But the dot got bigger than a drone, bigger than a plane. And then she could see it, clear as anything. The thing was still high up, but large. Disk-shaped, a massive floating swirl of a thing, perfect in symmetry, the body of it pearl white with blue streaks that flowed over its surface like waves. The thing hummed so loudly, it throbbed in Patrice's ears.

She had seen something like this a thousand times. But never in the sky. Never that big. The hum pulsed, and the outer skin of it pulsed as well, the blue streaks moving out from the spiral center.

A giant seashell, Patrice thought. A seashell in the sky, not obeying gravity, humming in her bones. Naming it didn't make her feel any less afraid.

She looked over at her father. His mouth was open, his chest rising and falling, reminding her of someone blowing into a paper bag. He instinctively grabbed for her and pulled her close.

The words came then. The things she wanted to tell him. That she wasn't sure she believed in God anymore. That she thought she was in love but was deeply suspicious about whether it was love and whether it would last. That he, her father, was the reason for that suspicion. But the sound of the thing in the sky drowned out everything. There wasn't any room for her or anything else.

Patrice watched as some people down the hillside came out of their houses, listened as people screamed. She heard dishes fall inside the house and watched as the thing in the sky settled a few feet above the highest hill of Water Island, humming like a beehive. And all her worries pressed against her, building with the noise of the seashell in the sky.

She felt her mother's trembling hands on her, but they felt small somehow despite being so close. They gave her no sense of safety.

There was a dark shadow now over Water Island where it

hovered, and Patrice thought to herself, this was how change occurred: something on the horizon closing in. *She doesn't seem imposing at first, but then she's close enough for you to see the knife hidden under her dress.*

And then the rude stranger tells you her name.

A HISTORY OF INVASIONS

When the Ciboney arrived on what would become St. Thomas, they found an uninhabited island, its shores teeming with fish, its hilly terrain populated with small animals, mostly reptiles and birds. The animals stared uncomprehendingly at their new invaders.

The Ciboney settled at Krum Bay and began a life there. They fished along the bay in their canoes, dug out from cedar and silk-cotton trees. They sang songs to no one but themselves and their gods. The constellations above their heads shifted in the night like a large quilt pulled across heaven.

Five hundred years passed. The Ciboney lived and died and buried their dead. They dreamed of worlds beyond them, of things they could not comprehend in their waking life. They listened to the ocean waves' endless beat. There were others once, they knew. Other people.

When they saw the small canoes bobbing out on the horizon, they recognized that their distant relatives had returned.

The Arawaks were not terrible. When they drove the Ciboney out, they kept many of the women and children.

The Arawaks were luckier, too. They enjoyed their solitude for a thousand years, settling on St. Thomas, St. John, and St. Croix—the names that future invaders would give them.

They fished the ocean around their islands in canoes weighed down with their catch. They scoured the sea floor for conch, clams, and mussels. They cracked the backs of crabs. To the animals, nothing had changed. Strange creatures stole them from their homes to devour them.

The Arawaks planted cassava and corn and peas. They made cassava bread. They modeled little gods from clay, wood, shell, and bone and called them zemis. The zemis had grotesque faces but could control the weather, nurture crops, put babies in bellies.

The Arawaks lived their lives, singing of the places they came from, of the zemi spirits in their hands that helped control their universe. They remembered that there were other people once. But that was a long time ago.

When the Caribs finally arrived, they met the Arawaks living in small settlements. Used to conflict, the Caribs raided Arawak settlements in the dead of night. They ambushed hunters in the bush. The Arawaks retaliated as best they could, their own violence waking from its long slumber. But neither tribe was successful in extinguishing the other.

An uneasy equilibrium settled between the two tribes, the Caribs and the Arawaks coexisting for another one hundred and fifty years.

And then one day, the tribes saw boats bobbing on the sea, with *large wings like bats about to take flight and pointed spears at their fronts. Boats much bigger than theirs and infinitely stranger.*

• • •

Five years after arrival

Jackson rubbed at his eyes. He got up, stretched, and went to the fridge, pulling out a cold Heineken and popping the top off with the opener attached to the freezer door. He brought the cool mouth of the bottle to his lips, taking a few big gulps as he walked back to the dining room table, nudging away the mess around his computer to make room for his beer.

Stacks of books lay everywhere around him, forming helical towers all along the table and rising from empty chairs. Copies of old maps hung on the walls, while others lay rolled up and scattered on the floor. Between the spiraling towers, a few empty green bottles stood as guardians.

He should straighten up, he told himself. Tomorrow. Tomorrow for sure.

He pulled his phone from his pocket instead and looked at it. There were no new messages.

He texted his daughter. *How is everything?* He watched the screen for a moment and then put the phone back in his pocket. He wouldn't be hearing from her anytime soon.

He could go back to writing? No. The computer screen was messing with his eyes again. Maybe he could take a walk. No, too hot out. He took another swig of his beer and stared at the maps on the wall.

Since his retirement, he had been doing research for this

stupid book. He struggled with what the book was actually about. It was definitely a history book of the Virgin Islands, he knew. A chronicle of invasions. First the Spanish and then the Danish and then the Americans. And finally, the Ynaa. Beyond that, well, he wasn't sure. The book had no soul.

He'd been reading about everything. Taking exhaustive notes. The book had taken over his life, stretched itself out in every room, leaving little space for anything else. He was pinned at the edges of his own existence, gasping for air.

Since retirement, he had moved out of his home and into this small apartment. Why had he done that again? To avoid uprooting Patrice from her life? She was gone now. Off to college for three long years. He barely ever heard from her.

So why was he still here? Why not just leave?

Jackson reached under the large stack next to his computer, to a folder filled with printed pages. He flipped through, finding the page he was looking for. At the top was the title of the most important chapter of his book: "The Immortal Witch." As he read the title, he reminded himself that he was not crazy. When he finished the book—*if* he ever finished—he would reveal something that would affect the entire world.

· · ·

Jackson taught Postinvasion Fiction at the University of the Virgin Islands on Wednesday nights. It was the only class of its kind at the university, so he got students from every major, though English majors still filled most of his roster.

The class was about fiction that directly or indirectly referenced the Ynaa invasion. Unsurprisingly, there were a lot of examples. The literary community, struggling to keep up with the change, was finding it increasingly difficult to make distinctions between conventional and speculative fiction in a world where they had collided so completely. It was giving rise to interesting discussions in literary criticism.

The class coupled those discussions with thematic exploration of several works that ranged in their treatment of the Ynaa. In truth, the term "postinvasion" was overly dramatic. The Ynaa did not *invade*, exactly. Not in their eyes, at least, and certainly not according to the stance of world governments. But the term had weight, and so it stuck in the academic community and in the general public at large.

Of his students, Derrick was the most engaged. It wasn't the first time Jackson had taught him. Derrick had taken his English class in high school before the Ynaa arrived. Since then, Derrick had attended two of his classes, the first a nonfiction seminar with the same focus. Jackson had the suspicion that Derrick signed up for the course mostly to ask him questions before and after class about his research. Jackson talked vaguely about his research into Virgin Islands history, and they often had heated debates about the Ynaa, but Jackson stayed off his more controversial theories— well, his *most* controversial theory, to be more precise.

On this Wednesday night, Derrick came late, so there was no preclass discussion. Jackson launched into his lesson. He noted, however, when Derrick slipped into the room ten minutes into his lecture and sat at the back of the class.

They spent most of the two-hour session discussing the film adaptation of one of the first examples of postinvasion fiction they had discussed as a class: a short story called "The Night After." The movie of the same name followed a young couple in the days before and after the Ynaa's arrival. The movie had no aliens in it, only referencing them through news footage—a common strategy used by literary types to separate themselves from the emboldened genre writers. But the connection featured prominently in the story's progression as the couple grappled with the end of their relationship while the world around them panicked under the existential presence of the Ynaa.

"I liked it," Derrick said, leading the class discussion. "But I wish they had dealt with the Ynaa more directly."

"Only *you* care about that," said Jacob from the front row. "Everything don't have to be about the Ynaa."

A few members of the class gave silent nods of agreement.

"I agree," Derrick said. "But then, why bring up the Ynaa at all?"

"If you love them so much, ask them to take you with them when they leave," Jacob said, turning back to face Derrick in the back row. "I tired arguing with your stupid ass, dehman."

A few students chuckled. Derrick started to speak, but stopped when Jackson clapped his hands. "Watch your mouth, Jacob. And I still waiting for your last paper."

"It coming, Dr. P. I promise. It just so much work dealing with Derrick stupidness that I forget to write it."

More laughter.

"You all shouldn't be laughing. The next paper is coming up next Wednesday. Don't start looking down at your desks. It better be in my hands on Wednesday or there will be points off."

Moans. Half-mocking gasps of horror.

"That means you, too, Jacob. With all the mouth you have in class, you'd swear you passing."

An extended "Oo-o-o-o-o" from the whole class.

"How you gon' call me out like that, Dr. P?" Jacob looked so wounded, it could only be pretend.

Jackson sighed. "Get out of my class. All of you. I'll see you next week." As they got up, he added, "With your papers in hand!"

A few students fussed as they walked out, but most of them would have their papers in on time. Jackson was accommodating, but also hard when he needed to be. Jacob would likely fail the class, but that didn't seem to bother him much. He was the first one out the door.

As expected, Derrick lingered. "Why you didn't jump in for me?"

"I jump in for you too much. The students are going to jump on you worse if I keep that up. Besides, my words can't change their minds if yours won't."

"You still could support me."

"But I'm not always sure I agree."

"How you mean?" Derrick looked affronted.

"Sometimes, I wonder if equal is really fair. It is our Earth, not theirs."

"But it is a good place to start."

Jackson reached into his bag and handed Derrick a sheaf of pages. "It has already started. And no one is seeing things your way. Especially not the Ynaa."

Derrick glowered, but he took the pages without a word. He skimmed the first one and then carefully read a few paragraphs on the second. "What's this?"

"A theory I have."

Derrick watched Jackson. "Seems far-fetched."

"They knew so much from the get-go. How else could they know so much? Speak our languages? Know who to contact on arrival?"

Derrick laughed. "You been hanging out with me too long."

"Or I'm onto something."

"And if I ask the ambassador about this?" Derrick handed back the pages.

"Tell me what she says."

"More likely to get my head ripped off than anything. If this is true, I doubt she'd want it getting out." Derrick gave Jackson a good long look, and Jackson felt suddenly as if he had given something away, though he didn't know what. Something like concern passed over Derrick's face. "You okay? With everything?"

"What do you mean?"

Derrick folded his arms, eyeing Jackson. He was a man now, wide shouldered and tall. Taller than he, Jackson had just realized. Derrick's hair was short and well managed, unlike Jackson's bushy gray beard and Afro that he only absently tried to maintain. The years between them could not be more apparent—at opposite ends of their adult lives, with different concerns, both brought together under this singular interest. Before all this, Jackson had hardly held a conversation with the boy. That had been Aubrey back then. She was the one who took a liking to Derrick immediately. "Such a good kid," she used to say.

"I'm fine," Jackson said, looking away from the young man. "Really. Just this damn book."

"Okay." Derrick patted him on the shoulder. "Take care of yourself."

The feeling of Derrick's palm remained even after he turned to leave—a phantom presence, an echo of touch. He had felt so apart for so long, the little bit of contact actually made him feel substantial instead of how he usually felt, as if he were slowly fading away into nothing at all.

Jackson's phone buzzed, and he took it out expecting to see his daughter's nonchalant reply to his earlier text. But that was not what he got.

How you been, Jack? Want to
meet up?

• • •

Jackson had tried to reach out to Lisa a few months after Aubrey.

As all such mistakes began, he had been drinking. When he called her, he asked her, slurring through the words, whether she wanted to come over. He was sprawled on the living room floor of his apartment, unpacked boxes scattered around him.

Lisa told him she would be over in an hour.

Her knocking woke him from his drunken sleep, still lying where he'd made the call. When he answered the door, her expression immediately changed.

"I want you," were his first cringeworthy words to her.

She looked him up and down but didn't come inside. "You sure about that? You even know who you talking to right now?"

Jackson kept nodding long past what could ever be construed as normal. "I'm sorry," he said. "Don't let my appearance ..." He trailed off, losing the thought.

"What happened to not wanting to get involved?"

"I'm single. And you single."

That was not the right thing to say. Lisa turned and walked away.

Later, Jackson had apologized a few times via voicemail and

text, sent her a message once or twice asking how she was doing. He received no reply.

Jackson watched the message on his phone for a few seconds before responding with a yes.

You busy tonight? I know you
teaching at UVI.

Class is over. Where do you
want to meet?

Bella Blu. Already there. Having
an after-work drink.

Bella Blu was a restaurant in Frenchtown. When Jackson walked in, he immediately saw Lisa at the bar.

"How you been?" he asked her as he sat down.

"Okay. And you?"

He smiled, watching her. She had cut her hair short and was wearing a long-sleeved shirt tucked into tight-fitting jeans. "I'm okay," he said.

"I didn't like how things ended with us," she said. "I wanted to apologize."

"It was my fault."

"We both could have handled it better."

Jackson nodded, his shame easing a little. That was a very diplomatic answer.

He ordered a Cruzan rum and Coke, and they talked on, catching each other up on their lives. Lisa told him about her stories. She had submitted a few to *Callaloo*, a Caribbean magazine, but hadn't gotten any acceptances. She was still waiting on a response to the latest story she sent out. Jackson told her about his project, his book about invasions.

"You know she's in Frenchtown right now," Lisa said. "The ambassador. Heard some people talking about it outside. She over at Sandy's." Some thought occurred to Lisa, and she said, "Don't go getting no ideas, now. I like you breathing."

Jackson took a sip of his drink and offered what he thought was a reassuring smile.

Lisa shrugged and changed the subject. "So how are you really?"

"I'm good." He stirred his drink with the tiny straw and slid his finger along the outside of the glass, wetting his fingertips with condensation.

"Just good?"

He didn't look at her face but could feel her eyes on him. "You know," he said without elaborating.

"I was wondering if you could look at my work. I miss your great feedback."

Jackson watched Lisa. She was smiling at him. He looked down at her hand and saw what he had missed. A wedding band.

Lisa followed his eyes, her smile thinning.

"Yeah, sure," he said. He swirled the ice in his glass, the watered-down remnants of his amber-colored drink sloshing at the bottom. "I'll look at it. Send me an email."

Lisa opened her mouth to speak.

"Can I pay for this?" Jackson asked the bartender. He slid a twenty on the table—way more than the drink required. "I have to head out. But send me that story when you can."

Lisa didn't say anything when he got up.

As he left the bar, the winter night air blew through him, giving him a chill. Jackson had been stateside only a few times in his life. He didn't enjoy it. His blood was already too thin for winter nights in the tropics.

Jackson walked over to his car and fumbled with his keys. Then he stopped. He put the keys back in his pocket and stared at his face in the glass, the image made clear by the gleam of the streetlight overhead. He chuckled at the scraggly old man peering back at him. He could feel his old knees groaning under the flesh.

He swayed a little and considered the prospect of going home. To nothing. To no one. Only that stupid book. He felt the weight of it crushing him again. When he was a younger man, he had written essays and short stories. Aubrey liked them, urged him to do something with them. He didn't. And she stopped pushing. He had unearthed them when he moved out of the house, rereading them just in case he could use them somehow. They were terribly dated. He wanted to ask Aubrey whether she thought they were worth revising, making new. But by then anger had fortified itself between them. Now, after all the years, all he felt was desolation and loneliness stretching on before him—a shadowed road with no one but him on it. And he was disappearing, too.

Standing there, swaying under the streetlamp, Jackson entertained a dangerous thought. Perhaps he wouldn't wait for Derrick to ask the ambassador. He tried the idea on and found that the voice in the back of his head, the one that warned against making stupid decisions, was tuned all the way down. Jackson realized something then. After so long in his marriage, that voice sounded just as much like Aubrey's as it did his own. She had become that warning. They had become that for each other, a guard against the impulses of their worst selves.

But she was gone now, and there was no use listening to ghosts. He turned and headed over to Sandy's.

• • •

Frenchtown lay close to the water, right on Charlotte Amalie Harbor. Jackson could smell the sea, strong in the air, as he walked down the row of restaurants on his way to Sandy's. He passed Rum Shandy, hearing laughter from the people inside, and the swell of the music from the speakers. Pie Whole was quiet from the outside, but the smell of fresh dough greeted him.

Cars lined the street, packed tight together. Even on a quiet night, it was hard to find parking in Frenchtown. Jackson had gotten lucky and found a spot against the Griffith Ballpark fence. As he passed other cars, he looked inside the ballpark, where a group of expats were kicking around a soccer ball. A blond-haired guy with long legs shot the ball high into the air. A stout brunette girl with strong thighs and pronounced calf muscles whipped down the field in pursuit, spitting up dirt as she ran. On the bleachers, Jackson could see a few island boys sitting, lighting up, the smoke curling up from the ends of their blunts. The palm trees on the far side of the field swayed like dancers in the night breeze.

Sandy's was only a two-minute walk from Bella Blu, but Jackson took his sweet time getting there. He pushed open one of the double doors, and the sound of lively chatter greeted him. Sandy's was a dive compared to Bella Blu, but it had a homey feel that made it much more inviting. Clever sayings and old-timey photos of St. Thomas hung on the walls. "Warning," said a sign in big, bold letters. "The consumption of alcohol may cause pregnancy." "No trespassing," said another. "Violators will be shot. Survivors will be shot again." A crocodile skull dangled from the ceiling. Jackson had no idea of its authenticity. In the back were two pool tables, which almost always had people playing on them. Tonight was no exception.

The chairs that curved around the U-shaped bar were empty except for an older white man at one end, and a younger-looking woman at the other. The bartender was busy pouring drinks for a couple who stood near the door.

Jackson watched the woman on the far end of the bar. She had her dreadlocks pulled back into a ponytail of sorts, the thick knots falling behind her like the dormant limbs of some many-tentacled sea monster. She looked sullen but at ease, a Greenie in one hand. Even from where he sat, he could see those piercing light-brown eyes that seemed to glow faintly in the bar's low light. Her skin was dark like Jackson's, but it gleamed as if she were some goddess who had stepped into the world of men only the day before and had not yet begun to age. The softness of a child, the physique of a woman. Her black tank top exposed arms corded with muscles.

Seeing her powerful arms, Jackson finally considered the prospect of losing his head. He felt the skin of his neck go taut, could almost feel her hands on him, the flesh tearing as easily as bread. He knew that the Ynaa were powerful and not opposed to harming humans, and he recognized the same self-assuredness, the same discreet threat, in the woman across the bar. Just like other Ynaa he had glimpsed on island, she carried herself with the promise of violence. But no one mistook Mera for just any Ynaa. No other Ynaa fascinated and terrified the islanders the way she did.

At the moment, most of the people in Sandy's seemed at ease

with the ambassador's presence, but Jackson knew better. He knew what hid under the smiles and conversation: the same quiet terror that was making his legs shake as he took his seat at the bar. He ordered a Greenie, and the bartender slid him a long-necked bottle of Heineken, cold and sweating with a little foam peeking from its lip.

Jackson let it settle and then took a swig while giving the ambassador quick glances. Soon, he gave up all his ambitions, measuring himself against the intimidating creature and finding that he was not up to the task. There would be no confrontation, no revelations this night. His sane mind had prevailed.

Sandy's had tables all around. Most, but not all, were empty. The couple at the bar had gone into the back room to watch a group of older men play pool, but a gang of young people were talking loudly at a corner booth. Every now and then, one of them looked in the ambassador's direction. Another couple ate their dinner quietly at the other end of the room, behind the ambassador's back. They, too, kept their eye on her, sneaking furtive glances.

The older white man smiled in Jackson's direction, and Jackson recognized the dirty-blond hair and missing teeth. He was a friend of the bar's owner. Jackson used to come into Sandy's a lot when he was teaching at Charlotte. The man was always here then, chatting up the owner, an older white woman with a loud voice and a warm smile, whose name actually was Sandy. She had lived on island most of her life.

The white man lifted his glass to Jackson. "Ain't see you in here in a while," he said in the island lilt.

Jackson smiled. The man was either a local Frenchie, which wouldn't be surprising here in Frenchtown, or an expat who had lived here long enough to pick up the talk. Jackson figured it was the latter, since he could detect a bit of awkwardness in the way the words rolled off the man's tongue.

"Yeah, it been a long while," Jackson said. "Been busier lately with all that been going on."

The man nodded and glanced at the ambassador. Jackson nodded back, assuming that the glance was intentional. The man tilted his head and smiled big, revealing a mostly complete set of teeth. Then he returned to his drink. Jackson quietly finished his beer and ordered two more.

After the third Heineken, he switched back to a rum and Coke. Without meaning to, he continued his careful observation of the ambassador.

"Another drink?" the bartender asked the ambassador. He was white and definitely an expat but had been working at Sandy's for several years now. He had a laid-back disposition that Jackson liked. And he seemed completely at home with the ambassador, which impressed Jackson.

The ambassador looked up at the bartender, smiled, and said, "Yes, give me another one."

The bartender nodded.

Most other Ynaa could not pull off an act like this. Even in their human skin, they couldn't be mistaken for the real thing. They were too slow, too jerky in their movements. Not the ambassador. She could pass for an islander if only her face weren't so infamous.

The bartender gave Mera the Greenie, and she held it in her hand as if to drink, but then put down the bottle. Jackson watched her do this, looking for something that would give her away, reveal what she truly was. He didn't realize she had turned her eyes to him until it was too late.

He felt cold dread move through him before his body reacted, and then he quickly averted his eyes. He felt the seconds tick by as he fixed his attention on a painting above the heads of the dining couple behind Mera. He waited. After some time, when he couldn't take it anymore, he allowed himself a quick glance at her. She was still watching him, with no expression at all. Something in her gaze caught him. He had stared into her eyes and turned to stone. Ants crawled up his back, and he was powerless to stop them. The world around him disappeared into those eyes.

Before he screamed, she pulled her attention away, releasing him. As if nothing had happened at all, she returned to her drink, staring into the middle distance between them, going back to whatever thoughts were occupying her mind.

Jackson felt hot behind the ears. He looked around, embarrassed. No one was looking at him, but the room was quiet.

He found a conspiracy in that silence. Perhaps he had drunk too much, but something broke in him then. His heart thumped with panicked rage, and the urge flooded back into him, filling all the spaces his terror had left. He wanted to run into traffic, to tip over a cliff, to slide the knife against flesh to watch it bleed. He heard Aubrey's voice in the back of his mind, begging him not to. And he found himself arguing with the voice, shouting back against it.

She had embarrassed him. And she knew she had done so. It was a very human thing to do—*too* human. How dare she! Who did she think she was? It was their Earth, not hers, not the Ynaa's. Who gave her the right to be here? Who gave her the right to deceive them all?

And who are you to lecture me now that you've left me? I loved you and you left me.

The words came out easily, a continuation of the argument in his head. "You been here a while, haven't you?" he asked, the question loud enough for everyone at the bar to hear.

Mera turned her eyes and head slowly this time to look at him. Not quite normal. Not quite human. It was a deception. He knew the truth.

"You been on Earth for centuries," he said, pressing on.

The bartender stopped polishing the glass in his hand. The older white man perked up, and the couple at the near table swung their attention Jackson's way. The background pop rock music seemed louder now since even the young people at the corner booth had stopped talking.

As if in answer, Mera got up and took a hundred-dollar bill out of her purse and put it on the bar, the movement so calm that Jackson shrank back in his seat, afraid of what would come. She smiled graciously at the bartender and moved slowly toward Jackson's side of the bar. His body tensed, his heart thumping hard and fast. He closed his eyes, listening to the soft footsteps approach. He could feel her closeness as she walked behind his chair. He waited in that tense silence for what felt like a long time.

But nothing happened.

When he opened his eyes, she was already headed toward the door, her back to him. Before he understood what he was doing, he got up from his chair. He rushed toward her, reaching out and grabbing her by the arm.

"Wait," he said.

She was careful when she turned. It was graceful. Slow. So human now. So painfully human. When she spoke, it was quiet, a secret for only the two of them.

"You can go back," she said, her eyes never leaving his. "You can take your hands off me and drink your beer. And I'll leave in peace. Nothing else will happen."

Jackson's eyes were wide. His body shook. Nothing about how she said this was odd at all. It was gentle. But he felt all the hairs on the back of his neck stand up. A chill slid all the way down to his legs. He let go.

"Good night," she said, and left.

The room sat in silence for a few seconds longer. Then murmuring crept back into the space. Soon, talking, though hushed, had resumed. Jackson had no difficulty guessing the subject of that talk. He returned to his chair and sat back down, staring forward, too afraid to leave.

Quietly he drank two more beers, his head low and shoulders high, sweat trickling down from his armpits. When the conversation in the bar felt as though it had returned to its normal tenor, he paid his bill and slipped out, the voices trailing behind him like a thunderstorm at sea.

• • •

Jackson slammed his fists on the door, too drunk to feel the pain, only the euphoria of his rage.

"Who this Jeep belong to?" he asked, his voice quivering. "It hers? She in there with you?"

It took several minutes before Aubrey answered his knocks, his yelling. The lights came on, and he heard footsteps inside the house. When she opened the door, she was in a nightgown.

He remembered the gown from when he lived here. He remembered how it clung to the slender curves of her body. Until this moment, he hadn't realized he missed it.

"What you doing?" she asked. "How you get up here?"

"I drove."

"You drove," she repeated. She looked at him for a short while, then stepped out the door and closed it behind her. He made space for her, almost falling backward, steadying himself at the last moment. "Look at the state you in. How you driving on the government roads looking so?"

"You worried about the government roads more than me?"

She came close, making an effort to keep her voice low. "I worried about *people*," she said. "People. You know, all those other folks sharing the road with you? What you thinking, Jack?"

His mouth hung open at the use of that name. He quivered. "Why you do this?" he asked. "Why you let this fucking woman come between us?"

Aubrey looked back behind her as if she expected Alice to be standing there. Then she turned back to Jackson. "It too late for you to be yelling. People trying to sleep."

"I not yelling!" His St. Thomian English was strong in his hot rage.

"You are."

"I love you!"

"Oh, Lord." Aubrey reached out to touch Jackson's hand. "Jack—"

He recoiled at the touch, pulling away. "She in there with you, ain't she?"

Aubrey looked him right in the face. "Yes."

Jackson gaped. No words came for a while. He looked around himself as if just realizing where he was. Tears burned in his eyes.

"Let me come home," he said, and when she didn't answer, he repeated it again. "I want to come home."

"You want me to move out?"

"No," he said, his voice cracking. "No," he repeated. "I want to be home with you. Not her. She don't belong here."

Aubrey stared at him. It wasn't a cold stare or an angry one. It was full of pity and sadness. "I don't …" she started, and then she stopped. She tried to hold his hands again, and this time he let her. "I can't," she said. "I'm happy."

Jackson's whole body felt hot. He cycled through a series of responses, finding none that could do the complex alchemy he needed. No words that he could find would make happen what he wanted. No words would undo what had clearly already been done.

"I want you to be happy, too," she said.

He chupsed his teeth, making the long sucking sound that indicated complete annoyance.

"We made a beautiful daughter," she said, ignoring his frustration. Her eyes were intense on him. He remembered how much he loved that steadying intensity, how much he felt as if he were crumbling in its absence.

"We did good," she said. "Let's keep doing good."

Jackson stared at her, not fully comprehending at first. Then, through the fog of his drunkenness, he understood what she meant. His body shook in rebellion. He did not accept this. He could not accept this. But then he gave up, from an exhaustion so deep it went beyond the body and deep into his soul.

"Okay," she said, understanding something he hadn't communicated verbally. She held his hand tighter. "Come inside and sleep this off." She pulled at his hand, leading him into the house.

Quietly, the rage within him burned out at last, and he let her.

• • •

Through the night, Jackson's dreams were filled with faces. It was as if the entire history of his island spoke to him from the darkness of his fitful sleep. Her voice was loudest of all. *You can still go back.*

Where? he kept asking in that purgatory between sleep and wakefulness, but he found that her voice only repeated the plea.

You can still go back.

• • •

Jackson had come across Mera by accident during his research. The earliest appearance was from the journal of Dr. Hans Balthazar Hornbeck, a Danish man appointed to be district physician of St. John in 1825, back when the Danes still owned the Virgin Islands. In Hornbeck's early years as a physician, he noted stories of a woman who healed slaves on the island. He got a description from a slave boy he had been treating. The woman was slender, with smooth dark-brown skin and piercing amber eyes. Another patient described her as stout, with a mane of locked hair. Hornbeck himself never met the woman, but noted in his journal that he would have "loved the privilege of meeting the witch."

Several reports from physicians on St. Thomas, St. John, and St. Croix referenced a powerful obeah woman healing sick slaves. "Obeah" was the term used to describe women with healing or cursing powers and a natural inclination toward magical arts. It was all superstitious nonsense, Jackson thought at first, but the possibility soon began to nag at him.

The stories were always decades apart, the descriptions of the woman always different. Neatly groomed short hair or long locks. Tall or short. Heavyset or lean. None of the contemporaneous accounts coming from more than one island. Another account from Rev. Henry Jackson Morton, several years before the Emancipation Proclamation of 1848, described a woman who would visit sick slaves in their homes, offering remedies with miraculous healing properties. He would be praying for sick members of his black congregation only to find them healed days later by an "angel of God," according to those healed. Later, she would return to help heal slaves dying during a cholera epidemic.

Both "demon" and "angel" were used to describe this woman, depending on the disposition of the person telling the story. Police reports in St. Croix in 1875 described the woman as a nuisance, "encouraging heathen beliefs among the blacks." In contrast, descriptions of Mary and Maria Thomas of Garden Street in St. Thomas were kind, describing the mother and her later-appearing daughter as old-fashioned medicine women. These accounts were easy to apprehend because there were so many accounts from the 1930s through the 1960s. In the 1980s, a woman from the St. Thomas Historical Society gathered spoken accounts from witnesses, along with opinion articles from the *Daily News*, about the "women on the hill." Both the affluent and the poor praised the women for their healing abilities.

The account that really raised Jackson's suspicions was one written in 1913 by Danish journalist Olaf Linck during his visit to the island. Linck's contact on the island was Dr. Christian Winkel. At the time, Winkel was St. John's physician and police superintendent. The journalist met him at his home, where they drank cocktails made from Johnian rum. Afterward, they rode horseback across the island, visiting one of the four still-running plantations, the Lameshur, where Dr. Winkel and Linck agreed to spend the night to treat a sick man named Oliver.

Oliver, a black man in his midforties, slept fitfully in a back room of the plantation house, trying to fight off an unspecified illness. Dr. Winkel watched over the man until late in the night. According to Linck's account, the man was a much-respected project head on the plantation, who kept operations going smoothly. For many blacks on the island, plantation work was still a mode of employment. Whatever had gotten hold of Oliver had kept him from his work for a full two weeks.

Winkel broke the news to Mr. White, the overseer of the plantation. The man would not live. "Whatever it is," Dr. Winkel said, "won't be cured. He is destined for the next world."

Mr. White stared at Dr. Winkel. Linck said the man's expression changed, became "darker." Mr. White was a local St. Johnian, born on the island. He knew things about the place that Dr. Winkel, a recent expat, could not know. When he spoke, his voice was soft, barely above a whisper. "I will send for someone."

Late that night, a woman came to the plantation. Linck's description was detailed, the best Jackson had come across. Long dark locks. A strong face and amber eyes. Tall for a woman, with a presence that Linck described as otherworldly. "Like someone who did not belong anywhere on this earth." Her voice was soft but not weak. It commanded the attention of everyone in the room.

Mr. White took the woman to the sick man. She stood over the bed and observed him for long minutes. What was written in the account had none of the flare of obeah stories told second- and thirdhand. The description mentioned none of the usual trappings of witchcraft—no animal bones or secret words spoken into the night. The woman put her hand on the man and closed her eyes. Linck recalled how hot the room was, how all the men were sweating in their clothes in the candlelight, yet the woman was as dry as if she were sitting in a cool breeze.

She opened her eyes not long after closing them. "Give him some water. He will come out of this just fine."

She got up and left. From a window on the first floor, Linck watched her walk into the night. The darkness outside didn't hinder her; she walked confidently down the path away from the plantation, the moonlight at her back. The next day, Oliver was completely healed.

Jackson had gathered a lot of his research from historical societies on the three islands. This account was written in *Gads Danske Magasin*, a Danish publication. It was the most convincing piece of writing he had found. The description also felt familiar somehow, as if someone had presented a blurry photo that, if squinted at just right, would reveal a face. When it finally clicked, the face staring back at Jackson was the ambassador's.

• • •

You can always go back, said the voice. In the darkness, eyes were on him, and out of that abyss came grasping hands.

• • •

Jackson woke up with a crick in his neck and a pounding in his head. He groaned and shifted on the living room couch, trying to find comfort for his old bones.

He could hear someone rummaging around in the kitchen.

"Hey," he called out.

The rummaging stopped. No one answered.

Jackson tried to sit but gave up. "Hello?" he called out again.

"Yes," said the person. It wasn't Aubrey.

He got up then, enlivened by his surprise upon hearing this other woman's voice.

"Morning," he said, stumbling through the greeting.

The woman came out from the kitchen and into the dining room. She had morning head, the frizzy mane wild around a freckled face, but it looked natural, almost deliberate. She smiled nervously and reached out to grasp Jackson's hand. He shook her hand and nodded, offering a smile of his own.

"I'm sorry. I didn't mean to wake you."

"You didn't."

"Alice." She pointed to herself in a way that Jackson found endearing.

"Jackson."

She smiled fully, showing teeth. The sun from the screen door caught her brown hair, and it flared red. Jackson had no trouble understanding what Aubrey saw in the woman. She had a warmth that complemented her obvious beauty. He buried a new upsurge of anger.

"I was going to make tea," she said. "You want some?"

"Okay."

She went back to the kitchen, and a few minutes later the kettle was screeching alive. She brought him a mug filled with water and a tea bag. At his request, she put two spoons of sugar in the mug.

He used to make the morning tea, he remembered. Aubrey

was not a cooker of breakfast. She liked to relax in the mornings. So he had taken up that responsibility. And now here was this woman, doing what he had done. He pictured himself throwing the mug to the floor, watching it break, looking up to see her astonished face. *You don't belong here*, he would say.

Instead, he thanked her. "Where's Aubrey?" he asked.

"On the porch. She likes sitting out there in the morning."

"To watch the sunrise," he added. How dare she try to tell him what his wife liked. His ex-wife, he corrected himself. She hadn't been his wife for a long while now. He took a sip of his tea.

She sat on the chair to one side of the couch. "I wish we had met sooner."

Jackson looked at her. She was smiling at him. Was she serious? Did she think this would be civil?

Then Jackson remembered Aubrey's words from last night. They came back to him between the throbs of headache. *We did a good thing. Let's keep doing a good thing.* He had so many voices in his head. They wanted so much from him, things he couldn't give.

Jackson didn't smile or answer Alice. Instead, he just stared at her for a long time. Alice returned the stare. The smile slowly left her face, but she seemed oddly at ease under his gaze, the nerves from before completely gone.

"She says she is happy," Jackson said after a time. "Are you happy, too?"

"She is an incredible woman." She still wasn't smiling. It was a statement without any hint of triviality. She was being sincere.

"She is," Jackson agreed. He forced a smile to his face—all he was capable of at the moment.

A smile bloomed on Alice's face in return, warm and true. It made him feel ashamed at the falseness of his own.

The sliding door creaked open, and Aubrey stepped in. She froze, watching both of them.

"Everything good?" she asked.

Alice turned from Jackson and smiled at Aubrey—a huge smile that wrinkled her eyes nearly closed. "Yes. Everything's good."

Jackson turned. He didn't smile but said, "No trouble here."

Aubrey's shoulders eased visibly. She walked into the kitchen to fix herself a cup of tea. Alice followed.

Jackson watched them in the kitchen, their voices low, uneasy smiles on their faces. He figured if he weren't here, they would be much different. They were containing themselves for his sake. He wished he were invisible then, so he could fully take in what he would likely never get to see: the two of them unhindered by his presence. It was an odd feeling, like stepping outside himself and looking back in. The view was different from this vantage point. He had mistaken his place in this story. The realization filled him with both terror and a little relief, the relief faint but present. He hoped the feeling would someday give him a measure of peace.

His phone buzzed on the living room table. Jackson picked it up hesitantly and then chuckled when he saw who it was. A text from his daughter, as if no time had passed at all, instead of actual days.

What's up?

LET THEM TALK

Derrick started deleting the hate emails. He could spot those at a glance: the reliance on caps lock, the multiple exclamation marks, the slurs hastily written in near-unintelligible text-speak. They were directed mostly at Mera, though every once in a while, one would be for him. The *traitor*.

The office was small. Derrick's desk was huddled against the south wall, and Mera's much larger desk was on the north, yet only a few feet separated them. The large east-facing windows emptied morning sunlight into the room. Illuminated dust particles danced in the still air. Between the desks, a chair sat empty, casting a long shadow.

As Derrick went through the emails, he could feel Mera's eyes on him. This he had gotten used to, even come to love.

The knock on the door was soft, spaced out. Derrick buzzed the visitor in. The door creaked open just a bit.

"Inside?" asked the man.

"Yes, come in, please," Derrick replied.

The man came in reluctantly. He was short and round, with scraggly facial hair. A yellow button-up stretched around his large gut, the bottom tucked forcefully into a pair of gray cargo pants. The man was drenched, his whole back dark with sweat. Derrick assumed he had been out there for a while, working up his courage, or else had walked some distance in the hot sun.

Mera looked at him but didn't get up from her chair. She was used to this: sweaty St. Thomian men, sometimes women, coming to meet her and give her a piece of their mind.

"Good day, sir," Derrick said, his voice as formal as he could manage. "Can I help you?"

The man's words came out slow. "I got a complaint to make."

"Okay," said Mera. "Let's hear it."

"One of your friend—them kill my dog. Rip him clean in two."

"And how do you know this?" she asked.

"I see it! How else?" He flinched, seeming to regret his forwardness.

Mera motioned for the man to sit in the chair in front of her desk. "How did this happen?" she asked.

The man's eyes darted from the chair to Mera, to Derrick. Derrick gave an affirming nod, and the man made his way hesitantly across the small office to the chair. "Well," he started, "the dog was on the porch with me, and one of your friend, them came strolling up the way. The dog start barking, as dogs do. He run up to meet the man." Derrick could see the man's glance shift from his lap to Mera's face. "Your friend reach down and grab the poor dog, tore his bottom half off and throw it on my porch. Then he keep on walking like nothing happen."

"So your dog wasn't on a leash?" she asked.

"He in the yard with me. What he need a leash for?"

"It sounds like he left your yard to attack this man."

"It weren't no man. It was a demon like you." Derrick and the man seemed equally surprised at his response. The man shrank back. "He was just trying to protect me," he added softly.

"And the *man* was just trying to protect himself. There is nothing I can do."

"But, Miss—"

"Isn't there a law about keeping pets on leashes?"

The man didn't answer. The silence stretched on.

"Well, then," Derrick said, ready to let the awkwardness end. "I think we are done here?"

The man got up and walked to the door. On the way out, he shot Derrick an evil look. Derrick pretended not to see the malice in his eyes. "Sorry, sir. Have a good day."

The man didn't say goodbye, just left. Derrick would hear another story through the grapevine soon—from Louie, probably—about the ambassador's assistant who did nothing to help his own people, the word "ambassador" oozing sarcasm and scorn.

Derrick went back to deleting emails. When he finished, he started on the voicemails that always stacked up after a long weekend. After removing the slanderous ones, he made the necessary appointments for those who wanted to meet the ambassador, talk to her, make their complaints. He would have to call them back, slip into his friendliest voice, and set up the appointments, trying his best not to let their animosity affect his cordiality.

As he listened to the voicemails, he looked at Mera. She was staring out the window, statuesque, her skin glistening in the natural light coming in. Brown human skin, like his. A clever trick, he thought.

Derrick finished the string of messages quickly. There would be no appointments to make. He settled into the silence between himself and his boss.

Derrick didn't mind Mera's silence. It felt like an old learned silence that seemed to stretch both backward and forward in time, drawing in and out like the tides. In the quiet, he imagined he could feel her silence on his skin, the essence of her solid and real, giving him goose pimples—like reading a poem and pulling something from it that wasn't on the page.

As he watched her, unmoving in the morning sun, her isolation became clear to him. Her difference. He recognized that she didn't fit, that she was an outsider even among her own people. All from the quiet. All from the feeling he got just sitting in the room with her. He recognized it in himself, too: his own isolation, his own difference. They were different. This was completely clear. But with Mera, he could just be what he was.

Not that he didn't have burning questions. Most days, Mera never moved from her chair. No one would come in, and Derrick would spend his time busying himself or appearing to be busy. When did she eat? He never saw her go out to lunch. He would take his break, and she barely said a word. And when he returned, she would be there.

And why be there when she could set up appointments from home or wherever and just come in when she needed to? Was it to appear available for the locals, to give them a sense of comfort that she would always be there to help them through their grievances? The last thing Derrick would describe Mera as was comforting. Not that he was complaining. The job paid really well. But why even have an assistant just to sort emails and voicemails? She could do that just as easily on her own. She wasn't doing anything, anyway. So why was he really here?

He had spent months thinking about this. It was the background noise in his head most days when he got restless. He had planned to ask any number of times, but he would look at her, and the courage would rush right out of him.

Today he would, he decided. He would ask. He wasn't letting another damn day slip by.

He opened his mouth to speak. Moments passed in that blanket of silence he couldn't breach. He closed his mouth again and turned back to his screen. He spent the next hour playing Tetris.

He tried again a few times, each time getting right to the edge of speech without crossing. Mera even looked over at him once, which made all the words fall right out of his head.

It was a few minutes before his lunch break when Derrick finally mustered up the courage. The words came out loud and cracked.

"Why did you take this job as an ambassador?" He cleared his throat.

Mera seemed to ignore the question at first, not even budging in acknowledgment of it. Derrick felt the sudden fear creep over him. Her kind was prickly, and the wrong words could land you in the hospital. Or worse. He swallowed hard and waited.

She turned. "I appointed myself to help ease our people into the assimilation process, get your people used to us."

"Assimilation? Do they even have any *interest* in assimilating?" Derrick hadn't kept an edge of disbelief from slipping into his tone, which he realized by the way she regarded him. A look that said, *I see you.* He held his breath.

"No, they don't. Not yet."

Derrick eased. "Then why do this? You can't help my people or give them justice. And your people are unwilling to change. Why take the abuse? Why accept the blame?" Any comments about her lack of approachability would go unspoken for now, he decided.

Mera's face remained impassive. "To teach a new lesson."

"What lesson?"

She moved only slightly, a tree in a weak wind. "Why did *you* take this job?"

"Because of the money. Highest-paying starting position on the island." This was *one* of the reasons Derrick took the job, but not the whole reason. He wouldn't be telling her that, either. Not now. "Why did you hire me?"

For the first time, Derrick saw a perceptible emotion visit Mera's face. Disappointment? About what, he could not imagine. She frowned, a soft exhalation escaping from between her lips. "You were to be my bridge. My bridge between worlds." And then she went back to her window, stiff, like an elder iguana perched on a branch.

He wanted to say something about this, but what? Feeling unsure of himself, he changed the subject. "Well, what do you do for fun?" He waited intently for her to come alive again, not really knowing where he was going with the conversation.

"For fun?"

"Yeah, for fun."

"I swim. I like the water." She was ready to return to her window.

"What about going to the club or the movies?"

"People are usually wary of me at night. And those things don't interest me."

Derrick ignored the first part. "Have you ever been to a club?"

"No."

"So how do you know they don't interest you?"

She gave him a look. Derrick decided to look back with the same intensity. He felt his arms tremble and his palms grow clammy. But he kept his face calm and friendly.

"You don't need to do something to know it is not for you," she said.

He remembered a conversation with his best friend, Louie, a Puerto Rican whose family had moved to the island a generation ago. He and Louie had often talked about Derrick's job and the people who would call and come in to complain. Louie would give him the latest gossip on how people felt about the ambassador and her assistant. It was always bad, of course.

On one occasion, Louie smiled and said, "You should take her out sometime. Then they'd *really* talk."

"Nah, dehman," Derrick had said. "Can't do that. These people would destroy me."

"No, they wouldn't. They gon' think you's her pet. And you already know how them aliens does go on when they lose a pet. Nobody gon' cross she. Not if they have a lick of preservation."

Derrick swallowed hard. He smiled at Mera, steeling himself. "Let me take you out," he said.

Surprise. *Real* surprise. "What?"

"Let me take you out. To a bar. Not a club."

Derrick observed Mera. He felt the pull of both attraction and fear, felt the sweat coming down from his hairline. He understood the fear. It was a sign of sanity. The attraction, however, he did not understand. Not fully.

"Come on, just once, as coworkers."

"I'm your boss."

"Is that a no, then?"

She considered him, her eyes lingering uncertainly on his. "Okay. When and where?"

"After work. Fat Turtle."

• • •

If Derrick was honest, he would have to admit that more than monetary need made him work for Mera.

He had spent his youth looking up at the stars. When he was ten, he made a habit of going out into the yard and peering up at the sky. He did this for hours, eyes glued to the slow-changing canvas of black specked with white, the island sky so clear that he was sure he could see every star in existence. It made him feel small, and everything around him trivial by comparison, a little ground of pepper in the sands of the universe. He would reach his hands up to the sky and squeeze his fingers into a fist, imagining that he pulled the stars down to him so that they knew he existed and he mattered.

Then, when the stars finally did come down, he was painfully disappointed. He was seventeen when the Ynaa arrived, and aside from the miracle cures and their deceptively human appearance, they seemed cold, *oppressive*. He felt inconsequential. A pepper grain in a beach of sand.

It took two years for him to become eligible to be the ambassador's assistant, and another two years to work up the courage. He had wanted the job because he was curious, but there was more to it than that.

He was sweaty the day of his interview, suffering from a case of nerves that could not be calmed. She didn't seem to notice. Her office was a tiny room crammed in a little corner of the Legislature—a reluctant gift from the governor of the Virgin Islands, though it was made explicitly clear to everyone that Mera would play no part in island politics. Derrick wondered how true that was, knowing that she and her kind had everything to do with the current politics of his little island world. But he didn't think about any of that stuff until after, none of the social and political aspects surrounding aliens from space with diplomatic immunity, none of the uproar over their appearance, or the suspicion about their gifts. And more personally, how his grandmother would react once she found out he was working for the devil.

Instead, Derrick spent most of the interview just staring awkwardly at her. There were questions, he was sure of it, and he had given short, inadequate answers. But he had come away only remembering that she had a really nice face, trick or not. Almost kind.

He also came away with that same feeling he had as a kid, out in the yard in front of his house, staring upward into the infinite black. He had that same vibrant emotion of feeling small yet hopeful. He desired to pull her from her heights, right down to his level, to cross the immeasurable distance between them.

She called him a few days later, thanking him for coming in, and gave him the job. She expressed her hope that it would work out. After months, he had been the only one to answer the ad. Filled with excitement, he accepted the job.

There was an inappropriateness to this excitement that felt shameful. This woman was not human. For a while, shame won out. But he had to admit—to himself, anyway—that he always desired to be her equal, to break the taboo that kept them at arm's length. The job was just the perfect excuse.

• • •

They left a bit early together, Mera not far behind him but keeping a little distance. Even with that, they caught confused and judgmental looks from the people they passed, a few from people he knew. He kept walking without a word. This was the way of it, no matter what. And Derrick wasn't trying too hard to hide the fact that they were leaving together.

The Legislature was on a small peninsula right up on the ocean, the building surrounded on three sides by parking lots, two of which hugged the water. Derrick and Mera walked around the back, where the lot turned to gravel and the cars lined the open edge. In some places, beyond the parked cars were rocks leading into the ocean waves; in other places, there was only a sudden dip into the sea.

Derrick was parked in the latter area and had to walk the small space between his old Honda and the ocean, the weak waves beating half-heartedly against the rocks below. When he reached the door, he stopped. Overhead, seagulls soared, their calls mixing with the distant honking of car horns. Out on the water, a pelican plunged from high up. Derrick watched it lift its head, a silver fish flapping in its beak for an instant before disappearing into its throat pouch. He still marveled at the sight.

As he turned back to the car door, he caught Mera observing him, and that sudden feeling of smallness returned. Did she see him the way he saw the pelican, as some lesser creature? Some quaint marvel?

Pushing the thought from his mind, he got into the car and unlocked the passenger side so Mera could get in. She opened the car door, its old hinges creaking, and got in without a word.

Derrick awkwardly moved all the junk near her feet onto the back seat. "Sorry about the mess."

Just then a group of people passed. Their voices were hushed, and their eyes were too deliberate in avoiding the car. Mera whipped the seat belt around her chest. The whir of the woven polyester unreeling, and the soft click of the metal tongue into the buckle were the only sounds in the quiet car.

"You're taking a real risk here," Mera said.

"What about you? Aren't you taking a risk?"

"If you mean socially, there is little risk for me. My people already see me as a *sselree*." Seeing Derrick's inquisitive stare, she added, "A lover of the weak."

So you are *an outsider*, he thought but didn't dare say. It was enough to know that he was right about her.

He knew of the Ynaa's famous arrogance, had known since he first saw one of them speak on television. "We will help you, and for it, you will give us a place among you," that one had said before waving the microphone away as if it were a pesky fly, the cameras flashing on his dark almost-human face. And in those words, Derrick had heard, *We will save you because you are weak, and we will take because we are strong.*

His phone rang. His ringtone was an old tune from a local reggae artist. "*Bat, bat, bat them off,*" the phone yelled, a racket of percussion and brass accompanying the vocals.

"Sorry, let me get this," he said, smiling.

It was his grandmother. "Bring me some cooked food, no?"

"Grams, I can't do that right now. I out with somebody."

"You'n tired gallivanting in the streets? Come quick, child."

"Grams—"

"I raise you up and you can't bring me a plate of food? Ungrateful children these days, I tell you."

"I'm a grown man, Grams."

Grandma chupsed her teeth, making a loud sucking sound through the phone. "Come on, child. I not feeling up to slaving at the stove."

"Fine. I gon' bring some ribs and rice from Texas Pit."

"Chicken."

"All right. Chicken."

• • •

Derrick stopped at Texas Pit, a food cart along the way, and then went up the hill to Upper John Donkoe, where he lived with Grams and his little sister. He raced up the narrow, winding roads as fast as he could, making the necessary hairpin turns to avoid flying off the soft shoulder. He got to a two-way road barely big enough for one car and had to squeeze past a Jeep. The low-hanging arms of trees reaching out into the road knocked against his car *rickety-tick-tick* as the driver's-side tires roughed it over soft earth and hard rocks.

He pulled into his driveway. "I'm really sorry about this. My grams—"

Mera waved him off in a surprisingly human way. "I'll be here."

Derrick grabbed the food and sprinted down the concrete stairs that led to their apartment. He met Grams on the porch. She sat staring out into the dense tree line in front of their apartment, her hand resting on the small coffee table beside her. She was in her nightgown, her wavy graying hair lank on her shoulders. Her thin lips were pursed. Something was wrong.

She barely looked up at him before saying, "So I heard about poor Mr. Anderson today."

"Who?"

"The man who came by your job. Poor man had to bury his dog in two pieces."

Derrick placed her food on the table. "How you know about that?"

"This island is thirty-two square miles of people talking. How could I not?"

"Did it get 'round that his dog wasn't on a leash? That it attacked that man and—"

"*Demon*," she said, cutting him off. "No man could tear a dog down the middle with their bare hands. Is a devil, he is."

"Grams, they're aliens."

"No such thing."

Derrick knew that it made no sense to argue. He could see the conversation in all its variations, and it would boil down to the simple truth that separated them. They each did not believe the other's version of the world. It wasn't something that could be resolved with talk.

"Okay, Grams. I have to go."

"I hope you not going out with that one from work."

Derrick didn't bother to ask how she knew. Grams had her spies, and even if she didn't, there was no shortage of people ready and willing to call her up and tell her what her grandson was up to every minute of the day. It could have been any of the people he passed as he left work, or any random person who peeped him on the way home. He had a feeling it was somebody from the Legislature, however, because of the timing of her call.

He tried to smile. "We're just going out to listen to some music, Grams."

Immediately, he wondered why he even answered.

"You best stay your butt in this house."

"Enjoy your food, Grams. I'll be back later tonight." He walked toward the stairs.

"Where you think you going?"

"Grams, I'm twenty-two years old. I going out."

"If you leave this house tonight, you better find yourself a new one in the morning."

Derrick knew his grandmother enough to know when she was serious. People like Grams did not back down from being challenged.

Still, he had already chosen long before this. He'd made a million decisions before this one, and they all pointed to Mera.

When he left, he could hear his grandmother yelling from the bottom of the stairs. "They *kill* people!" she was saying.

This was true. But maybe Mera would be different.

• • •

They drove down Waterfront, a four-lane street that cradled Charlotte Amalie Harbor, and the biggest thoroughfare on the island. The sky was mostly a creamy pink like the inside of a conch shell, a mist of orange against the horizon, edged with the purple tint of coming night. Streetlights as well as house lights dotted the hillside. The palm trees that lined the street every few feet swayed in the trade winds coming in from the sea. The Danish-style buildings along the harbor whizzed by, their arched doorways and red roofs reduced to dark blurs in the setting sun.

Derrick turned his phone to silent. He rolled the window down and took in the moment. The air was cool and salty, the breeze stroking his face as they sped along at forty miles per hour. Mera was quiet. Except for the unfocused image of her in his peripheral vision, it felt as if he were alone in the car. He didn't fill the void with words. He let the wind do the talking, its loud and endless breath filling the silence.

This was his island, a little green rock in the Caribbean Sea. And now it was hers, too. This woman with her dreads flowing down her back like cats' tails, brown skin like his. And beneath that, what was she? Not human. So close, but still not. And if he didn't care, what did that make him?

Derrick pulled into Yacht Haven Grande's parking lot. Yacht Haven was a private harbor for the rich, with a collection of high-end stores for tourists. Pristine white yachts bobbed side by side along the 180-foot concrete pier, their names etched in beautiful black letters on their sterns. The *Drifter. Wind Rider.* The *Blue Dolphin.*

Fat Turtle was one of several seaside bars right along that stretch of human excess. Derrick and Mera made their way past the Louis Vuitton store, Gucci, and Bad Ass Coffee. Then they were there.

The bar was filled with an older crowd—men and women in their late forties and fifties, who came in to unwind after work. A few groups of tourists were sprinkled throughout. As they walked up to the bar, Derrick met eyes with a black man with short, curly white hair, wearing a satin tropical shirt too colorful to be anything but a gimmick. No doubt a shuttle driver for tourists. Only taxi drivers and tourists wore shirts like that.

The man seemed to recognize Mera. Derrick avoided his glare.

They found a seat at the bar, and Derrick ordered them drinks. Passion-fruit Cruzan rum and cranberry for him, Heineken for her.

"Didn't think you would be a beer drinker."

"I'm not, really. Just try it on occasion."

"Can you get drunk?"

"Yes." She gave him a smile that surprised him.

"I would pay big dollars to see you drunk."

"Well, tonight will not be the night." She gave him another smile. This one stuck and lingered.

Was she flirting with him? He wasn't sure.

"I'm sorry," he said. "It is just hard for me to wrap my mind around what you are. I've never been able to."

"I'm not a demon."

"I know that."

"And I don't kill."

"I know."

"You want to ask me something, so ask it."

Derrick hesitated. He hadn't been thinking to ask her anything. Not right now, anyway. But he could guess at what she meant. He had wanted to ask Mera that question a hundred times. The Ynaa never gave a real answer, and he assumed that she would be no different.

"To teach," they would say when asked. "To teach the lesson."

Derrick remembered the one time he had seen with his own eyes the lesson being delivered. It had been late at night. He was leaving Shipwreck Tavern, a bar near Havensight Harbor, where the cruise ships came in to let off tourists. A man, drunk on his ass, stumbled into one of the Ynaa, cursing and pushing.

This one had towered over the drunk man. He had a hard

jawline and small eyes—perfectly human if you were drunk or
not paying attention, clearly Ynaa if you were aware of their
mannerisms. The Ynaa had wrinkled his nose and bared his teeth.
Animal rage, the first warning. The drunk man had stumbled
back and swore. "What the fuck you gon' do?" he said. A crowd
had gathered on the tavern balcony. They understood what was
going to happen.

Softly, the Ynaa placed his hand on the man's shoulder and
arm. Then his grip tightened and he pulled, tearing bone from
socket, meat from meat, blood spitting from the wound. It was so
fast. Only seconds. The Ynaa threw the man's arm down on the
ground, the splashy thud somehow audible amid the screams of
the crowd. Derrick had just stood there, a statue of himself. The
Ynaa, now covered in blood, continued walking as if nothing had
happened. By the time the ambulance came, the man had bled out.

"Why do the Ynaa kill without remorse?" Derrick asked.

The bartender heard the question and jerked back, suddenly
having business at the other end of the bar.

Mera nodded, paying no attention to the frightened bartender. "Our world was mostly water, spotted with large islands.
We had five intelligent races that competed for life, resources,
and territory, all of which became limited as the populations of
each grew beyond their shorelines. The growth was unsustainable
without conflict." Derrick watched Mera take a swig of her beer.
"We learned to do things to ensure *our* survival."

He waited, but she added nothing. Finally, he nodded. "I get
it," he said, hiding his bitterness.

When the Ynaa arrived, they came speaking human languages
and bearing gifts. Cures for diseases, energy technologies that
solved Earth's sustainability problems. In exchange for some time

on the planet. The nations of the world were awestruck, thankful, and afraid. They accepted the offer, knowing they had no choice and grateful for the opportunity to save face.

As another gesture of good faith, the Ynaa chose to stay where they landed. The United States, in continuance of its absentee landlordism over the Virgin Islands, wasted no time agreeing.

At first, the killings were few enough to occasion only quiet whisperings. "You hear about the killing up Ras Valley?" someone would say, and everyone would know who had done it, just by the details. Soon, though, the trend became more apparent and more terrifying. People spoke up. And then they would hear the Ynaa response. The lesson. People needed to learn the lesson, they'd say. They said this with the open condescension of adults speaking to little children.

"And you're different?" Derrick asked Mera.

"I've learned a new lesson."

"A *new* lesson," Derrick repeated, chewing on the words.

"Yes."

He leaned forward in his chair. "How did you acquire this new lesson, when the rest of your kind didn't?"

"My work with the humans."

"As ambassador?"

Mera nodded, her face tightening.

"You've only been here a few years. How did you learn so fast?"

She let the question hang. Then she smiled, the corners of her mouth curling slightly, the muscles in her face relaxing. Her eyes fixed on Derrick's, and he felt the tremble creeping up his spine. They both knew that the conversation had morphed into another one entirely.

"Your drink," Mera said. "It's empty. Should we have another?"

Derrick nodded and, controlling his body to affect calm, waved down the bartender. The bartender warily returned and took his request for another rum and cranberry. It came quick, lemon biting the top of the glass. He removed the lemon and gave it a good squeeze, dropped it into the glass, and stirred with the cocktail straw.

Mera requested another Heineken from the skittish woman, then returned her attentions to Derrick. "Tell me about the women you've dated," she said, smiling.

He blinked. What was really happening here? For the third time this evening, he considered Mera, trying to figure out how her mind worked.

"The women," Derrick repeated. He sucked at his drink through his cocktail straw. "What you want to know? My relationships were all failures."

"But there's more to the story than that, isn't there?"

"There was one who decided that my agnosticism was too big a deal to simply overlook. One who spent most of her time asking me to try coke she'd bought by sneaking cash from my wallet. One I couldn't bring myself to love and couldn't figure out why. One that cheated. One I cheated on. One that left the island because she hated the Ynaa and didn't want to be anywhere near you and hated me for not wanting that, too. That one was the most important one and the first of my many failed relationships."

As he talked, Mera leaned in.

"It doesn't really help that I am now working for one," Derrick said. "Not been having much luck with women after taking this job."

"I'm sorry to hear that," she said. She seemed genuine. She

was so close now that he could touch her if he moved at all. It was distracting.

Over the next half hour, Mera asked him about his family. Dad was dead, he told her. Mom left right after Lee was born—to Florida or the Bahamas, depending on who you asked. Been raised by Grams for most of his life. How did his dad die? Hypoglycemia. His sugar got too low; he slipped into a coma and never woke up. She apologized. He told her it was okay. It all happened a long time ago.

She touched his hand briefly.

"I want to know more about you," he said.

"Okay." Mera downed the last of her beer and waved down the shaky bartender again for another. "I'll tell you."

He started to ask a question, but she cut him off. Then she told him a story.

It was 1827, and an earthquake had hit St. Thomas. After the earthquake, the water rolled back past Water Island. In those days, people didn't know what they knew now. A couple of dozen people ran out into the ocean, picking up flapping fish with their hands and stuffing them into shirts, sacks, metal pails. One of those people was a middle-aged woman named Amelia, her name inspired by the town where she was born: Charlotte Amalie. She was a beautiful woman, Mera told him. Part Carib. Long dark hair to her back.

"When the water came back in, she was still out there," Mera said. "They pulled her drowned body from the water along with the rest."

As she told the story, tears filled Mera's eyes, making them look like deep puddles, the pupils glistening. Derrick placed his hand on hers. She accepted the gesture and blinked a few times. A tear broke free from her eye, drying on her cheek so fast it couldn't be normal. Derrick tried not to gasp but realized that his mouth was hanging open.

"Don't ask me anything else," Mera said. "For now."

"Okay." Derrick kept his hand on hers. Something had just happened. An exchange. They each had given a piece of themselves in sacrifice to the other. It was obvious that Mera had given more.

Derrick took a moment to look around the bar, realizing how close the two of them were, how completely he had lost awareness of his surroundings. People were sitting at the bar and at the tables around the bar, many of them making quick glances his way. Let them, he decided. He tried to locate the man from earlier, the one with the stereotypical shirt. He found the table, but the man sitting there was different. Same short gray hair, yes, but thinner in the face. A sharp jaw. Small dark eyes. An animal terror burned through Derrick.

Mera followed Derrick's eyes. When she saw the man, her body tensed, too. She placed two crisp hundred-dollar bills on the bar table—far more than enough for both of them. "Let's go."

• • •

Out in the parking lot, Mera picked up her pace, so fast that Derrick struggled to keep up. When they were only a few feet from his car, he heard someone call out to them.

"One moment," the voice said.

Mera didn't turn, so Derrick didn't, either. He picked up to a jog to narrow the distance between himself and Mera.

"Didn't you hear me?" the voice said just a moment later. But it was not right. It was too close. Derrick could hear it practically in his ear. He spun, and the face looking down at him smiled. Inches from him. Close enough to tear his arm from its socket.

Derrick stumbled back, losing his balance, falling. By the time he hit the ground, Mera had moved to stand between him and the man. An unreality swept over Derrick, as if he had plunged into a parallel universe that didn't make complete sense. Nothing he had ever seen moved that fast.

The tall man took a step back, putting his hands up. "It's okay," he said. "It's okay." His gesture looked so distinctly human, it sent Derrick scrabbling away from the two of them, crawling backward on all fours.

The Ynaa man stared down at Derrick, amused. "Didn't mean to frighten the poor boy, but you two were pretending not to hear me." The Ynaa's eyes stayed on Derrick, giving him no room to do anything but tremble. Something like recognition appeared on his face. "I've seen you before, haven't I?"

Mera stepped closer to the other Ynaa. Finally, he looked away from Derrick.

"Don't do this," Mera said, a strong edge in her voice.

"I'm Okaios," the Ynaa said, returning to Derrick. "A friend of your ambassador."

"Derrick," he said. *Your ambassador?* He tried standing, but his trembling legs didn't get the message the first time. He tried again and barely managed to find his footing.

"Pleasure to finally meet you," Okaios said. "Officially, I mean."

"Go to the car," Mera said. She didn't turn, so it took Derrick a moment to catch on that the command was meant for him. When he realized it, he turned to go.

"Wait," Okaios said, his voice deep, a growl to it. Derrick turned back to face him. "I have a question."

"You don't," Mera warned.

Okaios ignored her. "Did she also tell you why we're here?"

"What do you mean?"

Okaios tried to get closer to Derrick. Mera stood firm, blocking his way. "She's been so open tonight," he said. "So careless." The words hissed out in a way that could not be mistaken for human. "Just want to make sure she didn't betray herself. Betray us. Betray you."

"No, she didn't."

"Good," Okaios said. "I'm relieved. I would have had to keep that quiet if she had."

"Go," Mera said again.

This time, Okaios said nothing to stop Derrick from heading to his car. Derrick could hear them talking behind him, but not in words he could understand. The language hissed and whistled in ways unfamiliar to his ears. Still, he could hear the edge in Mera's voice. The threat. Okaios' threat had not been lost on him, either. He opened his car door and tried to shut them out of his experience. He wiped the sweat at his hairline.

Sitting there, he replayed the whole thing, trying to figure out the quick succession of events. He hadn't had time to process Mera's revelation before being launched into whatever had just happened. At the very least, he had avoided something terrible, even though he wasn't sure what or how. He wiped the sweat away again, but it was everywhere.

When the passenger door opened, Derrick watched Mera climb into the car. She looked calm mostly, but he thought he could detect an underlying emotional turmoil she was trying desperately to hide.

Without a word, Derrick started the car and pulled out of the parking lot.

• • •

The drive up to Mera's house passed mostly in silence except for Mera's directions, which were simple and curt.

When they pulled onto the dirt road up Northside, Derrick finally broached the subject. "What was that about?"

"You were there. I'm sure you can figure out enough of it on your own."

"I could, but—"

"I really can't tell you anything else." Then she repeated the phrase again: "You were there."

The car rocked and shook as Derrick drove over the uneven road. The headlights revealed just enough of what lay ahead that he could avoid the worst of the dips and bumps. Night bugs flew past the high beams.

The road swerved to the left, and a driveway revealed itself in the bush, a large house beyond. Derrick crawled to a stop and turned off the ignition.

"I knew him. I saw him kill someone once."

Mera nodded. She didn't seem surprised. "Then you know the danger."

"Now I do."

"I'm sorry."

"For what?"

"Risking you."

The lights in the front of the house came on, revealing varnished double doors. The government had leased the house to her, Derrick guessed. So far removed from the rest of her people on Water Island. Apart from the islanders, too. Hidden at the end of a long dirt road.

"It's okay," he said, understanding some of Mera's isolation. Like him, she didn't really belong anywhere—an island on an island.

She opened the car door and stepped out. Derrick did, too, deciding to walk her to her door. He didn't quite manage that. He followed behind her quietly, his head lowered. The night whipped at him, the air cool though somehow not welcoming. The trees and the bush around them rattled like a million tiny bones. Crickets chirred endlessly. The mountain frogs whistled like birds.

When Mera turned to tell him good night, Derrick leaned in and kissed her. He hadn't known he would do it. He just did. Nothing happened at first. He just closed his eyes and kept his lips on hers, not moving. He noted that her lips were unexpectedly soft and warm, but he was afraid to push any further. After what must have been a few seconds, Mera's hands reached up and tightened around his forearms. He felt his own heat rise, and he tried moving his lips to nudge hers into the dance of a long, passionate kiss. Her lips didn't oblige. With gentle force, she pushed him back. Though it was gentle, Derrick could do nothing to counter it. When he tested, it was like pushing against a brick wall.

Derrick opened his eyes and saw Mera staring at him. He could not read her expression. She gave nothing away.

"I'm sorry," he said.

Mera smiled. "Good night."

Derrick released the breath he hadn't realized he was holding. "Good night."

Mera took her hands from his forearms, and without any preamble, she turned, unlocked her door, and stepped inside.

In the long minutes that followed, Derrick stared at the door. The whirlwind of the night had finally numbed him to his own emotions. He couldn't tell what he actually felt, though he could sense the tumult within that would eventually come.

When he got home, he would have to take his stuff off his grandmother's porch. He would have to call up a friend— Louie, probably—and sleep on his couch for a few days while he found a place to live. There would be other consequences, too. Tomorrow, he would have to deal with the fallout from tonight. Eventually, everyone would know. People would talk. And other things would happen that he couldn't possibly imagine.

He told himself it would be okay in the end. Let it happen. Let them talk. He could live with that. His choices were his, and he had made them with both eyes open.

Walking back to his car, he thought of Mera, the heat of her lips still on his.

I'll be your bridge, he thought. *Between worlds.*

MOON

Aubrey was in her garden again. Weeding, by the look of it. Lee always got up the stairs before her grandmother, and most mornings she would meet Aubrey messing around in her garden, watering or weeding or cutting open a yellow passion fruit to eat.

Lee had been seeing a Jeep parked next to Aubrey's house. But she never saw who it belonged to, and she wasn't close enough to her landlord to ask. She knew that it wasn't Jackson. He had been gone for quite a while.

"Good morning," Lee said.

"Morning." Aubrey stood up for a moment to wipe some sweat from the back of her neck.

Lee watched her. She couldn't get over how young Aubrey looked, plucking the bits of bush away from her hibiscus tree every morning. She had the most beautifully muscled arms.

"You want some passion fruit?" Aubrey asked.

Aubrey was always offering passion fruit from her garden, or mangoes from the tree in the back of the house when they were in season. Lee would go downstairs with a bag full of mangoes that she would devour over the course of a week, only to get it refilled the next time she saw Aubrey.

"No thanks," Lee said.

Aubrey plucked one from the passion-fruit vine and walked over and handed it to her anyway. "Maybe you'll want it later," she said, smiling.

"Thanks," Lee said.

Just then, Derrick's busted-ass jalopy rolled down the steep hill. Lee looked at the ramshackle mess, still unwashed, still looking as if it had been built from scraps of rusty galvanize. Aubrey gently touched Lee on the shoulder and returned to her garden.

Derrick parked next to Grams' much better-looking electric hatchback. He had to be one of the few people on island still driving a gas car.

"You look like a boy," he said as he got out of the rattletrap.

Lee was wearing a New York Yankees cap and a fresh pair of Jordans. The baby-blue blouse of her uniform was half out in the back. Her skirt could be girlie if worn by someone else—anyone else—but on Lee, it might as well have been basketball shorts.

She never bothered to answer her brother when he pointed out her tomboyishness. She didn't sense judgment in his words—merely the playful teasing of an older brother.

"Where's Grams?" Derrick asked.

"Downstairs."

"You know what she's going to tell you when she gets up here, right?" He looked at her hat.

"Nothing as bad as what she is going to tell you."

Derrick laughed, but it sounded hollow. He seemed tired, weighed down. "I guess so."

There was the sound of a door closing, and Grams appeared at the foot of the stairs. She had a bunch of bags in her hand. Lee watched Derrick's body twitch with the impulse to help, but his feet stayed frozen in place.

What a punk, Lee thought but didn't say. She poked Derrick in the side.

"You need help?" he blurted out.

Grams continued climbing the stairs without answering.

Lee moved her eyes between the two, her stomach tightening. She wanted to head to the car, but she wasn't sure whose car to go to.

When Grams made it to the top of the stairs, she handed Lee one of her bags. She wore one of her long dresses, with red and blue floral patterns all over. It looked like a curtain, which it likely had been in a previous life. Grams took one look at Derrick before focusing on Lee's hat.

"Take that off." She didn't wait for Lee to do it herself. She took it off and stuffed it in her old worn black leather bag, cracked and sagging from years of overwork. "And tuck that shirt in."

Lee did as she was told.

"Grams," Derrick said. "Can we—"

Grams glared at him. "Lee, get in the car." She handed Lee two more bags.

Lee tried to move toward her grandmother's car, but Derrick grabbed her by the shoulder.

"I can give her a ride to school," he said.

Grams didn't even bother to look at him this time. "No need, boy. Lee, do what I told you."

Derrick's grip slackened, and Lee pulled away and headed to the car, still listening to the conversation.

"Can't we talk about this like adults?" Derrick was asking.

Lee stopped and turned toward them to see Grams' face. Grams' mouth was all twisted up in anger.

Grams sucked her teeth, walking toward the car. "Get in, Lee."

The car was locked, but Lee didn't bother saying anything. She wasn't going to be the one to incite any further rage. She simply waited for her grandmother to notice and let her in. When she finally did, Lee hopped in, stealing one last glance at Derrick's disappointed face.

• • •

Driving along Waterfront on the way to school, Grams talked at Lee about everything from her brother to the light bill. Lee mostly ignored her. She stared up at the early morning sky and the birds flying there. She followed a tern as it flew across Charlotte Amalie Harbor and out to sea. For a moment, she saw the Ynaa ship, quiet as sleep, perched on top of a thin white column, casting its long shadow over Water Island.

And that was when she thought of her.

• • •

Lee and Angela had been friends since third grade. They met at Ulla F. Muller Elementary School at the base of Contant Hill, where the kids wore blue-and-gray uniforms. From the beginning, they were close friends. Sleepovers on the weekends. Inseparable during school hours. Even joined majorettes together, teaching each other to twirl the baton in preparation for the Children's Parade during Carnival. Angela's mom got used to calling Lee her other daughter. Lee would smile big, remembering the mother she had lost so long ago.

As time went on, they stayed in each other's orbit. Depending on the year, the relationship changed. During eighth grade, when Lee was starting to look good to the boys, her curves filling out, Angela revolved around Lee, hoping some of that magic would rub off on her. By ninth grade, Angela had developed a wit about her and started spending more time doing her hair and putting on lip gloss, and by then the boys were singing a different tune. Lee took her place, a moon around Angela's world.

Lee thought it best to stay where she was. She got into sports. She started running all the guys on the basketball court, which pissed them off. "Fish!" they would yell out, and Lee would have to land them flat on their ass before a principal or a hall monitor showed up.

Angela got into older and older boys as time passed. And not the good boys, either. These boys were up to no good: getting into fights, tucking knives into their socks. While the entire world was getting its mind blown by the prospect of superior alien life, these guys were planting flags on school hallways for their respective motherlands. Savan. Ghettos. Round de' Field. There was a turf war every week. Angela started doing a dance between two guys from rival spots, and things really got scary.

"I don't get it," Lee said after one of Angela's beaus got stabbed in the side and had to be taken to Schneider Hospital.

"Don't get what?" Angela said, not really paying attention. Her eyes were swollen from crying, her lips quivering.

"These guys you keep dating." Lee gave her the look she always gave when she thought Angela was being stupid.

Angela looked back at her, and for a moment it seemed as if some good sense was waking up inside her. But that lasted only a moment. Angela chupsed her teeth. "Of course *you* wouldn't get it."

"Okay," Lee said, looking away as a strange heat erupted from out of nowhere inside her. She found it hard to breathe.

Tenth grade brought its share of boys. Lee made no protest. By midyear, Angela had shacked up with a senior. She was smitten. Head-over-heels gone for this guy. He had a car and everything. Had a habit of riding into school with his thousand-dollar speakers blasting. He was old, too. He had spent three years in twelfth grade. His name was Woody. The mythos around his name was true, Angela confirmed.

Lee started seeing Angela a lot less. During that time, Dian, a mutual friend of theirs, was pressing Lee hard, but Lee wasn't having it. She remained caught in Angela's orbit, an ever-diminishing sliver of moonlight in Angela's growing world.

• • •

"You gon' see the grave tonight?" Jessica asked.

They were sitting at their usual spot, a row of benches in an open area right next to the soda machines.

Lee nodded. "Yeah."

"When a'you going?" Milton asked, his face made up as if he'd been hit with a bad bellyache.

"Wait, that's tonight?" Dian asked.

Lee gave him the look of death.

"Yeah," Jessica answered, rubbing Lee's back. "I was going to go around six."

"Can't believe it been a year already," Dian said, trying to save himself. "That shit feels like it just happened."

"For fucking real," Milton agreed.

"A'you know if Ms. Robin hear you talking like that," Jessica cut in, "she would flip."

"Nobody cares how many flips Ms. Robin does," Dian said.

Lee rolled her eyes. It was lunchtime, and Ms. Robin was nowhere in sight—the perfect time for a guy like Dian to be as bad as he wanted to be.

Students were everywhere, but the noise didn't seem to register above a whisper for Lee. She was lost within herself. She felt like a piece of rock floating through space, unanchored and alone.

There was more talking, but Lee couldn't hear what was being said. Her heartbeat throbbed in her ears. People walked back and forth in front of them. A girl and a boy held hands and laughed. Dian and Milton continued to move their stupid mouths as Jessica rubbed her back. But Lee was there only in body, the rest of her lost in memories.

• • •

Two things had happened at the end of Lee's tenth-grade year. The first thing: a boy from her school got himself killed by one of the Ynaa, on Polyberg Hill, just yards from the high school gate.

Anthony, already known for getting into fights and being suspended frequently, spotted the female Ynaa ahead of him.

She was tall with dark mahogany skin, hair almost completely shaven clean. She looked human, of course—they had looked human from the moment they stepped out of their ships. But there was always a way about them that people could feel and understand if they were paying attention: the walk a little too stiff, the facial expressions a little late and too infrequent, the movements a little too slow.

Anthony, egged on by his friends, decided he would hit the Ynaa over the head with a stick. His friends watched as he ran up behind her, hitting her so hard in the back of the head that the stick splintered.

He tried to run away, but the Ynaa responded with unusual speed. She turned and hit Anthony in the face with the palm of her hand. There was a sound like a branch buried beneath a pile of wet leaves breaking underfoot, as Anthony's head snapped back past its natural limits. He fell, his head flailing loose as if attached by rubber tubing. Cars screeched to a stop as the whole street's breath caught. The trees stirred weakly in the breeze as screams rose up from the quiet.

The second thing: The night before Anthony's death, Woody was driving Angela home after a night of partying at Duffy's out in Red Hook. They were driving fast down Waterfront when Woody took his eyes off the road and missed a swerve in the street. The car went flying straight off the dock and into the water.

Woody freed himself and swam back up to the surface. Angela, however, was unable to unbuckle her seat belt. By the time they pulled the car out of the water, she was dead.

What made Lee beat Woody's ass when she saw him in KFC (thus earning her own personal ass-whupping from Grams) was not the fact that they had found alcohol and weed in his system. What had pushed her over the line was that she knew, no matter what anyone told her, no matter what Woody said, that Angela's precious boyfriend was hitting her when they drove off Waterfront. This she based on previous signs of abuse, specifically the whole week Angela took to wearing sunglasses despite the protests of all their teachers.

What made it worse was that Anthony's death, something Lee couldn't possibly have cared less about, had completely overshadowed Angela's accident. People took to the streets in protests. Anthony's mom was all over the local news, tears streaming down her face, begging for justice for her son. The governor put out letters in the *Daily News*, urging people to calm down while they made arrangements to mitigate the suffering of Anthony's family.

Mera, the alien ambassador, apologized for the "unfortunate chain of events," explaining that her people had a cultural tendency to respond with extreme violence when threatened. "This is not an excuse," she said, "but an explanation." Grams and Derrick argued every day because of Derrick's decision to work for said ambassador, neither of them budging an inch. The whole island echoed Grams' animosity. They began calling him "traitor."

And as all this happened, as people marched and cried and apologized and fought and prayed for the swift death of all Ynaa everywhere in the universe, Lee locked herself in her room, playing the scene over and over in her mind. Angela with her lungs on fire. Angela clawing at her seat belt. Angela screaming but not making a sound, the water bubbling out from her mouth as she struggled to free herself. Angela's eyes—as her heart stopped, as the nerve endings in her brain expelled their final burst—staring out into the dark. No light. No savior. No moon in her sky.

• • •

After school, Lee got a call from Grams. "I coming to get you, so stay at school."

Lee assumed this had something to do with preventing her from getting a ride with Derrick. "Grams, I going to Gela's grave today. I was going to get a ride home from Jessica."

Grams was quiet for a moment. "I need you home with me. I not feeling good."

"Today's the anniversary, Grams."

"I need you. Stay at school. I will be there soon." She hung up.

Lee was fuming, of course, but also not surprised. This was the kind of shit she expected from Grams. And though Lee was a second daughter to Angela's mom, that same fondness, that same unconditional love, had not been present between Angela and Grams. Grams had never approved of Angela. "She's rude," she would say. And when Angela got out of hand with the boys and the misbehavior at school, Grams' dislike grew boundless. In their ninth-grade year, Grams came home and caught Angela smoking a blunt on her porch, and whatever hope remained was dashed away in that instant.

Naturally, when Lee came to her crying, Grams gave her granddaughter some semblance of compassion. At the funeral, she hugged Lee the whole time. "It's going to be all right," she kept saying. "She's in heaven." Lee buried her distrust of those words. When she thought of heaven, all she could see now was spaceships. And even worse, she doubted that her grandmother thought heaven was the place Angela would go.

As if to confirm Lee's suspicions, Grams' sympathy for Angela soon evaporated. Before long, Lee's mourning became an annoyance. Five months after Angela's accident, Grams opened the door to Lee's room and stood there staring at her.

"You think you the only one ever lost somebody?"

Lee knew who Grams was talking about. Her son, Lee's father. And her husband, Lee's grandfather. Lee didn't bother to mention that she had lost them, too. "Leave me alone," Lee said, but Grams was already walking back down the hall to the living room. She had said all that she had to say.

Grams arrived at school fifteen minutes after Lee received the call to stay put. Lee could have pleaded, but pride held back the words. When they reached home, Grams sent Lee out into the yard to pick some lemongrass, to make bush tea. As she escaped into the yard, Lee cursed until the heat welling up inside her made her dizzy.

The yard was choked with dense bush in every direction. She had to push her way through to reach the lemongrass that grew wild next to a kasha bush. When she tried to rip some lemongrass out, her hand got cut on one of the thin, sharp kasha thorns.

"Shit!" Lee yelled. "I hate these fucking things."

"You okay, girl?" said someone. A woman, but not Grams. Or Aubrey. A light-skinned woman with curly hair stood on the upstairs porch—Aubrey's porch—staring down at her.

Lee stood there for a second, frozen.

"You were talking to yourself a second ago. Now you got nothing to say?"

Lee smiled, preparing her most polite self, grateful it was this woman and not her grandmother who had heard her cursing. "Sorry. I didn't see you there."

"No worries."

Lee's hand bled. She brought her hand to her lips and sucked at the blood. Then she realized what she was doing and stopped.

"I do that, too," the woman said, smiling. "You need a bandage or something. I'm sure Aubrey has some in the house."

"No. I'll get one when I go back inside."

The woman didn't say anything. She just stood there smiling, arms leaning on the porch railing.

Lee turned back to the lemongrass. This time, she managed to pull it right out without a problem. Derrick used to cut the kasha away from Grams' lemongrass. It would always come back after a month. Now Lee would have to do it.

Lee heard the sliding door open upstairs, and for a second, she thought the woman had gone back inside. Then she heard Aubrey's voice.

"Hey, what you doing out here?" Aubrey asked.

"Nothing, just talking to your neighbor's granddaughter," said the woman.

Lee turned just in time to see the woman kiss Aubrey on the cheek. Aubrey pulled back a little. She touched the woman on the arm, and the woman turned to look at Lee. Aubrey leaned on the railing, putting some space between them.

"Oh," said Aubrey. "I didn't know you'd be home so early."

"Grandma is feeling sick, so she came and picked me up right after school."

"You eat that passion fruit yet?"

The fruit was still in Lee's bag. She had forgotten all about it. "No. But I will when I get back inside."

"I'm Alice," said the woman, a little too loudly.

"She's a good friend," Aubrey said.

Lee smiled. Alice looked quickly over at Aubrey and then back at Lee. "How old are you?"

"Sixteen."

"A beautiful age. You must be driving the guys crazy."

"No, not really."

"We won't keep you," Aubrey said, touching Alice's arm again, quick and gentle. It reminded Lee of the way Aubrey had touched her shoulder that morning.

"Okay, okay," Alice said. "Get that cut bandaged up," she said to Lee. And they both went back inside.

Lee stood there staring up at the porch for a few seconds. Then she remembered Grams. She looked at the bunch of lemongrass in her hand. More than enough. She went back inside.

When Lee came in, she threw the lemongrass onto the counter before heading to the medicine cabinet for Band-Aids. After covering up the slice the kasha had given her, Lee returned to the kitchen, where she slammed some pots around before finding the right one and made her grandmother the bush tea, letting the tea leaves and lemongrass sit in the pot as the water boiled.

"Come rub me down," her grandmother said.

Lee stomped from the kitchen to the bathroom for the vapor rub and then to the living room, where her grandmother had kicked up on the couch in front of the TV.

Grams moaned in relief as Lee rubbed the overwhelmingly minty goop all over her chest. The icy burn filled her nostrils. As her grandmother groaned, Lee rolled her eyes, pushing back every wave of anger that threatened to rush forth into the world.

She brought the tea, and Grams drank it down with the

loudest slurps known to man before falling asleep on the couch. When Grams started to snore like a motorbike revving up, Lee knew that she was out cold.

The news played on the TV. The Ynaa had graciously given another piece of valuable technology: a solar cell 40 percent more efficient than the one humans currently possessed. This particular program did not sing praises. Some conservative talk-show host went on about how these supposed gifts were going to be used somehow to destroy everyone. He pointed to the fact that there were now over a dozen cases of contact violence as proof that the Ynaa meant to kill them all, proclaiming, "These 'gifts' are just to fatten us up for the slaughter."

Lee sat across from her grandmother, in an old leather chair, its arms cracked open to reveal the yellow flesh underneath. She dragged her fingers along the cracks, gently lifting the hard skin occasionally and pulling away little pieces of the hard brown leather. After about fifteen minutes of sitting and trying to figure out how one could ever fatten up a human for slaughter using solar technology, a thought came to her.

She opened her phone and went through her list of contacts. When she reached her brother's number, she pressed CALL.

"What's up, sis?"

"I need a ride to Gela's grave tonight. Can you come get me?"

For a moment, there was quiet at the other end of the line. "Grams know about this?"

"Does she need to?"

Another silence. "All right, what time?"

"In an hour," she said.

"An *hour*?" He sighed. "Okay. See you in a bit. And be ready."

Lee put down the phone and immediately walked over to

where her grandmother slept. She reached down into the bag next
to the couch and pulled out her hat.

• • •

Derrick arrived within an hour. As she walked up to the car, she
saw Mera sitting in the front seat. Mera turned and smiled. To
Lee, it was like watching a statue come to life.

"Hey, Lianna," Mera said. "How are you?"

"I'm good. You?"

"I'm all right."

The reply surprised Lee. It was such a human thing to say,
and it didn't seem to fit with her understanding of the Ynaa. To be
honest, any reply would have surprised her. "That's cool," Lee said
finally, not knowing what else to say, and got in the car.

"Strap in," Derrick said.

"Whatever, monkey brains," Lee said, folding her arms. She
looked out the window at what she now knew to be Alice's Jeep,
parked in the same spot.

Derrick chupsed his teeth and put the car in reverse. "You
welcome."

Lee had met the Ynaa ambassador only twice, both times
when Lee caught the bus up to the Legislature to wait for Derrick
to get off work. As she entered the office, Mera would smile and
say hello before getting back to whatever she did at her desk.

Lee would watch her.

When Mera moved, she seemed perfectly human. Not like
the others. She could have blended in wherever she went. She was
quiet, but that wasn't a big deal. Lee was quiet, too.

When Mera wasn't moving, however, it would get weird.

She'd get really still—so still, you couldn't even tell whether she was breathing.

Derrick had once let slip that he thought Mera was there before the ships came. How had she managed to fool anyone back then, sitting still like that?

Lee had asked once, after working up a sufficient degree of courage, "Did you used to do that when you were pretending to be human? Be still like that?"

Derrick had looked up from his work disapprovingly. "*Lee!*" he whispered.

Mera woke from her hibernation, and for a moment there was a flicker of surprise. "Yes." And after a moment's pause, "When I had to play dead."

"Oh," Lee said.

People had their theories about Derrick and Mera. Lee heard it from every direction. And worse, people were starting to ask her about it. "They work together," Lee told people. "That's all." But she had a brain. She knew that wasn't the whole story.

"You don't expect us to believe that," said two of her younger cousins after church one day.

"That's their business, not mine," Lee said, walking away.

"Derrick's behavior," Lee's grandmother had told her that same afternoon, "is an abomination. Unnatural!" Apparently, it was the talk of the congregation. There was always some shit the old heads at church were going on about.

Lee had heard that word a lot growing up: "unnatural." For many things. It hung oppressively over her. What was unnatural about loving someone? She never got a good answer on that. And as far as she knew, there weren't any scriptures condemning inter-planetary love affairs.

"You mind us waiting for Lee?" Derrick asked as he sped up the little hill in front of Grams' house.

"No," Mera answered. "Of course not."

Lee wished she could see Mera's face. She tried looking in the side mirror but could see only her shoulder.

"How you holding up, Lee?" Derrick asked.

"What you mean?" Lee asked back, playing with the bill of her Yankees cap.

"I'm sorry I didn't ask this morning. Didn't know it was a year already."

"Don't worry about it," Lee said. "Thanks for picking me up."

Lee glanced up to see Derrick looking at her through the rearview mirror. He was trying to read her face. She smiled and waved at him. He turned his attention back to the road.

"Grams see you when you leave the house?"

"Nah."

"She gon' lose her mind when she wake up and you'n home."

"Grams gon' be just fine."

"Hmm," Derrick said, nodding his head and pushing out his lips. "Okay. If you say so."

Lee rolled her eyes. "You worried what she gon' do when she finds out it was you who took me out the house?"

Derrick didn't say anything. He gripped the steering wheel tighter and flicked on the low beams. It was starting to get dark. Lee could look out the window and see the bats already in the darkening sky, swooping and swerving for their meal of mosquitoes and moths. She rolled down the window and felt the cool breeze hit her face. The wind blew into her ears, and it sounded like someone blowing into a microphone. Houses passed by on one side of the road, some still wearing blue tarps from Hurricane Irma. It had been years, and some people still had not fully recovered.

The car jerked to the right as Derrick swerved to miss a pothole at the last second. The road was filled with them. St. Thomas: pothole capital of the world. Even an alien invasion couldn't make her people get their act together.

Lee swore as Derrick swerved around another hole.

"The only time anybody drive in a straight line is when they're drunk," Derrick said.

"And when they beating up their girlfriend," Lee said quietly.

No one said anything for a long while. Lee waited for someone to speak into the mike, but there was only the wind against her ears, like the sound of distant rolling thunder.

• • •

"**H**ey," Derrick called as Lee was getting out of the car. "You need me to come with you?"

Lee looked at Mera, sitting motionless in the front seat. "Nah, I cool."

"Okay, well, we gon' be right here. Take your time."

Lee could see a small crowd already gathered by Angela's grave, and another, much larger one closer to the graveyard entrance. As she walked, she read names and dates off the graves. *Oliver Thomas. Died 1960. Michael Todman. August 2015. Rachel Aberdeen. 1945.*

Lee wondered how they made room for all the dead. The island had roughly fifty thousand people and only two decent-size graveyards. And centuries of dead folk. Soon, she imagined, they would have to stack people like dominoes. They had already done just that for family members. Some sites had three graves of concrete stacked one on top of the other. Lee wondered who would get the spot on top of Angela.

As she approached Angela's grave, she read the tombstone. *Angela Mary Gifford. May 28, 2023.* The words *Beloved Daughter* were etched in an attractive cursive into the gray marble tombstone. Below it, the carved outline of Angela's face. Two bouquets of flowers were right next to the tombstone, a framed picture of Lee and Angela smiling, cheek to cheek, beside the flowers. Five people were gathered at the grave. Milton, Dian, Jessica, Angela's mother, and a man next to her who must have been another family relative.

Lee smiled at Angela's mother. She only nodded and returned a brief smile, and then, as if Angela's tombstone were televising important moments of Angela's short life, her mother stared back down at the grave.

"Who's that with your brother over there?" Jessica asked.

Lee looked over in the direction of the car, as if she didn't know what Jessica was talking about. "Mera."

"Oh, snap," Dian said. He opened his mouth to say something else.

"If you like your teeth, you should keep it behind your lips," Lee warned.

"Yeah, yeah. Nice hat."

Lee didn't respond. Angela had apologized when she gave Lee the hat. It was a gift, and a symbol of turning over a new leaf. "I know I been distant lately," Angela had said. "I won't be anymore." She had died the following week. And all Lee had was this gift, the precursor to a stolen promise.

From her location, Lee could make out some of the people

over at the other graveside. She knew immediately that the larger group was there for Anthony's one-year anniversary. They were a day early. No doubt, there would be another, larger remembrance ceremony tomorrow. Someone sang an old church hymn Lee didn't recognize. But she did recognize the woman shaking in the arms of two men. Anthony's mother.

"You remember when Gela slapped that pahnah for lifting up her skirt?" Milton asked. "I swear, the whole of Building A heard that fetch."

"That slap was heard around the world, mehson," Dian said.

"Yeah, dehman." Milton's eyes had a faraway look. If Dian was hopelessly in love with Lee, Milton had it for Angela to the power of ten. "She was something else."

Lee looked up and saw that Angela's mother was watching her, the same old familiarity in her eyes. "Come here, daughter," she said finally. Lee went, and Ms. Gifford put her arms around her and began to cry.

A long moment of silence followed as Lee tried to find words to say that might ease her surrogate mother's pain. "I love you, Gela," Lee said loud enough to carry to Ms. Gifford's ears. "We miss you." Silently to herself, Lee said, "I love you more than you know."

A raspy rendition of "Amazing Grace" started up from the other crowd and carried on the wind.

Ms. Gifford held Lee tighter and trembled. Lee thought there was a message in that embrace that she could receive, so she found herself holding on tighter as well. It felt as natural as gravity.

Several minutes passed in that peaceful embrace.

A calm before a storm. Lee really shouldn't have been surprised when it ended.

When the singing from the other group cut off, replaced with the yelling of a dozen voices, Jessica was the first to turn. Her eyes widened. The chill of anticipation swept through Lee. Looking over Ms. Gifford's shoulder to the other crowd, she needed only a moment to put it together.

"Shit."

WHAT THE UNIVERSE UNDERSTANDS

This would be the second time Mera got herself killed. It was July 1792. Cane season.

Back when it was still the Danish Virgin Islands, Mera stood out on the sweltering fields of La Grande Princesse Plantation of St. Croix, cutting sugarcane with the other slaves.

She looked out over the plantation as she worked. The hot air above the ground created a mirage effect, a world underwater, the ground and sky swirling together. Tamarinds hung from the trees, roasting in their shells.

The sun-weathered slaves swung their sickles in rhythm. *Swash, swish, swash.* They sang along to the susurrant pulse, singing of places and lives past.

A baby cried. The child's mother worked across from Mera. The mother paused from her work to tend to the little boy resting near her on a piece of dried calfskin.

"Come here!" yelled the white bomba watching over their group. He motioned the woman over to him, curving his index finger like a coiling snake.

The mother went, staring up at him on his brown donkey.

"Why you keep messing with that baby?"

The mother was from an Akan tribe and only spoke Twi—a ship girl newly branded and seasoned. She stared up at him, frightened, saying nothing.

"Well?" he said, getting louder.

More nothing.

He sighed. "Turn around, then."

The other slaves in Mera's group continued their chanting song, their sickles moving in rhythm. But they kept their eyes on the bomba and the woman.

Whap! The whip hit her on the forearm. She turned immediately with a whimper, her back now facing the bomba. *Whap! Whap! Whap!* She fell to her knees wailing, her voice echoing over the vast fields of cane.

"Be quiet and get back to work!"

The woman understood "work." She got up, still moaning, and returned to her sickle. The sunbaked baby, as if inspired, joined his mother with a new bout of crying.

Perhaps it was the gnawing rage that threatened to consume Mera. She had watched too many similar beatings, seen too many broken bodies pulled from their beds before dawn by the steady bleat of the conch shell to spend their days, from sunrise to sunset, with their backs bent into the endless stalks of cane. Or perhaps it was the memory of Siba.

Mera dropped her sickle.

"Hey!" the bomba yelled.

She walked over to that bomba on his donkey.

"What you up to, girl?"

She kicked the donkey so hard in the ribs that it toppled over like a wooden chair caught in a strong wind, trapping the pot-bellied man beneath.

The bomba screamed out, but she shut him up quick. She stomped on his neck hard, crushing all the inner workings. He gurgled and spat blood; his eyes rolled back in his head. A gentle breeze filled the silence. Only the trees talked.

Then Mera walked off the field, past the astonished slaves and back to the slave village. She found her hut, with its wattle-and-daub walls and thatch roof, and stooped to get through the low doorway, disappearing into the dark, dirt-floored room within.

A little after noon, while some of the slaves were still on break, Mr. Schimmelmann came with ten angry white men and called Mera out of her little shanty.

"Get out here!" Mr. Schimmelmann yelled.

She came out fast enough, and they shackled her and carried her out to a big locust tree near the plantation's main road.

Mr. Schimmelmann's wife, the mistress of the plantation, was pregnant. He was not about to let any woman inspire an uprising, especially since his almost four hundred slaves outnumbered the whites twenty to one.

He ordered another slave driver—since the dead one had forfeited the pleasure—to give the woman two hundred lashes of the whip. This one was black. He kept looking back at Mr. Schimmelmann until the plantation owner angrily ordered him to whip her right away. The bomba quickly returned to Mera. She stood completely calm, as uninterested in the events as if she had no involvement in them at all. The bomba cracked the whip twenty times against her dark, naked back, each stroke more furious than the one before. But her skin did not break.

"*Obeah!*" said the bomba with the whip, panting like a winded dog.

"Witch!" another yelled, backing away a few steps.

A few men approached Mera at once. They stripped off the rest of her clothes and strung her up from the locust tree, wrapping the woven rope tight around her slender neck. Mera could feel the fibers as the rope tightened, a boa squeezing.

Several white men pulled her body up to a decent height and then tied the rope around the tree trunk.

Mera hung there with her feet swinging, her toes pointed and trying to touch the ground below. She watched the men as they continued to whip and curse her for her wickedness.

"Devil!" said Mr. Schimmelmann as he spat out dry bristles of sugarcane. Red-faced, he bit into the cane stalk again and chewed, subduing his nerves, beads of sweat collecting on his upper lip.

The plantation was in an uproar. Other slaves came to see the obeah woman who would not die. Two Yoruba tribeswomen conversed in excited whispers. The white men hooted and hollered. Schimmelmann's wife and daughters stayed inside their majestic plantation house, staring out from behind white-curtained windows.

Mera continued to watch the whole thing as if she weren't a part of it. At one point, she lifted her hands over her head and pulled herself up just enough to laugh at them. Eventually, she got bored and let her head hang off to the side. She closed her eyes and was very still. She didn't even bother to move as they continued to whip her.

Hours after sunset, when everyone had gone off to bed, she opened her eyes again. No one had dared pull her down. She lifted her hands over her head again and tore the rope. She landed on her feet and started walking down the dirt path to the sea, feeling the salt wind against her naked body.

She would have to repeat this process again. In a decade or two, she would go to another island and impersonate a slave fresh off the newest ship in from the West African coast.

• • •

When Mera came in to work the morning before she would accompany Derrick to the graveyard, he was not there.

She didn't think anything of it at first. But then an hour passed. She called him on his cell, but he didn't answer. She left him a voicemail.

Mera knew he was avoiding her. It was obvious why.

To pass the time, she busied herself answering calls and emails. The emails were easier to do. She gave carefully worded answers to people's concerns. Many were about the recent unrest. Protests were a regular occurrence now, coming up on the anniversary of a young boy who had been killed. Many of the people emailing the office wanted to be assured that the Ynaa would not react aggressively to the situation.

Mera lingered on one email in particular, from a mother of three boys. The woman begged Mera to speak on the behalf of humans, ask the Ynaa not to respond to the unrest by murdering any more young men.

My boys are good, she wrote. *They deserve a full life. All our boys do.* There was a message between the lines of her message: the acknowledgment that most of the killings by the Ynaa had been of men and boys, and the deeper acknowledgment that those killed had been the more aggressive of the locals, engaging in outright altercations with the Ynaa.

As Mera sat puzzling over a reply, she spoke through her mind to her reefs. They sang back in the language of information.

We're close, they were saying through a million points of data. *Very close.*

The reefs were the Ynaa's greatest technological accomplishment. Little superintelligent cybernetic cells, used in everything from the building of megastructures like their calcium carbonate cities and ships to the management of Ynaa physiology on the submicroscopic level.

Mera usually kept the link between herself and the reefs on throughout the day, pulling them to the front of her mind when necessary, pushing them to background noise when she needed. She had practiced this for hundreds of years, so that the habit had become second nature. She was good—better, she had learned, than any other Ynaa—when it came to this particular application of the reefs.

At her urging, the reefs relayed updates on the hundreds of thousands of test samples she had obtained during her time on Earth. Cells from several hundred species of animals, plants, and fungi. Samples of bacteria and viruses. Cells from humans, both healthy and not. Mera requested minor adjustments, poked at bits of data that looked promising, demanded further investigation from her reefs where there were gaps in knowledge. Her reefs obeyed, singing to her as they did the work. *Close*, they said. *So close.*

Mera pushed the reefs to the back of her consciousness. *I'll do my best*, she finally wrote in response to the woman. A bullshit reply. A nothing answer.

Mera knew that her best would not be good enough. She had been helpless to stop all the previous violence, unable to speak out against the Ynaa and unable to speak fully on behalf of the humans. In the beginning, Mera had used what little authority she had to negotiate for extensive background checks and heavy restrictions on officials and tourists visiting the territory. She'd exhausted the rest of her influence by limiting Ynaa movement to the three US Virgin Islands, a concession the Ynaa agreed to only because a high-profile incident might threaten their timetable.

Those early actions bore mixed fruit. The tourists proved to be well-behaved, since they could just leave and go home. But the people of the Virgin Islands, with little means to flee from the oppressive encroachment of the Ynaa, became the sacrifice for the larger peace she had worked to create.

If she replied to the woman by saying she would stop the Ynaa from acting against the locals, she would be lying. If she told the Ynaa to stay away from them, she'd be dismissed. She could force it, but then she would lose her position, replaced with someone who would be less sympathetic to the locals. She could hold her research ransom, but it was too late for that to do any more than slow the Ynaa down. They would discover it anyway, but the delay could spell disaster for the humans, and again, she would be removed, unable to help in whatever little ways she now could.

She might warn the locals to stay in their homes, but that would have unintended consequences, causing greater unrest. The governor was terribly corrupt and couldn't be trusted, nor could she expect him to create any policy that wouldn't imme-diately implode on everyone, human and Ynaa alike. In truth, she could do nothing but watch the train hurtle down the track and hope for better judgment to prevail. Or finish her work fast enough for the Ynaa not to do any more significant harm. She focused on this last option but worried that she would be too late.

And yes, she had tried one other thing: Derrick. But that, in the end, was a foolish idea.

Telepathically, Mera found Derrick's vitals through the reefs she had passed to him when he kissed her. His readings came back to her, steady and safe. Alive. She would keep it that way.

Come with me, a voice in her mind said.

Mera ignored it.

● ● ●

In the summer of 1732, Mera walked out of the bush of St. John to begin her first life as a slave.

The Jerson plantage had two windmills, a curing house, and a boiling house near the cane fields that stretched across the St. John hillside for a couple of hundred acres. The fields sloped down a little despite some effort to level the land. At the top of a small hill stood the plantage house. It wasn't large, but it was neat and well kept, with a foundation of stone and mortar. A winding dirt path led up to the place. Downwind from the plantage house was the slave village—several rows of little thatch-roofed huts.

A minor plantage of insignificant status. Mera had studied the place and found it perfect for her purposes.

A bomba spotted her first as she approached the Jerson plantage from the far edge of the cane field. By the look of puzzlement on his face, he knew that she wasn't one of theirs. He hurried out to meet her.

"Stop," he said in Danish. "Where did you come from?"

Mera said nothing.

"Who do you belong to?"

Mera watched the man. He paused to wipe sweat from his forehead. He let his gaze travel the length of her. She was completely and deliberately naked, not wanting to offer any hints of her origin. The bomba seemed to have no feeling about this. He noted each part of her body distantly.

"Come with me," he ordered. Mera obeyed.

He walked her up the path to the main house. There Mr. Jerson sat in the shade, fanning himself with a plantain leaf. He was a long, thin man with a severe jawline and large, quick-moving eyes. He watched her up and down as well, smiling at her, his eyes lingering on her breasts.

"She is a fine one," he said, also in Danish. "She'll be good for work."

"She won't tell me where she's from," the bomba said.

"How did you get here?" Mr. Jerson asked her directly.

Mera said nothing. She lowered her head.

"Don't look away, dare girl." He got up from his chair and lifted her face to him. "You a maroon from another plantage?"

Mera shook her head, contorting her face in practiced confusion.

Mr. Jerson laughed. "It's all right. Don't get yourself worked up."

"Maybe she from off a shipwreck?" the bomba asked.

Mr. Jerson turned his quick eyes on the bomba. The man lowered his head and took a step back, slumping noticeably and drawing in his shoulders.

"Maybe she did," Mr. Jerson said after a long moment. "Is that right, girl? Did you survive a shipwreck?" Mr. Jerson mimed the movement of swimming through water. His long arms swooped in and out of imaginary waves.

Summer in the Caribbean also meant hurricane season. Mera knew that ships occasionally got trapped in storms or seized by pirates. She smiled sheepishly and nodded at Mr. Jerson.

The plantage master seemed satisfied. He grinned, revealing a missing tooth on the bottom row. "See to it that this one gets situated. Get her working in the fields as soon as you can. I'll visit her later to see about her progress."

The bomba grabbed her by the hand, still making himself small, and quietly took her away.

That night, Mr. Jerson visited Mera in her slave quarters. He knelt down to enter and called out to the dark.

"Are you awake?"

Mera watched him quietly. She got into a sitting position on the slab of wood she used as a bed, figuring he would hear the movement and know that she was awake. She was staying in the quarters of a man who had recently died. She could still smell the sickly stench of the disease that took him.

"Don't be afraid," he said, his voice low and gentle, as if he were coaxing a child.

"I've been thinking," he said, still gently, "you had no chains on you."

Mera could see perfectly in the dark, but even blind, she could have smelled Mr. Jerson. His scent was a sharp mix of sweat and alcohol, so close to her now in the small dirt-floored room. She readied herself.

"You must have been a prize to your last masters, or you'd

have been in chains. No branding scars, so you must have had a sheltered life. Also means you must speak at least one European language. Am I wrong?"

He placed his hand on her shoulder. She took a quick breath and tried to shift her body away from him as if frightened.

"Shhh." He put his hand to his lips. Mera could see the sweat beading on his face.

"Don't worry," he said, this time in English. "I will take care of you—give you a good life as a loyal slave. Put you up in the house to make and serve food. Your life will be easier."

Not a bad guess. The English colony of Tortola was only ten miles away.

"What do you want?" Mera asked in English.

"Nothing at all," Mr. Jerson said, smiling at his great intuition. "Just to be near you."

His hand went from her shoulder down to her thighs. He applied gentle force, trying to ease her legs apart.

Mera grabbed his hand and squeezed so fast, he had no time to protect against it.

He sucked in air sharply. "What are you doing?"

"I won't be going to your house," she said in Danish. "I'll be staying here. And you won't be causing me any trouble. You won't tell anyone about this or you'll be dead before you say the words."

"What!" he screamed out. He tried to get his hand free. Mera held firm. "How are you doing this?" he asked.

Mera spoke to the reefs on the surface of her skin. They passed to him, biting at the free nerve endings in his arm. For the next hour, Mera educated Mr. Jerson on her capacity to keep promises.

• • •

A little after noon, someone knocked on Mera's office door. She knew that it wasn't Derrick.

When she buzzed the caller in, the door inched open, and a tall man stepped through.

"Afternoon, as the locals say." The man smiled and let the door close behind him. "What? No pet today?" He frowned. "I was looking forward to seeing him."

Mera recognized the man, of course, though he had changed his face since they last met. Several hours or days in a reef bath could make an Ynaa into anything he desired.

Underneath the disguise, the real Okaios still hid, the whorl of tentacles on his head stretched and flattened against his skull, his paper-thin gills visible only as creases on his neck, the claws shaved down and tucked under rounded, deceptively delicate fingers. At night, he might still glow a little if excited enough. As he walked casually across the room, Mera noted how natural he seemed in the disguise. So many of the other Ynaa looked uncomfortable, as if they had been stuffed inside a jar and wrapped up tight. Okaios looked quite comfortable in his human skin.

He sat in the chair in the middle of the room and crossed his legs, his right foot kicking out in a sort of rhythmic tic. His pointed dress shoes shone.

"Nice office," he said.

Mera nodded. She let her eyes travel across the small room before settling on Okaios again. "What do you want?"

"To talk about recent events," he said. "The protests—"

"You caused."

"I didn't kill that poor young boy." Despite his sorrowful delivery, Okaios smiled.

"But you were the first. *You* set the trend."

He put his hand to his chest as if hit by a bullet. He grimaced just a little, as if in pain, but his lips curled with self-satisfied pride.

"And how many times since then have you killed?" Mera added. She let the question rest at his feet.

Okaios didn't bother to pick it up. "Father O wants to know what you are doing to rectify the situation," he said in Ynaa. His voice came out low and whistling—layers of sound on top of each other. Impossible to do with just human vocal chords.

"And he needed you to come here to ask me that?" Mera said, code-switching as well.

"No," he said, tapping his hand against his creased dress pants, matching his rhythmic kicking. "But you were on my way."

Ohoim didn't need a lackey to tell Mera anything. He could do it over any number of communication channels without ever leaving Ship Tower. She bristled inside at whatever mind game Okaios was playing.

"I can't do anything," she said, switching back to English. "My hands are tied. I can't make the Ynaa behave. I can't make the humans any less angry at your misbehavior."

"*My misbehavior?*" Okaios said. "You don't mean just me, right?" He stopped kicking, his body going completely still. Then, with an exaggerated gasp, "Ah! You mean *us*. The Ynaa. Not *you*."

Mera checked herself before speaking, drawing in her anger before it could betray her. "I am not the problem."

"You're not?" Okaios asked, as if the statement were the most revelatory thing he had heard all day. "So carting that boy around to bars has no effect on current tensions?"

"Not nearly as much as tearing someone's dog in half."

Okaios ignored the accusation, instead turning his head to look at Derrick's empty desk. "Where is the boy, anyway?"

"He has the day off."

Okaios turned serious. "You shouldn't lie. It's easy enough for me to find out."

Mera watched him for a moment, noting the faraway look in his eyes, as if his attention had been drawn elsewhere. Fear rushed through her. She tried not to change her facial expression. She kept her breath even and slow, whispering through her mind to her reefs.

"You know how many planets I've been to?" Okaios asked, the faraway expression breaking just long enough for him to dart an intense look at Mera—an indication that he truly wanted her to answer the question.

"Dozens," Mera guessed. *Safe*, the reefs replied. *Safe*.

"Hundreds," Okaios corrected. He mouthed something that was barely words at all, and then added, "Most of them empty. A few populated only with microbes and other simple life."

Mera tightened her fists. No way to know anything but *safe*. No way to get there if a threat sat lurking where her reefs couldn't see, but close enough to do harm. She felt the rocks rushing toward her, the froth of violent waves.

"You know how many I found with abundant life like the rock you found here?"

"None," Mera said, holding her voice back from shaking.

"Two. And you know what I did?"

Mera sensed he didn't need an answer, so she waited.

"I collected samples. I did my research. So I could find *Yn Altaa*. The one true goal. *Yn Altaa*," he repeated, almost singing the words. "I spent one thousand combined years on those rocks. And nothing. Nothing at all."

Mera thumped her finger on the desk. She whispered again and again. *Safe* came back, over and over.

"How many planets have you been to?" he asked.

"One."

"Just one."

"I got lucky."

"Not yet. There's still time to fuck it up." Whatever he was doing, Okaios stopped. He refocused on Mera and smiled. "I'm not who you should worry about," he said. "I'm a friend."

Mera watched him. *Alive*, the reefs said.

"Hurry up and finish your work before the universe notices what we're doing here," he said, standing up. "The enemy's eyes are on us."

Mera followed him as he walked to the door and opened it.

"And be careful with that pet of yours," he added right before slipping out. "This world is filled with fragile things."

When the door closed, Mera got up. She grabbed her keys and waited the appropriate number of minutes. Then she left the office. As she walked to her car, she texted Derrick again.

I'm coming.

• • •

For the first few months, Mera kept to herself, trying not to make Mr. Jerson any uneasier than he already was. The man spent a lot more time inside the main house since their encounter, and

Mera didn't want to frighten him further and risk getting him replaced by someone she couldn't control as easily.

She also didn't want to develop relationships with fellow slaves. Her ability to mimic a human seemed to be holding, but taking on a particular background and wearing it convincingly would be trickier.

Still, despite her efforts to hide out, she aroused the interest of some of her fellow field slaves. Men, mostly. And one in particular, who, she knew, would eventually introduce himself.

During the midmorning break, he approached her as she ate.

"Where are you from?" he asked in his native Twi.

She considered him but kept quiet, eating a bit of boiled plantain from her clay bowl. She didn't like the stuff and would sneak away at night to get fish from the sea, but she had to keep up appearances.

The man waited patiently, watching her eat. He held his bowl of salt herring and sweet potato in his hand, paying no attention to it. After a while, he said, "Not Akwamu, then. Adampe?"

"Yes," Mera replied in Adampe.

He watched her longer than the comfortable span for humans. "Are you telling the truth?" he asked in Adampe, careful not to sound accusatory.

"I am," she said, mimicking the language from her study of it. "Though I was taken when I was very young. I don't remember my time there, but my mother has kept the tongue."

"And where is she now?"

"Gone."

He chewed on her answer and seemed to decide not to press further.

Mera knew his tongue, too, but decided it best not to fabricate a story that he could easily dismantle with knowledge unknown to her. She worried that this ruse wouldn't last long, either, but she had already committed. There was something she liked about the man. Perhaps it was his confidence, the gentle, assured way he approached her, with both respect and a direct- ness she found atypical of the humans she had studied. He was an Akwamu noble, she was sure. He had taken the time to learn the tongues of nearby tribes. He himself might have had slaves from those tribes.

"You know Danish, then?" he asked in Danish, although with a heavy accent.

"I do," Mera answered, accenting her own Danish just a little.

He smiled at her. Apparently, she had passed the test. "May I eat with you?"

Mera didn't answer right away, considering the situation again. It would be dangerous to develop a relationship with this man. But it would also be advantageous. She could learn more things in actual interaction than by piecing them together through distant observation. A calculated risk, and a necessary one.

She nodded, and he sat beside her.

• • •

Following protocol, Mera had sent regular updates to the Ynaa. Physical and genetic descriptions of the planet's diverse life, human cultures, and a few of their languages—everything she could gather about the world, along with her own thoughts about the creatures living on it. Mera had spent most of her time in the Caribbean, particularly in what would become the US Virgin Islands, but she had sent dozens of stealth probes all over the planet to monitor other locations and collect biosamples. As a result, she knew more about the world than any human living on it. She was familiar with the humans' defenses, knew many of their secrets.

Something Mera had sent to the Ynaa—perhaps many things—had piqued her people's interest. When five hundred Ynaa arrived in a midclass research ship, Mera was just as surprised as the humans.

Of course she had asked why they came, but the answer was unsatisfying.

"To make sure you don't betray us," Ohoim had said.

"Why would I betray you?"

"Time away has a negative effect on some Ynaa."

As expected, he did not explain what he meant, but Mera understood the danger of seeming too attached to the humans. She had her fears confirmed when she learned of Okaios tailing her the other night. Their conversation today had made it clear.

When Mera knocked, Jackson took a few minutes to open the door. She could hear movement inside the house—two pairs of feet rushing back and forth, the soft closing of a door.

The door opened, and he seemed genuinely surprised to see her. "I'm sorry. Wasn't expecting anyone. Fell asleep on the couch." He smiled, a bead of sweat moving down the side of his face.

Mera smiled back. "No problem." She watched him coolly.

"Oh," he said, "come in." He made space for her to pass through the doorway. She did, and he closed the door behind her.

"I'm sorry for the mess," he said, motioning her to the couch. There were empty beer bottles on the table, and two that still had beer in them, the outsides of the glass sweating with condensation. "You know how it is," he said, and then laughed. "Well, maybe you don't, but my house is always cleaner when I know in advance that I will be entertaining."

Mera smiled and sat on the couch. "I understand. Don't worry."

Jackson sat on a seat across from her. He looked nervous. "I wanted to apologize about, well ..." He trailed off, looking at her.

She gave him a smile. "It is okay. You didn't hurt anyone." *Even better, you didn't hurt yourself.*

"I'm sorry anyway," he said.

Mera kept the smile but offered no further reply.

"So what brings the ambassador to this lowly doorstep?" he said, easing back in his chair.

"I was looking for Derrick."

"Oh, yes," he said. "I know him. Wonderful young man. Good head on his shoulders. But what brings you *here?*"

Mera looked at the two bottles on the table. She also let her eyes wander to the dress shoes against the living room wall, and the bedspread on the arm of the couch. "He told me he was staying here," she said finally.

She watched what he would do next. He couldn't deny that Derrick was staying here; the evidence that he'd had company was everywhere. Nor could he challenge her on her statement. To do that, he would have to acknowledge that he had talked to Derrick about her, knew why she was here, and had prepped for her visit.

"He's out at the moment," Jackson said, a resigned shrug punctuating the words.

"Okay," Mera said. She got up. "Well, when he comes in, can you tell him I need to talk to him? He's not been answering his phone."

"That's weird," Jackson said. "I'll be sure to tell him you stopped by."

Mera walked to the door, Jackson following. She lingered, looking down the hall to the closed door at the end. Jackson took the bait, turning to look. When he saw the door still closed, he looked back at her, relief on his face. He twitched a little when he saw that she had been watching him.

Not giving him a moment to catch himself, she leaned in. Jackson twitched again like a cornered mouse. Her voice low, Mera said, "When he is ready to talk and not hide, he knows how to reach me."

Jackson jerked his head up and down in overeager acknowledgment. Mera left, not wasting any more of either his time or hers.

Twenty minutes later, while sitting at a stoplight, she got a text.

Where are you?

She smiled. Finally, Derrick had retrieved his good sense. She texted back.

By Emancipation Garden

Okay. I'll meet you there.

• • •

Siba woke up in a cold sweat. Mera reached out to touch his face, his sweat dampening her fingers. Even in the dark, she could see his wide eyes.

"What are you?" he asked.

Mera noted the *what*, not *who*.

She had been intrigued by the superstition of humans. Something strange came into their periphery, and they were ready to get on their knees and worship it—or run screaming. Apparently, Siba tended toward the latter.

Mera looked at him for a long time, not knowing what to say. What *could* she say? She couldn't talk away superstition. She couldn't reason with a mind unready for reason.

She smiled. "I am someone who cares about you."

Siba didn't say anything. He stayed frozen in place, his wild eyes staring at nothing. Only then did she realize that he was sleep-talking. Nonetheless, he seemed comforted by her words. His eyes closed, and his body relaxed. She put her hand on his chest. Some warmth had returned. She gently nudged him back to lying down. They had put pieces of cloth over the wooden slab to provide more softness. She bunched up some of the cloth and placed it under his head.

Siba woke up like this sometimes, but this was the first time that his blind horror had been directed at her specifically. Usually, he woke and screamed out the name of his wife and son. He had lost them back in Great Accra when the Akyem, Ga, and Kyerepong tribes took the city.

The Akwamu had risen to prominence as middlemen between the Danish and the other tribes. As their power grew, they abused it more and more, selling members of weaker tribes into slavery for more wealth and influence. They made enemies. Eventually, their enemies gave back to the Akwamu in kind, sacking their city, beheading their king, and selling their prince, Aquashi, to slavers. Siba and his family were sold, too. Siba and Prince Aquashi survived the journey to St. John. His wife and son died on the passage. Mera never asked the details of their death.

When Mera heard Siba begin to snore, she answered his question. She told him where she came from, about the bone pits and Ynaa Sky. She told him why she was here, that she had come in search of the one thing: *Yn Altaa*. And she told him her true name. After she was finished, she listened to his breathing.

Physically, Siba was a slender man. A gentle man. Mera could have destroyed him in an instant. It seemed a little odd that she was attracted to him. It was how *whole* he felt, how complete. A deep world inside him, more important than any outward strength. She watched him for a time, observing the quiet movements of his body. When she had taken in enough of him, she lay down next to him and went to sleep.

Over the next few months, a lot changed. A crushing drought passed over the island. St. John had had trouble with maroons for years, but the drought made it worse. Slaves were running off into the bush to fend for themselves. Every night, Mera could hear the tribal drums, announcing the comings and goings of maroon groups.

Many of the maroons lived at the abandoned Vessup plantage on the northwest side of the island. Another camp had been established at Waterlemon Bay Estate to the northeast.

At first, Siba showed no interest in joining the maroons. But then Prince Aquashi escaped his enslavement at Estate Adrian and disappeared into the bush. One night before bed, Siba told Mera of Aquashi's escape. He said it in such a way that she sensed some significance to it, the beginning of something, though he didn't say what. When Siba started hoarding food and sneaking out at night, she didn't ask why, because she knew the answer.

Then the proclamation from St. Thomas came to the ears of the slaves: runaways would be punished severely. Most maroons would lose a leg, but the ringleaders would be broken on the wheel, each bone of their body crushed by the executioner's hammer.

Word traveled to the plantations of St. John and then to the maroons in the bush. They beat their drums endlessly. And then everything changed. Siba argued with Mera every night. He wanted to leave for the bush. She urged him to reconsider.

"You're asking me to betray my king."

"Your king is dead. You don't owe his son anything."

"He is king now."

"No, he is not. The land you once ruled is far away from here. He rules over nothing now but water-starved bush."

Siba glared at her. He sat up and moved away from her. "You have no right. You are not one of us."

Mera could see him staring blindly in her direction. The crickets and night birds played their songs to the darkness outside.

"Siba …"

He didn't let her finish. He got up and left the hut. Outside in the crisp night air, he stood alone, staring into the trees and darkness beyond them. It was late. No drums played in the distance. Mera watched him from the stooped entryway of their hut. She didn't approach.

A few days later, the drums played for Siba—a summoning by his king.

"Will you come?" he asked.

Mera shook her head.

Siba didn't bother trying to convince her. He nodded, tears in his eyes, genuine hurt on his face. Then he left. He walked into the darkness, and the drums carried him away.

• • •

Emancipation Garden wasn't very big, but it had history. On one end of the park was a copper statue of a shirtless black man, a conch shell to his mouth, his puffed cheeks blowing. On the other end was a replica of the Liberty Bell atop a base of mortared stone. A bust of Danish king Christian V stood at the center of a bed of red flowers. Etched into a commemorative plaque was the date of emancipation: JULY 3, 1848.

The park, located across from the Legislature, was frequented by young people, tourists, pigeons, wild chickens, and the island's homeless. On this afternoon, schoolchildren were still hanging around in the park, their uniforms still on, though many of them had untucked their shirts from their pants and skirts.

"I was upset," Derrick was saying. They sat on a bench, Derrick's body tilted toward hers. He wore a plain blue T-shirt, which seemed a little jarring to Mera since she had only seen him in dress shirts.

Mera didn't say anything in response to the confession. She knew he had been upset.

"It's difficult," he continued, looking down and then away from her, "since you have all the power here."

"Do I?" Mera asked. She considered the statement, not entirely sure what he meant by it.

"Yes," he said, not seeming to realize that his words needed more clarification.

"I don't understand."

"A symptom of your power."

Mera felt something rile up under her skin. The words chafed against her, waking her from her numbness. "I'm sorry," she said. "I shouldn't have agreed to go out with you to begin with. It was inappropriate."

Derrick laughed bitterly.

A feral chicken pecked at something in the dirt near Mera's feet. She let it get close. Over the long years, she had raised a few chickens for their eggs. She remembered her first chickens, from the garden she shared with Siba.

"What am I to you?" Derrick asked.

Mera cycled through a few answers to the question. Finding no good response, she settled on a terrible one. "A valuable assistant."

The flare of anger on Derrick's face confirmed whatever he had been thinking.

"A tool," he sneered. "I'm a good tool."

Mera said nothing.

"And now you've closed off any possibility of me being more."

"It's dangerous."

"You've told me that already." Derrick stood up, spooking the chicken. A homeless man sitting on a bench stared at them.

They had been lucky so far. Except for the homeless man, no one was really paying attention to them. Now Mera saw the schoolchildren look their way. They recognized her at once. One of the kids, a tall boy, actually took a couple of steps back. A girl's eyes went wide before she caught herself and looked away.

The group of five started whispering, careful to keep their eyes and faces averted. Mera could hear them even from this far off. "That's the ambassador." "We should go." "Who that with her?" "The traitor. Yeah, that him right there." "How she letting him raise his voice to her like that?" "I heard they kill people for shit like that."

One of the kids caught her eye. "She looking. Oh, no. We should go." And then they all left the park.

As all this happened, Mera had said nothing to Derrick. When she returned her attention to him, he was watching her.

"There are people who might hurt you to hurt me," she said. "We have to restrict our relationship to the office."

"You said that already, too."

"Some of the Ynaa see my weakness. They might decide to *teach* me through you."

"Without provocation?"

"We've been known to interpret abstract threats as concrete ones."

"My life is mine," Derrick said.

"That doesn't mean I'm going to let you throw it away."

Derrick folded his arms. An impasse. Mera let the silence rest.

The day before, Derrick had asked her again to go out. She had refused. When he responded with "maybe next time," Mera clarified. No, she would never go out with him again. He hadn't said anything then, just gathered his things and left, looking wounded. She felt bad about it, but not enough to change her mind. She reserved the right to make that decision. She had never agreed to anything beyond that one night.

When Derrick spoke again, it was barely above a whisper. "I have feelings for you. Do you have feelings for me?"

He met her eyes so intensely, she almost looked away. When she didn't say anything, he stepped a little closer to her and repeated the question, his voice even lower than before. Mera was still sitting, so she had to crane her neck up a little to look him in the face. A crown of leaves shifted above him, the wind spurring them to life. The park had all but emptied while they talked, even the homeless man choosing to move on to a safer locale. The chicken had drifted back over toward them, however, pecking at the dirt again, clucking quietly to itself.

Derrick waited, his expression not angry or prodding. He just looked resigned, shifting his weight from one leg to the other. He maintained a respectable distance, choosing not to step any closer to her.

"I don't," Mera answered.

Derrick nodded, his face unchanging. "Okay," he said, sitting down beside her. Again, Mera let the silence rest between them.

Minutes passed without either of them saying anything. Mera watched the chicken peck at bits of discarded orange peel. In her nose, she smelled coppery blood. In her ears, the ocean crashed.

Derrick's phone rang. He looked down, checking the name, and then answered.

"What's up, sis?"

Mera tried not to listen to what Lee was saying.

"Grams know about this?"

Derrick's face hardened for a moment. His shoulders tensed. Mera watched.

He let out a sigh. "All right, what time?" he asked. He paused and listened. "'Kay, see you in a bit."

Derrick hung up. Then he turned to Mera. "I got to pick up my sister for this thing."

She nodded. "I figured that out."

"Will you come?"

"What?"

"Will you come with me?"

Mera blinked. "Why?"

"There's something else I want to ask you."

Mera tried to read Derrick's face, but he gave nothing away. After a moment, she relented. "Okay. Just this last time."

• • •

The insurrection began with Sodtman's plantation, in the early morning hours of November 23, 1733.

Sodtman woke at the yell of a slave. The Dane rushed outside with his gun, only to be seized from behind by several maroons. They disarmed him and dragged him back inside. They all gathered in the dining hall and set Sodtman on top of the strong mahogany table at the heart of the room. The maroons ordered the house slaves to light candles. Two maroons held his stepdaughter. Heat hung all around them, the air ripe with the stench of unwashed bodies and terror.

The maroons asked him to dance. When he refused, they sliced at his legs with sharpened cutlasses. His blood leaked all over the mahogany table. Enlivened by his screams, they crowded in, hacking deeper into his legs, his arms, his sides. His young stepdaughter watched his blood paint the room. She screamed and fainted.

Finishing him off was only a formality. They removed his head. Quietly, the two maroons held their hands to the stepdaughter's mouth, pinning her body to the floor. She woke up kicking. It didn't take long for her to stop.

At the same time, several maroons approached the island's military outpost, disguised as bearers carrying bundles of firewood. The men at the outpost, not suspecting a thing, let them in. The maroons took cutlasses from their bundles and went to work on the soldiers.

On the north side of the island, the maroons followed the path from plantation to plantation, killing every white person they could find. A mother was hacked to death, a newborn in her arms. Someone lifted the screaming baby from the bloody mass and swung it by the feet against the stone wall, the wet thud ending the baby's cries.

Loyal slaves either fled or died with their masters. A doctor was spared, along with his two sons. Another man was given clemency because he was well liked. In the south, many of the slaveholders, warned in advance of the carnage, had time to flee.

Women and children were transported to a cay off the coast, to protect them from the maroons, who had no boats to pursue them with. The remaining white men, forty in all, fortified themselves at the Durloo plantation, which had several cannons. Twenty-five faithful slaves were given guns to guard the plantation and protect their masters. The maroons, lacking the necessary weapons, failed to seize the plantation. And so the rebellion had ended in a stalemate.

Mera heard all this at a distance. She heard the two cannons fire when the maroons took the outpost. She knew from the unease of the other slaves that the rebellion had begun, but her plantation ran as usual for most of the first day even after Mr. Jerson and his family slipped quietly away.

By the next day, many of the slaves had wandered off to join their preferred group of maroons, had run off into the bush to hide, or had tried to join the men defending the Durloo plantation. Mera stayed where she was. She tended her garden as best she could, and slept in her hut. She carried on as if nothing was happening. She whispered to the reefs in her ship to be ready for her return.

Siba came to her two nights later. The scent of him announced his presence. He was unwashed, his skin covered in dirt. Blood was on his hands.

"Come here," Mera told him, and he obeyed.

He didn't talk. He only shook in her arms. She didn't need to ask him what had happened. His body spoke the words.

"I won't go with you," she reminded him. "But you can come here when you need me."

He made a noise, a small one that trapped itself in his throat.

It took him a long time to fall asleep, but at last his shaking subsided to heavy, even breaths. A few times through the night, he startled awake for a moment, but Mera would whisper to him that it was all right and that she was there and he was safe, and he would drift off again.

She never told him that she loved him. She regretted that very much.

•   •   •

"I'm sorry about the crowd," Derrick said. "I didn't expect so many people to be here."

They were parked in an area between the two sides of Western Cemetery. The small pathway barely amounted to a road, but several cars were parked along it. A large gumbo-limbo tree grew out of the dirt to one side of the path, fused to the walled entrance on one side of the graveyard. Derrick was parked at the end of the path, near the road.

Behind her, Mera heard the quiet roar of passing cars. In the graveyard, she saw Lee standing over her friend's grave. Several people were standing with her. A larger group, maybe two dozen, crowded around another grave. They stood much closer to the path than Lee and her companions. Mera could hear a woman sob. People continued to trickle toward the larger crowd.

Derrick hadn't said anything to Mera during the drive to pick up his sister. After Lee got in the car, Mera hadn't expected him to broach the subject. But now they were alone again. She shifted her attention to him. He was looking ahead, staring at the back of the car parked in front of him.

"I know you can't tell me why you're here," Derrick said. He hesitated, finding his words. "But can you tell me when you'll leave?"

"Very soon," Mera answered. Two men walked past the car, and she watched them take the path in the direction of the large crowd. When they were about halfway there, one looked back.

"You leaving with the others?" Derrick asked.

"Probably."

"But you don't have to?"

Mera shook her head. He was circling around something. She waited for him to spiral down into the real question.

Derrick took a deep breath and said, "Could you take me to Ganymede?"

Mera shifted back her attention to his face. He looked serious.

"Just to see it," he added. "I've always wanted to go there. Since I was a boy."

"*That's* what you wanted to ask me?" Mera smiled, showing teeth. "Okay. When all this is over, I'll take you to Ganymede."

Derrick didn't look satisfied.

She continued to wait, listening to someone sing "Amazing Grace." The beautiful voice, a woman's, swelled with passion, the edges of it breaking off in anguish.

When Derrick's words finally came, they tumbled out all at once. "This job is much more than what's on paper. I've accepted that. I've stayed on, knowing that. I'm sorry I overstepped boundaries, and I'm okay if we don't develop a true friendship. But I don't want to pretend anymore like all I'm here to do is answer your emails. If you want to build a bridge, this needs to be more. Even if my title doesn't change, the way you treat me must.

"I know you have to make decisions. But don't base your decisions on what you think I can or can't handle. Please give me the full respect of an equal. Make your decisions based on what *you* can handle."

Derrick opened his mouth as if to add more and then stopped. He had raised his voice a little at the end—not in anger, but with passion. Now he forced that passion back down, causing his body to shudder just a little.

The words had been heavily accented with St. Thomian vowels, the dropping of *t*'s and *g*'s at the ends of words. He didn't slip into St. Thomian grammar, however—a habit he never indulged in her presence. On one hand, it was a gesture of professionalism; St. Thomians commonly maintained a standard version of their English in professional settings. But it was also an indicator that Mera was an outsider. She was not one of them and would never be.

And she had long ago lost the feeling of belonging among the Ynaa. In truth, she belonged nowhere, and now she had brought someone else into that space with her. And in that space, she had created a microcosm of the outside: the Ynaa above, the human below.

"I'm sorry," she said, looking at him. "I was wrong."

"We both were," he said, staring back, intensity in his eyes.

They didn't notice the song cut off and the crowd start to disperse. Hearing yelling, Mera finally shifted her attention just in time to notice part of the crowd spill out from the graveyard, filling the space that the cars hadn't taken up. She watched a young man boldly pick up a stone from the edge of the path.

"Derrick, get down!"

Mera reached to open the car door. If she could get to the man, disarm him and put him to sleep, perhaps she could quash what was to come. But he hurled the stone before she got out of the car. Mera turned back, the door already slightly open.

Phantom blood wet her face. Gasping, she blinked the memory away.

Too late. She had just enough time to see Derrick staring stun-faced as the windshield shattered. She stiffened as the rock hit him. He grunted and fell back in his chair, sliding down in his seat. His head cocked to one side; his eyes rolled back in his head.

Mera flung the car door open. She moved faster than she should toward the young man. He was already bending down for another rock. As he stood up, she caught his arm and pulled the rock from his hand. She threw him into the surging crowd, knocking the front line back. Many of them scattered, while a few stood frozen in fear.

"Get back!" she yelled. It came out low and gravelly, like a growl.

A man knelt down and pulled the young man back. The frozen people in the crowd fell back as well. From a safer distance, people yelled at Mera. "You don't belong here." "You kill his brother." "Go away. Leave us alone." "You devils." "You demons." "His brother is dead. His brother is *dead*."

Lee approached Mera from the side. Mera whirled on her and stopped herself inches from the girl's throat.

Lee didn't flinch from the narrowly avoided attack. "Is Derrick okay?"

Mera looked back at the car, the broken windshield. "Help me get him in the passenger's seat."

A few small stones peppered the car as Mera and Lee returned to it. They got Derrick into the passenger's seat. Mera put her hands on him, releasing as many reefs as she could. Blood was pouring from the wound in his forehead, covering his eyes, nose, and mouth. Lee buckled him in and took off her shirt, wrapping it around his head.

Mera started the car as Lee hopped in the back, her chest and bra stained with Derrick's blood.

They reversed out into the street as stones continued to pop and patter against Derrick's car. An SUV honked furiously, almost rear-ending them.

"Come with me," Mera said as the tires squealed in forward drive. She had lost track of time and space. In her frantic perception, the world ahead looked like ocean, the road like rocks jutting out of a white sea.

• • •

The rebellion lasted six months. In that time, two Danish attempts to retake the island failed, along with one British attempt. The maroons were adept at guerrilla warfare, but they had neither the strategy nor the weaponry to seize Durloo or to fully engage the better-armed Europeans.

In May, the French came to the aid of the Danish, with a

ship of two hundred Frenchmen and a free-Negro corps perfectly capable of hunting the maroons through the bush.

Unlike the Danes and British before them, the French were systematic and ruthless. For a month, it was an extended cat-and-mouse game: the maroons fleeing, the Frenchmen and free Negroes pursuing.

A few weeks in, the French began to find bodies. Maroons had begun killing themselves as their desperation turned to despair. The French cut men, women, and children down from trees or collected the bodies of maroons who had shot themselves with their remaining bullets.

Ram's Head Peninsula was a particularly attractive destination—a cliff face that gave cornered maroons a final escape into the sea. Located on the south side of the island, the area was frequented by torrents of wind that threatened to toss a careless person into the rocks two hundred feet below. A part of this cliff face resembled the head of a ram, horns and all—something a suicidal maroon could catch a glimpse of on his way down.

Mera tracked Siba to this spot, ahead of the pursuing Frenchmen. When she found him, he was alone. The smell of death hung in the air. Not far away, two women had hanged themselves. The bush was littered with the corpses of the hopeless, who had sought death to avoid a worse one.

Siba stood near the edge of the cliff, his gun pointing down the path where the Frenchmen would arrive.

When he saw Mera, tears came to his eyes. "My wife," he called to her in his delusion. He had been gone for over a week. To be with his king, he had said. His king was not with him now, having chosen to flee with others into the bush. Siba was tasked with keeping the Frenchmen at bay.

The shouts of a dozen men rang out as they came up the path.

"Don't do this," Mera said. "I can take you to the sea. I can protect you." Waiting under the water was her small ship. "I can take you home," she said, grabbing his arm. "To Great Accra."

"My home is gone," he said. "My king is here. I must protect him."

Mera shook her head. She came close. The wind gusted loudly, straining even her superior hearing. She held his shoulders and squeezed them harder than she intended. "I do not understand this. Don't you want to live?"

She saw in his eyes hope mixed with hopelessness. She couldn't understand it. His eyes were those of a madman.

"Come with me," Siba said. He had stepped closer to the edge now, and Mera, finding herself suddenly repulsed by him and afraid, had let him.

To ward off the enemy, she said a mantra in her mind: *Never do the universe's work. Live to spite it. Live against all else.*

Siba put his hand out to her, his eyes wild. "Come with me," he said again. "To the other life."

"There is nothing else," she said. "Only here, now." She stepped away from him again. She had forgotten her plan to take him with her. She was confused, frustrated, and terrified. She had never felt this way before.

He looked past her, to where the men approached.

Mera turned to see the men pointing their weapons at them, yelling, their voices muffled and distant in the angry wind.

She turned to look at Siba, and he, too, had his weapon pointed.

"No!" she yelled through the wind.

Too late. She felt the blood wet her face. Siba fell backward, where there was no land to catch him. On instinct alone, Mera leaped after him. Again the universe conspired against her. Gravity kept him ahead of her. The jagged rocks jutting from the white foam of the crashing waves rushed up to meet them both, Siba arriving first. Mera could only watch as his spine cracked. She whimpered as his head shattered into a plume of blood and bits. The next wave crashed, carrying the body away.

When Mera hit the rocks, her reefs protected her. She rolled off into the water. As she sank under the surface, she could see Siba, the blood spreading around him like a dark cape.

She pushed herself to him and cradled his body in hers as the blood surrounded them both. She allowed herself to cry then, but her tears were indistinguishable from the blood and the water. Around them, a congregation of drowned maroons swayed and weaved like stalks of seaweed in the current.

• • •

Months later, when Mera resurfaced on St. Thomas, she learned that the great king Aquashi had been captured by the French, each bone in his body broken on the wheel, his head removed after death and impaled as a warning to other slaves.

She visited his head one night. Below it, in Danish, was a plaque written in blood: *There are no more slave kings. Only masters.*

• • •

Mera and Lee were sitting beside Derrick's bed when he finally opened his eyes.

"Hey, monkey brains," Lee said. "Good thing you wake up, 'cause I was about to get some ice water."

Derrick smiled and looked to Mera as if awaiting a smart remark from her as well. She kept her mouth closed. Gone was the earlier frenzy she had lost herself in. Instead, she presented as her usual calm self, though her stomach felt tight and her teeth ground together. It was not much of a disguise for her inner turmoil if Derrick knew what to look for.

He touched her hand, revealing that the disguise was as weak as she imagined. Mera felt the impulse to pull away, but she didn't follow it. The storm inside her spun furiously.

"What happened?" Derrick asked.

"You were hit in the head," Mera replied.

"There was a riot at the graveyard," Lee added. "A bunch of people visiting Tony's grave." She didn't need to explain further.

Derrick nodded, seeming to understand the whole context. "Graveyards are dangerous places."

"You should get some more sleep," Mera insisted. The reefs she had put into his body were still working to heal him. She controlled their work, since he didn't have the ability to control them himself.

"I'm not going to sleep," Derrick said stubbornly. "I want to know what else happ—"

Mera sent a command to the reefs, and they put him to sleep in the middle of his protest.

"What the hell was that?" Lee asked.

"Don't worry," Mera said. "He will heal better while sleeping."

"That's not what I asked," Lee said, glaring.

Mera watched her calmly in return. "It's an Ynaa drug," she said, opting for a simple explanation. "It will not harm him."

"It better not."

"You need me to take you back to your grandmother's?"

"I'm not leaving him here alone with you."

Mera smiled, pleased to see that boldness was a Reed family trait. "Okay," she said, getting up. "Watch him. You can take the room next door if you get tired."

In the doorway, she risked one more look at Derrick. He slept peacefully, as if he had not been awake only moments before. Satisfied, she left the room.

• • •

When Mera was young, her mother took her to see the Pits of Yn.

It was down on the Sa's surface, far beneath the floating city of Ynaa Sky. Mera had never gone to Yn or any of the other large islands of Sa. Her mother told her this was where the other races lived. The weaker races.

Her mother sang to the reefs on the walls of their ship. The walls disappeared, billions of tiny eyes reflecting back to them the world they were descending into. Mera could see the sky outside, the ocean beneath, as if they were standing in midair.

Ynaa Sky, above them to the west, shone with her pearly blue-white walls swirling up to high pointed spires. Blue-white calcium-carbonate ships soared around Ynaa Sky like birds.

Below them to the east, Ynaa Water reached out of the ocean with large spiky red, blue, and green limbs, a rainbow tree bustling with activity. Under the water's surface, a coral metropolis descended all the way to the ocean floor. A family of brown-backed fera swam nearby, the vast shadow of their bodies clearly visible in the midday sun, their tall fins cleaving the surface and trailing white foam.

In front of their ship, Yn revealed itself. They had not strayed too far from their home island. The large green back of Yn rose from the deep ocean as their small ship came down from the clouds of upper Sa. The island rose high above the ocean on this side, a cliff of smooth dark stone reaching up to an elevated plateau.

As they passed over the green trees of their old home, her mother told her the story she had heard a hundred times in Ynaa Sky.

"A long time ago, our people were almost destroyed by a large flood. The great waters of Sa rose and drove us inland, where there were beasts we had not encountered before. Back then, our people lived on the border of the land and sea. We had never encountered the deep jungle."

Mera could see the green trees stretching out to the horizon. She knew she had come from an island like this, but had not been aware that it was so large. From this height, she could see pockets of large flowers, their petals massive and drooping. Large canai dipped down into the flowers' throats, feeding from them with long tubular tongues. The hair on their backs and wings undulated, and the tips of their wings glowed like dying embers.

"Whatever these beasts were," her mother continued, "it didn't take long for us to understand the danger. They hunted us at night. They dragged us away to their lairs. They ate us. We could hear them eating us."

Mera felt frightened. She hadn't felt frightened by the story in a long time.

Her mother continued, the tendrils of her head dancing to

her words. The streaks of orange below her black eyes woke and widened, spreading their fire. "We sat stupidly for a long time in that horror, until we decided that this was a lesson we needed to learn. The only lesson."

"I don't believe you," Mera said. "It's just a story."

Her mother hissed through sharp teeth. She put a cold hand on Mera's back. Her sharp nails pinched a little, but Mera didn't dare show intimidation.

"I used to believe it was a myth, too. A story to scare children, to convince them of why so many of us left Sa for the black sea, in search of the one thing. But then I saw the bones."

It didn't happen right away. Her mother, Ssasharen, had no trouble waiting in the silence until it did. Before long, the trees fell away abruptly. In their place were pits dug into the red earth. Mera could not see how deep they were, because they were filled with bones—huge bones, the ribs of monsters Mera had never seen in Ynaa Sky. Purple vines coiled around the yellowed bones like remnants of ancient skin.

"It wasn't as long ago as you would think, Ssasmeran," her mother said. "And they aren't the only bones down there."

As they got close, Mera could see the little ones, too. She recognized some of the twisted shapes. The long backs of the Angaars. The broad skulls of the Mndei. Dead races of Sa who had come into conflict with the Ynaa during the Sa Expansion. Races that had left their home islands to make bigger maps, only to meet their end. Mera had heard those stories, too. Now she was looking at their bones.

"So we could be safe," her mother said as if in response to the unvoiced question. Her nails dug deeper. Mera felt her face flare from the pain, her stripes pulsing.

"To continue," her mother said. "Because if we hadn't done what we did, *we* would be in those pits, with purple vines choking our bones." Her mother released her. "We had no choice. The universe understands only strength."

As Mera lay in bed, she repeated her mother's words in her mind, comparing them to what she believed now. That world, that version of herself, felt like a lifetime ago. How much had changed since then? Mera had spent more time on Earth than on Sa. Even at the time, the Ynaa had changed their physiology. They were no longer the smaller, weaker version of themselves that came out of the jungle. Mera had gone further. She had become an entirely different race, the reefs' alterations to her body far more extensive than the superficial changes to her brethren.

Back then, her mother's words had felt so powerful, so important.

Mera knew better now.

She had seen her own strength fail. She had clung to Siba's corpse in a coffin of salt and water. She had arrived too late to save Amelia from the wave that swept her away. She had nearly lost Derrick while sitting right next to him.

The universe didn't care about strength. It didn't care about anything. Indifference looked like malice to creatures with something to lose.

Mera sat up in bed, the large house set out before her, quiet like a pit of bones. She got up and walked down the hall, stopping at Derrick's room. In the dark, she could see him. He had moved since she saw him last, shifting from his back to sleep on his side. Lee was not there. Mera entered, her footsteps careful.

"Thank you for saving me," Derrick said as Mera approached. She stopped.

"You're not as quiet as you think." He sat up in the bed with a groan.

"How are you feeling?"

"Better." He smiled in the darkness. "And fucking hungry."

"I can fix you something."

"You cook?"

"I've had a lot of practice."

Derrick laughed. "Was that a joke?"

She smiled but said nothing.

"I'll wait for morning," he said. "I just want to make sure you won't go back to protecting me from the world."

"I won't," Mera said, moving closer to the bed. Derrick followed her, tilting his head up to watch her face as she approached. She watched his eyes strain to make her out in the dark.

She stepped closer, leaning over him, so close that he didn't have to try hard to make her out. She lingered there for a moment. She could feel his hot breath. Her body responded with quickened breaths of her own, the human parts of her biology responding to his.

"What ..." He gave up when Mera's lips came down to meet his. The wave that went through her surprised her. It was a dangerous thing, what she was doing. She didn't care.

Breathing hard, she put her hand on his chest and pushed him back down on the bed. She got up on top of him, staring down into his eyes.

The kiss was a question. She waited for his answer.

Derrick reached up and kissed her. She allowed the kiss to happen, allowed him to nestle deep into her like an animal seeking warmth. Derrick shuddered, surprised by the intensity.

The night air crept in from the slightly open window. It filled the room, swirling under them and through them. Mera felt it, her skin puckering with new sensitivity. She took off Derrick's shirt and touched his chest. His body warmed to her touch, as if it were communicating in some special language of atoms and energy.

Mera pulled Derrick closer as if in answer, and with all her strength, she let go.

KING COCK

Jammie heard the fire engines first. Then he smelled the smoke.

It couldn't be.

He told Dana to get out of the house, then rushed outside to see his backyard on fire. The crackling flames were burning through his entire blasted weed farm.

Shit!

It was too late for the weed. The fire truck, by the sound of it, was making its way down Waterfront. It would take fifteen minutes tops before it barreled down the small St. Thomas road leading to his house.

Enough time to save his cocks.

Jammie took off his white shirt, stained yellow from years of use, and wrapped it around his neck. Taking one last breath of clean air, he tied the shirt over his nose and mouth. Then he ran into the smoke.

Jammie's backyard was fenced in, with a tight dirt path between his weed farm and his coop. The unkempt grass along the path had caught fire, and within minutes, the chicken coop would be up in flames, too.

He ran down the dirt path and jumped over the burning grass, flames licking at his legs.

By the time he got to the coop, his rooster Joliah was already dead. The poor bastard. King Cock, however, was going crazy in his cage, screeching in terror, his mane fluffed up beyond what Jammie had thought possible.

The heavy smoke was burning Jammie's eyes. He blinked away tears, unlatching the cage and reaching in for King Cock, barely thinking about proper technique. When he grabbed King Cock, the bird went nuts, pecking and clawing everywhere. Jammie was pumping with so much adrenaline, he didn't pay any mind to the fresh cut on his hand. He tucked the big rooster under his arm—an ordeal in itself.

Jammie could hear the sirens through the crackling flames. They were close. He scrambled his way through the tall grass along his fence because it was the only path left to him. When he cleared the fire, he pulled the shirt from his face and took in a gulp of smoky air. He erupted in coughs, his throat scratchy and raw.

King Cock went crazy again, scratching at Jammie's side. There was no shirt to protect him from the rooster's sharp claws and spurs as they dug into his flesh.

He winced and loosened his grip, and King Cock launched into the air and landed on Jammie's roof, then took off out of sight.

"But what fuck I seeing here!" he yelled. "Where the rass you going?" It made no difference. His prize rooster was gone.

Pressing his shirt to his bleeding side, he walked out to the front of his house just in time to see the fire truck pull up. Five men in full firefighter gear jumped down before it even made a full stop. Three men went for the hoses, and once the driver stopped the truck, they all ran past him in the direction of the fire.

Jammie felt dizzy, the world around him spinning furiously.

In minutes, the firefighters had hosed down the flames and returned to the front of the house. Jammie's backyard was all black twigs and ash, but the fire was out. The neighbors were out on the street, grateful for their collective good fortune. Two older women glared at Jammie and spoke in whispers.

"You know how this started?" one of the firefighters asked.

Sheila, most likely, Jammie thought. She had been livid when she found out about Dana. And she was the type to act out in this way. "Nah," Jammie said. "The smoke woke me up." Not precisely true, but it didn't matter.

"You got a permit for that farm in the back?"

"Yeah."

"You mind showing me?"

"Yeah, no problem." He reached into his wallet and handed over a card.

The man glanced at it and looked up at Jammie. "This is your driver's license."

"Shit, my bad. It in the house." Jammie staggered backward. "I can get it if—"

"No, it's fine," the man said.

"Pahnah high as fuck," said another firefighter, standing near the fire truck.

"Give me your address and number," said the first man. "We'll be contacting you."

• • •

When Jammie returned, bandaged and stumbling, Dana was still naked in bed, smoking from her glass hand pipe, serene as ever. She had not taken his warning to heart.

"What happened?" she asked in a tone that displayed no real interest.

"I'm going to have to go to court," Jammie said, undressing. "Some shit about a fine. It wasn't even my fault."

But it *was* his fault. He knew that a reckoning was due for getting with Dana. He just hadn't known what it would be.

Dana said nothing. She inhaled deeply from her pipe.

"I lost my cocks," he said.

"Oh?" Then nothing.

The weed farm was, in fact, legal. He really did have a permit. It was the cockfighting that would get him in trouble if anyone really cared.

The weed would grow back, and a burn was good for the soil. But King Cock, that magnificent bird, was irreplaceable. That loss, he would feel. Jammie was tired of losing things. In thirty-seven years, he had managed to keep only a weed farm and some fucking roosters. And now that, too, had literally gone up in smoke.

Jammie slid his naked body up against Dana. The room spun around him. He sighed, looking her over as if with new eyes.

"What under there, anyway?" he asked. "Under that skin." He poked her in the side.

"Don't," she said.

"I'm serious." He reached out and grabbed her breast. "This even real?"

Dana moved so fast, Jammie could still see the afterimage of her, lying calmly next to him. The image of her on top of him, however, felt more real. One of her hands was clenched around his throat. He could feel the pressure behind his eyes, as if they were going to pop right out of their sockets. That felt very real.

Dana's eyes were blank. Jammie didn't see a human anymore, but something else. Her face seemed to vibrate, and behind it he could see pitch-black eyes and fluorescent skin.

"Please," he managed to say. "Please."

Her face softened, and she loosened her grip on his neck.

At the moment, her body felt more real than his, her skin smooth and hot against his cold, numb collection of parts. His mouth was dry. He tried to speak, but his tongue felt like a heavy, lifeless thing.

Just as quickly, she returned to her side of the bed, calm again. Not surprising. Quick, flashing anger was typical of her kind. As was sudden calm. She lit her pipe again and inhaled. Jammie took a few minutes to catch his breath.

He had met Dana one night out at Duffy's. He was alone, dancing in the center of the dance floor, drunk and high out of his mind. She had been standing against the wall, watching him. They had locked eyes a few times. It was only at the end of the night, when she approached him, that he realized what she was. He had gone home with her anyway.

"I'm sorry," he said to the Ynaa in his bed. "That was disrespectful. No excuse."

"You won't do it again," she said as if she were naming an essential truth of the universe.

Jammie waited a few minutes before speaking again. "I could ask you something?"

"Yes."

"Why you leave your planet?"

"It became too small for us."

He didn't bother with a follow-up. This was all the answer he would get.

"What do you miss from home?" he asked instead. Warily he laid his head on her shoulder. His temples throbbed as if his head were resting on the chest of a hummingbird.

"The endless ocean. The salt in my gills. Coarse skin."

Jammie tried to picture her with gills and failed. Air filled his lungs and emptied again. He felt as if he could float away with one deep breath.

An unknown length of time passed as he vibrated through waves of high. When he came back to himself, he called out to her. At that moment, he realized that "Dana" could not be her real name.

"What?" she answered anyway, continuing the illusion.

"When you leave here, what will you miss?"

She pulled Jammie closer to her. For what it was worth, the human skin covering her own was soft to the touch. He felt comforted.

"What will I miss?" she said, stroking his cheek. "I can't think of a single thing."

HOMECOMING

When Patrice pulled into the driveway a little after noon, Derrick was already standing outside, the ambassador's house looming behind him. The house was white and had a red cross-hipped roof with several ridges and valleys. Extravagant and nonsensical and too big for just one person. The decadence annoyed Patrice beyond words.

She had to go down a tight, winding dirt road to get to the house—gravel, rocks, and potholes the whole way, making it impossible to drive more than three miles an hour. Northside was filled with big, expensive houses at the end of dirt roads. It was how the wealthy hid. The ambassador was now using the same strategy, for similar reasons.

"You came down for *me*?" Derrick asked playfully as she got out of the car.

Patrice stood behind her open door, maintaining some distance between them. Derrick was wearing basketball shorts and a V-neck. He looked good except for the giant bandage wrapped around the top of his head. "No. I was due to be home."

"Uh-huh," Derrick said, smiling. He sat on the hood of her car, and she watched him as he gave her a once-over, unsatisfied since most of her body was blocked from view behind the tinted driver's-side window of her mother's car.

"How could you be so stupid, Derrick?"

He shrugged and put his hands in his pockets. "I didn't think—"

"Obviously."

"What do you care?"

Patrice knew what he meant by this, knew the meaning behind the words. "You're still my best friend, Derrick. No matter what."

"No matter what," he repeated. "How's your mom?"

"Fine," Patrice said. "At home with Alice."

Derrick smiled.

She glared at him. "So where's the ambassador?"

Derrick stopped smiling. "Look, I'm not going there with you. I've had enough trouble with this shit as it is."

"Then stop doing it." She had said the words. But she knew Derrick. He would do what he wanted and damn the consequences. For all he went on about his grandmother's stubbornness, Patrice couldn't imagine another soul more stubborn than Derrick.

She moved out from behind the car door and closed it. He could see it now. He looked down and then up again.

"The fuck?"

Patrice didn't say anything.

He looked down again, this time lingering. "You've been busy."

Patrice looked away. "Look, you can't be messing with that"—she searched for the right words—"*individual*, Derrick. It's dangerous."

"You can't just drop a bomb like this and go on to lecture me about my love life."

"So it's true?" She felt a kick in her belly.

"Not really," he said. "A little bit."

"Oh?" She wasn't sure just how to feel about this revelation. What he was talking about was unnatural.

"What about *that*, though?" he asked.

"It was unexpected."

"The dude know about it?"

"What you think?"

"Don't know. Didn't hear shit about it until you showed up here."

Patrice had to stifle the desire to punch him. "I came to see if you were okay. That's it."

"I safe. You should come inside."

"I told you—"

"Trice, she not here. She went out this morning."

"I don't care. I'm not—"

Derrick chupsed his teeth and turned, heading for the house. For a moment, Patrice stood there with her arms crossed, trying to be stubborn. It didn't last. "You stupid boy," she muttered, and followed Derrick inside.

• • •

In senior year of high school, Patrice and Derrick dated. He professed his love in their junior year, not long after the Ynaa landed. The event had affected him deeply, he said. It had made him come to terms with his feelings about her. The first time he confessed this, Patrice laughed.

"You serious?" she asked. "Aliens invade, and you talking about *love?*" The invasion hadn't had the same impact on her. Mostly, she wanted to run away. Far, far away. When she didn't feel that impulse, she felt numb. The whole thing had knocked the wind out of her. It still hadn't come back.

"When would be a better time to confess your love to someone?" Derrick asked, not really asking. He thought he had already won the argument. "And they didn't invade. They *arrived.*"

This was one of the reasons she and Derrick were doomed from the beginning. The difference between those two words, the vast gulf between the two points of view they represented.

Patrice brushed him off at first. But Derrick was persistent. For the whole summer, he told her again and again. Each time, she would roll her eyes and tell him to shut up. She wasn't interested in relationships.

All the while, the aliens were setting up shop. You couldn't go anywhere without seeing them, monsters wrapped in human skin. You couldn't look out at the ocean without seeing their massive ship, a silver-blue blight over Water Island. And you couldn't read the paper without stumbling across a story of an islander torn to pieces.

On the second day of senior year, Derrick confessed again, and this time Patrice said yes. It was mostly out of exhaustion.

"If you're sure this is what you want," she said. She felt like a ghost floating through the world.

"This is what I want," he said.

They dated the entire year, and within a few months, she had remembered how she felt about him, too. Her old self, before everything changed, started to return to her. She felt semisolid, almost human again.

And then it came time to apply to colleges.

"I want to stay here," Derrick said. "Go to UVI."

"*What?*" They were on her bed, his head on her stomach, his feet kicked up against the wall. Patrice looked down at him in disbelief.

"I don't see the point in applying stateside. Right now, St. Thomas is the most interesting place on earth."

He was talking about the Ynaa. St. Thomas was interesting because aliens had landed here. Until then, she had assumed that Derrick would at least have entertained the thought of leaving, of forming a life away from all this, away from them.

"I'm applying stateside," she said. "Why didn't you say this before?"

"I don't know. I was thinking it through. I think you should stay, too."

"How could you be so selfish? You know I hate it here."

"I'm here."

"This ain't about you."

"Stay."

"No."

"Please stay." Derrick was up now. He was sitting cross-legged on the bed, looking at her with his dopey eyes. Patrice sighed. If he didn't understand this about her, he didn't know her at all.

"Whatever," she said.

"Is that a yes?"

She nodded.

That month, Patrice applied to the University of the Virgin Islands and five schools stateside. She got into UVI and two others: Florida State and the University of Pittsburgh. Florida wasn't far enough, so she enrolled at Pitt. On a hot day in July, she told Derrick. She didn't expect him to cry, and it caught her by surprise when he did.

"Why would you do this?" he moaned. "I can't believe you would do this!" Then he looked away, wiping at his eyes with the collar of his shirt.

They were sitting in his beat-up car, parked out in front of her house. Patrice didn't say much, only "sorry," only that if she stayed she wouldn't be alive and she desperately wanted to be alive. He didn't understand. He couldn't. He hit his fists against the steering wheel, and when he was too angry to look at her, he told her to get out of the car. She left quietly. If she was sad then, she couldn't truly feel it. She felt numb. She was a ghost floating through the world. Two weeks later, she got on a plane.

• • •

Derrick led Patrice to the living room. They walked through a long hall and then a dining area next to a ridiculously large kitchen. In passing, she could see that the countertops were of glossy granite. The ceiling in the house was high, each room entered through high archways.

The living room had the widest arch. It was lower than the other rooms, so you had to step down into it. They sat on the couch. It was a plush gray, matching the rug at her feet. On top of the rug stood a glass coffee table with generic home-and-garden magazines spread like folding fans. On the walls were paintings of pastoral scenes: ducks on a pond, a verdant hillside, palm trees silhouetted by a tropical sunset. The corners had giant vases with small palm trees, their leaves dark and waxy.

The whole place looked like a guesthouse for rich white expats coming down to the islands for the "tropical experience." Patrice just rolled her eyes and stared at the least offensive thing in the room: an attractive gray armchair next to the couch.

"Pretty nice place, right?" Derrick said.

"Sure."

He sat wide-legged on the other side of the couch. He faced her, his arms spread over the arm and back of the couch like a bird in flight, taking up as much space as possible. The baby kicked again in Patrice's belly. She adjusted herself to be more comfortable, tilting toward him and resting the side of her face on the back cushion.

"So what happened?" she asked.

"You'n know already?" He didn't wait for her to answer. "Some dude threw a rock through my car windshield. Cracked my skull."

Patrice looked at Derrick's wrapped head again. The wound under the white gauze didn't seem to be giving him much discomfort. "Who was the dude?"

"You hear about that kid from a while back, right? The one that got killed by one of the Ynaa on Polyberg Hill?"

"Yeah," she said. "Tony. Went to school with your little sister." "Nah, a year below her. Anyway. It was his big brother. They were having an anniversary ceremony at the gravesite. Saw me parked up and lost his shit."

"What were you doing down there, anyway?"

Derrick looked at her as if she should know the answer to that question. "We really should talk more often. You never call."

"It takes two, Derrick."

He shrugged. "Lee wanted to visit Angela's grave."

Patrice lowered her head, feeling a little guilty. She had totally forgotten about that. "How's she doing?"

"She safe. Was a little shaken up with me bleeding all over her, though."

"How's your head?"

"Want see something cool?" Derrick pulled at the gauze wrapped around his head, untangling it. If there was a wound there, Patrice couldn't see it. No indication of bleeding on the gauze, either. And no scar. "Mera healed it right after we left the graveyard. She felt really bad about it. Suggested I wear this for a while, though. Just to be safe. Didn't want to make people any angrier than they already are."

"Yeah," Patrice said. "I guess I'm just people, too, huh?"

"You came all this way to check up on me. Didn't want you to feel like it was a waste of a trip."

"Why did you go there with her?"

"Where? With who?"

Patrice said nothing.

"You still haven't told me about that." He looked at her belly.

"Not much to tell."

Derrick inched closer to her. The baby kicked like mad. Patrice held her stomach.

"Tell me anyways," he said.

By the time the ambassador returned to the house, Derrick was up to speed on everything—or the version of everything that Patrice lied her way through. The ambassador walked in so quietly, Patrice didn't notice until she appeared beneath the archway. Patrice jumped, her heart pounding in her chest. Derrick laughed and told her to relax. The ambassador sat in the chair beside the sofa where Patrice and Derrick sat.

"This is Patrice," Derrick said. "She came to check up on me."

"Nice to meet you, Patrice," the ambassador said. "My name is Mera."

"I know," Patrice said. "Everyone knows." She could feel herself shaking, which only made her angrier. "Tell me something I don't know."

"Like what?" Mera asked.

"Why you're here. Not the bullshit reason. The real reason."

"Trice …" Derrick started, concern in his voice.

"I'll tell you one day," Mera said with what looked to Patrice like smug amusement. "When it's safe."

"Sure, because this is about my safety and not your control. Your power." Derrick actually looked terrified, but the ambassador's expression didn't give anything away. She just kept up that damn smirk of hers. "I'll be leaving now," Patrice said.

"You sure?" Derrick said. "I think you should stay a bit."

"I have to get back. Nice meeting you." Patrice forced a smile.

"Wait, wait," Derrick said, looking from Patrice to Mera, to Patrice again.

Mera stood up. "I can leave if you two need more time."

Patrice really took the ambassador in then. She was not like the others. When she tried to be human, she could almost fool you. Mera was the same caramel brown as Patrice, with long dreads that she let hang loose around her shoulders. Her eyes were a piercing amber. Patrice could appreciate the mask for what it was. It had certainly had its effect on Derrick. She seemed human enough for Derrick to decide to work for her. And now this, whatever this was.

Patrice glanced at Derrick. He looked like a stray cat caught in the headlights. She took one look at his gaping mouth, his dopey eyes, and got up. "I'll see you later."

"Let me walk you out."

"No. Don't worry yourself."

Patrice made her way back through several arches to the door. She could hear nothing behind her, just the conspiratorial silence of two people with secrets. One person, anyway. Now the baby was fully awake and doing backflips. She stifled a groan. She had no idea what sex the baby was. She listened again for any sound from the big house. Nothing. She wished she hadn't wasted her time coming here.

She slammed the door on her way out.

• • •

The boy was a basketball player. She had seen him around campus before, so she recognized him at the house party when she caught him staring at her.

She stood in the middle of the basement, surrounded by a few girls from the cross-country team. He stood in a corner, huddled with some other dudes from the basketball team. The basement floor was already wet with booze, and Patrice's heels stuck dangerously to the gummy surface. She'd already had too much to drink.

It took him a while to come over, and when he did, he danced around the periphery of the cross-country girls, edging his way closer to her. He was tall and dark-skinned and danced okay for a Yankee. By the time he had worked up the courage to dance next to her, the DJ had switched from hip-hop to reggae. It was old stuff, a mix of nineties dancehall and some Sean Paul shit that had gotten popular in the early 2000s. It reminded Patrice vaguely of home, so she allowed herself to get into the music. When she felt him against her, her eyes were closed. This presumption she was used to. Black dudes from the States behaved much the same way island men did. Unlike most of the girls she knew back in high school, she usually responded to this aggressively, turning immediately and cutting her eye at the perpetrator. But that night, the music swelling in her ears, the faint feeling of home pulling at her edges, she allowed herself to be like those other girls. She let him be. She swayed her hips, and when the song called for it, she wined against him.

She lost count of the songs. With each one, they got closer and he pressed harder against her. She caught the eyes of the other girls on the team, and they smiled approvingly. The DJ played "Murder She Wrote," and she let the music take her over. She swayed slowly to it, allowed her whole body to pulse with the throb of the bass. He held her thighs, and she let him. She felt something shift somewhere inside her, a small candle being lit in a back room.

When she was younger, she believed in the value of virginity, that it was a gift to be guarded. She went to church every Sunday. She listened to the pastor speak on the value of chastity. She believed. She didn't question it. After the Ynaa arrived, she still didn't have sex. Even when she and Derrick had been dating for a while and he asked if they could, she still held out, still guarding that gift, even after she had given up going to church.

At the end of the night, she told her cross-country friends not to wait up. She let him take her home. They didn't talk much. He took his time, which she appreciated. There was lots of touching and kissing. She could smell the night on them, the beer, the weed, the sweat. She kissed his neck and tasted his salt on her tongue.

The moment of penetration just flowed from what had come

before. He hadn't reached for a condom. She thought about this only for a moment. She considered the consequences. But then she let him continue. It was unlikely that this one time would be a big deal.

Throughout all this, she was surprised at herself. Surprised at how easy it was. She clawed the ripples of his back. She wrapped her legs around him. There was no fire or brimstone. No manna from heaven. No shame. No salvation.

The next morning, she watched him get dressed, observing his body distantly. She acknowledged how beautiful it was but didn't want to do it again.

She gave him her number, with every intention of ghosting him. When he texted her, often late at night, she didn't respond.

One morning, she woke up nauseated, and soon it became a ritual to sit on the floor of her bathroom, her body hunched over the toilet bowl, the pain like rough hands pulling at her, tugging her insides apart.

When she finally spotted him on campus, he averted his eyes. By then she was wearing large hoodies.

● ● ●

When Patrice came back, Alice was still there, cooking in the kitchen. It smelled good. Patrice could pick up the scent of plantain, mutton, and peas and rice. It made her remember her hunger.

She went to her room and closed the door behind her. She sat on her old bed. It felt so small now. Her entire room did. There was still stuff on her walls—old doodles she had drawn during AP calculus and honors English. She looked at one of them, watched the aimless swirls wind in on themselves. At the time, she thought it was nice—beautiful, even. Now it looked like a child's drawing. She cradled her stomach and eased back onto her bed. She stared up at the ceiling, looking for patterns in the little knobs of the orange-peel drywall. When she was younger, she did this all the time. If she looked long enough, she could find anything up there, constellations of white against white, contrasted by a legion of shadows. She searched for one of her favorites and found it quickly: a side portrait of an old woman with no eyes and a crook nose. Patrice wondered what it would be like to be stuck like that, forever trapped behind drywall in a vacant room.

She was close to sleep when she heard the knock at the door. The person didn't wait for Patrice to answer. The door creaked open. Her mother.

"We need to talk about this," her mother said from the doorway.

"About what?" Patrice didn't bother to get up.

"Why you'n tell me about this?"

"Sorry."

"When's the last time you been to a doctor?" her mother asked. One day back and she was already mothering.

"A couple months ago."

"What!" Her mother stepped inside and closed the door. "We should go sometime this week."

"Mom, I'm fine."

"You're not." Her mother sat on the bed. "Who is he, anyway?"

"Just a guy. He not involved."

"What the shit!"

"Look, it's my business. I taking care of it."

"Don't look it."

"Do I ask you about your business?"

Her mother said nothing.

"No, I don't," Patrice answered for her.

"Trish," her mother said in that old way Patrice remembered, filled with that old familiarity. "You still angry with me?"

"I'm not angry." Patrice sat up, her back pushed against the wall.

Her mother sighed loudly. "Me and your father—"

"You and Dad is you and Dad. None of my business." She could see her mother's face now. She looked horrified. Patrice felt a pang of guilt. "I'll take care of it, okay? Don't worry."

"What you gon' do when the baby is born? You have another year of school. You know people up there? Can you pay for a sitter? For day care?"

Patrice knew people, but she wasn't close to anyone in that sort of way. "I'll figure it out."

"You keep saying that."

"She living here now?" Patrice asked.

Her mother stared at her for a long time and then looked down. "No."

Patrice watched her mother. She wanted to say something but couldn't think of a single thing.

"You have a name for the baby?" her mother asked. She wasn't looking at her. She was still looking down.

"No."

"You should transfer to UVI. I can watch the baby when I can."

"I'm okay."

"Come home, Trish." Her mother waited for an answer. When none came, she got up and straightened her dress. She left the room without another word.

Patrice decided that she needed to get out of the house. Get some air. It occurred to her that it had been a long time since she was in a room with enough air for her lungs. She passed by the kitchen on her way out. She grabbed her mother's keys from the counter as she did.

Alice was still cooking, stirring fresh vegetables in a large frying pan. It was a lot of food for just two people.

"Are you hungry?" asked Alice.

"No," Patrice said. "I'm good."

• • •

She stopped at her father's apartment. He opened the door and smiled at her. It was familiar and warm, and only then did she realize she missed it.

"Took you long enough to come see me," he said. It was a chastising statement with no sign of animosity. Sometimes, it felt as if she could do nothing to upset him.

"What were you doing?" she asked.

"Work." Patrice assumed that meant work on his book. He looked down at her belly and said, "You 'bout to blow."

She glared at him, but a smile quivered at the edges of her lips. She hadn't told him about her pregnancy. Even this didn't seem to upset him. "So no lecture? That sucks."

He laughed and let her in. She walked ahead of him, so she couldn't see his face when he said what came next.

"Lately, life's been nothing but curveballs. I'm not about to losing my head over the unexpected appearance of a grandchild."

"Okay," Patrice said. She looked back at him to find his face completely serene. "Should have told you sooner, then."

"You should have," he said, and in that was a hint of something like judgment. Then he smiled, and it was gone.

Her father's apartment was filled with empty beer bottles. He had always liked his beer, but this was too much. He looked healthy enough, but he had a belly, and bags under his eyes from lack of sleep. He was bulkier in the arms, which surprised Patrice. He must have been working out more to curb his anxiety. He was lying about how easily he was handling all the changes in his life. No number of push-ups could hide that.

They sat at the dining room table. Patrice had to push some of her father's books off the chair and onto the floor.

"Careful," he said. "Those aren't mine."

"What?" She kicked away some of the books near her feet and grinned.

"You think you funny, eh?" He laughed, which made Patrice feel warm. She needed this.

"So what you been up to?" she asked. "It can't all be work."

"Yes, it is," he said. "What else is there?"

Again she caught no sign of pain in the statement, but there had to be some there. Only people with a large hole in their lives filled it with nothing but work. But then, how did she explain the hole she felt? She didn't even try to fill it with anything. Perhaps having a hole was the normal thing, the default state of all beings.

"Nobody in your life?" she asked.

"What you mean?" His smile died then, which told her he understood the question.

"Mom's with someone," she added. "Shouldn't you be moving on, too?" This was dangerous territory. They both knew that Mom had someone, but they never talked about that.

"I'm not ready for that," he said. "Maybe someday."

In her father's eyes, Patrice could finally see what he was trying to hide—that knot of pain and bruised ego inside. She empathized with it, understood it the best she could, but she also reserved another, opposing feeling.

"You must get attention from women all the time," she said. "You sure you don't want take someone up on their offer?"

He watched her then. It was a hard stare. In it, Patrice saw a man, not her father or the man fitting himself into that role. He seemed to be turning the words around in his head, which she wanted. Anger curled his brow, which she was okay with. But then it went away, replaced with resignation.

"You blame me for what happened with me and your mom," he said softly.

"I blame both of you." Then she sighed with the same resignation. "I blame you more."

Her father got up and got a beer from the fridge. As he popped the cap, he started talking. He took a sip and held it out for Patrice. She made a face and shook her head, pointing at her belly.

He laughed, but it had none of the usual luster. It was just a weak attempt at easing the mood in the room.

Patrice didn't say anything. She waited for him to finish his thought.

"I love your mother. And I was faithful to her even when I didn't want to be." He paused to let that thought sink in.

Patrice smiled thinly, nodding for him to continue.

"And your mother was good to me for a very long time. She just wanted different things. I have to be honest. I was angry about that, but I'm not"—he paused to consider—"I'm trying not to be anymore."

"Good for you," she said.

"Your mother is happy. You can't hate her for making a decision that makes her happy. And you can't be mad at me for not fighting her."

"I'm not," Patrice said, but her father was ready for her. He gave her a knowing look, tilting his head down and raising his eyebrows. *You sure about that?* the look said.

Patrice swallowed the rest of her defense. She had the urge to pop his Zen bubble, tell him that the effect of the divorce on him was obvious to her, but she swallowed that urge, too.

She put up her hands in defeat and got up.

Her father laughed. "So you're leaving now?"

"I gotta be somewhere," she said.

"You're escaping," he said simply.

Patrice didn't take the obvious bait. She pushed in her chair, knocking around more books.

As she was walking out, he said loudly, "Girl, one day you gon' run yourself right off a cliff."

• • •

Patrice decided to go down to Yacht Haven Grande after grabbing a sandwich from the Frenchtown Deli. She and Derrick used to go down to Yacht Haven all the time when they were dating. She would call him up, at odd hours sometimes, and sneak out of the house, and they would get in his car and drive down there. They would go to the catwalk that overlooked the yacht dock and sit down at one of the metal cocktail tables and talk or stand and hold hands and watch the yachts from a distance, their lights revealing their beautiful interiors and giving the water beneath them a ghostly glow.

This was often when her parents were fighting all the time, and even more often when they stopped and the house was as quiet as a crypt. They wouldn't even notice that she was gone. One day, her dad packed a bag and came into her room to say he had found an apartment to live in. He told her that he loved her and that he would be calling her, and to let him know if she needed a ride to school, or anything else.

She asked him why, and he gave the bullshit answer you gave children when you believed they couldn't handle hard truths. He told her they just needed to take some time apart and not to worry, that things would work out.

"Sure," she said, knowing that things didn't just work out. Some things weren't mended with distance. They atrophied further. Their fibers stretched and tore.

Patrice assumed that it was her father who ruined the marriage. She overheard enough to know that he had gotten into his head that he needed to travel, that he wanted to work abroad for a while after she graduated from high school. She thought this was crap. She thought there was another woman and that her father was too much of a coward to say so.

Then she noticed how often her mother stayed away from home. She would come home from track practice to find an empty house with food in the oven. It was like this for months. Then one day, she came home and Alice and her mother were having dinner and watching TV. Patrice introduced herself, and Alice greeted her with a smile. She sat and watched the television show with them. Olivia Pope had finally unearthed the alien conspiracy. She stared into Fitz Grant's eyes long enough to see the nictitating membrane. Olivia gasped, and so did her mother.

Her mother reached for Alice's hand, squeezing it before letting go. The move was so fleeting, Patrice wouldn't have caught it if she hadn't looked away from the screen at just that instant. A quick smile curled Alice's lips and slid away. Patrice noticed how close her mother and this woman were on the couch, how comfortable and familiar it all was, as if they had done this many times before.

Later that night, she called Derrick and they went to Yacht Haven and stared out at the yachts, and she held his hand tight against her as though she would lose it if she weren't careful.

This time, there were no hands but hers. She locked them together tight and watched the yachts, watched a group of women laugh their way across the dock to a yacht where two men waited. She listened to their talk but couldn't make out much of it.

The catwalk was parallel to the yacht dock, which was a few feet out into the harbor. The two were connected by a narrow bridge with a large locked gate at the end. You had to be a yacht owner to get access. The water between the walk and the dock was relatively calm, slapping weakly against large rocks beneath. Lights under the walk gave the water the same cloudy blue glow. Patrice liked to watch the water, liked to search for the dark silhouette of some sea creature snaking its way through the murk. Most times, she was unsuccessful. Tonight appeared to be one of those times.

She would be having the baby soon. In two and half months, she would have another life besides her own to look after. Right now it was still under her skin, wrapped in membrane.

She hadn't told her mother that she had already sold most of her belongings. That she had collected a few hundred dollars from selling her stuff on Craigslist and eBay, to help cover those first few months of diapers and baby clothes. And that she had not booked a return ticket to Pittsburgh, though the fall semester was just a couple of weeks away. She wasn't sure she'd be returning, wasn't sure she would be able to survive up there on her own. She had to confess that she had wanted her mother to make the offer she did. She had wanted to be saved.

From Yacht Haven, she could see the Ynaa ship. The disk sat on top of a long, thin stem, blaring dizzying white light into the night sky.

A lot of people believed that the Ynaa would save them. Their arrival was so promising. Patrice never believed that. When she saw that thing come down, she felt only menace. And she was right. There were no saviors coming from space. Only intimidation and death. And there was no good news from heaven, either. The celestial bodies didn't shift a minute of a degree at the thought of the humans' plight on this spinning Earth, enduring this long occupation.

No, she decided. She was done with saviors. If she wanted to be saved, she was going to do it herself.

Patrice heard a splash below her. She looked down just in time to see the tail of something dark breach the surface and then disappear again. It was so quick, it could have been a trick of the eye, a phantom, a twin soul.

A THIRD OF THE STARS OF HEAVEN

Henrietta followed the receptionist down the empty hall of Schneider Hospital. The woman's keys jangled as she walked, mixing with the echoing clicks of Henrietta's blue church shoes. No other noises greeted them.

Henrietta watched her shadow stretch into each unlit room, her form made large by the ultrabright fluorescents of the hallway. One of the lights in the hall blinked on and off. She pinched her eyes shut to ward off dizziness. Her lower belly throbbed, and she stifled a groan.

To calm herself, she rubbed her hands together. The action did little to ease her nerves or the pain blooming in her belly. Two weeks ago, at least five patients occupied rooms on this floor. Where had they gone?

"Here we are," the receptionist said when she reached a door with a printed name etched deep into gold plating, the letters thick and dark so they could not be mistaken: DR. ANNA CALDWELL.

"All right," Henrietta said softly. "Thank you."

From inside, someone said, "Come in," and the receptionist opened the door. Dr. Caldwell was sitting behind her desk, waiting. Just then the phone down the hall rang.

"Go ahead inside," said the receptionist as she shuffled back to her desk, keys jangling all the way. "Busy day today."

Dr. Caldwell stood up behind her desk. "Please come in."

"Yes, well," Henrietta started, still lingering at the door. She took another look down the empty hallway. "I'm just a little nervous."

"Nothing to worry about," the doctor said.

Dr. Caldwell had a rather large smile. Large white teeth behind obscenely red lips. Lips that red were hardly appropriate for a doctor. Henrietta stepped inside and closed the door.

"Please sit," said Dr. Caldwell as she took her own seat. This bothered Henrietta; surely the doctor should have sat *after* she did. It was only good and right to do so when you had a visitor.

Dr. Caldwell was a stout woman. She looked to be in her forties. She had her hair pulled back in a shiny bun and wore big gold hoop earrings that looked tacky. After shaking Dr. Caldwell's hand graciously, Henrietta sat down. She clasped her hands on her lap and stared expectantly at the young doctor.

"It is a pleasure to have you in today, Mrs. Smith."

Henrietta squinted. She didn't know how to take this. Was this going to be a pleasant conversation? Weren't they about to discuss something quite serious? Henrietta crossed her legs. She swallowed hard. Her mouth felt terribly dry. She gave a polite smile and nodded.

"Oh, sorry," Dr. Caldwell said. She bent over in her chair to reach for something near the edge of her desk. Henrietta heard the sound of something slamming shut before the doctor sat back up with a Dasani bottle in hand. "Please have some water."

"Thank you," Henrietta said, taking the water. "I was very thirsty."

"Yes, I can imagine," said the doctor. "You must have had some difficulty doing so much walking to get up here."

"I took the elevator."

"Yes, still. At your age …" Dr. Caldwell smiled, saying nothing else.

Henrietta stared, blinking twice. She was not in the mood for this woman. She wished she would just get on with the actual conversation.

"The walk was fine," Henrietta said. "Just my nerves."

Dr. Caldwell had a manila folder in front of her. She opened it and looked through it, turning a piece of paper every few seconds. Henrietta saw the hideous red polish on her fingernails, gleaming even brighter than her red lips, and had to resist the urge to say the Lord's name in vain.

"Sorry," the doctor said, not looking up. "I'm just making sure I got this right. You took some tests last week, yes?"

"Yes."

"Pap test, was it?"

"Yes." Henrietta was confused. Didn't the receptionist say the doctor was expecting her? Wasn't this appointment written down somewhere in her notes? She should know the details of all this already. The last time she was here, it was a different doctor who ran all the tests.

"Excuse me," said Henrietta. "Where's Dr. Moses?"

"He moved away."

Henrietta waited quietly for more information. Dr. Caldwell looked up and noticed the look on her face.

"He left St. Thomas to go stateside. Seattle, I think. The hospital has been downsizing since the Ynaa arrived. Not a lot of demand for doctors."

Henrietta nodded.

"Okay," Dr. Caldwell said, closing the manila envelope. "You have cervical cancer."

Henrietta nodded again. She uncrossed her legs. She uncapped her bottle of Dasani water and took a sip. *Of course it's cancer.*

"Not to worry," Dr. Caldwell said. "We can simply proceed with treatment. We do injections here."

"I not taking no injections," Henrietta said, all formality gone in an instant.

"Or you can visit a clinic and get it in capsule form. We don't have it here. We're terribly sorry for the inconvenience."

"I not taking no capsules, either."

"Sorry?" Dr. Caldwell said. There was clear confusion on her face.

Henrietta said nothing.

"If you are concerned about the nano-synths, they don't stay in the body long. Once treated, they die and you flush them out."

Dr. Caldwell's voice was soft, too gentle, as if she were speaking to a child. Under all this, Henrietta could hear the island girl in her. She had gone off to school and gotten herself a Yankee accent. Now the doctor used it to talk down to her patients.

"Don't care what they do. I not going through with any procedures." Henrietta's St. Thomian accent was thick now, biting.

"Ma'am, I don't think you understand what you're saying. We

don't have the facilities for chemotherapy. And even if we did, your cancer is rather far along. You will die if you don't receive this treatment."

There she went with the "ma'am" stuff. Henrietta took a deep breath, placed the bottle of water on Dr. Caldwell's desk, and stood up.

Dr. Caldwell stood as well. "Ma'am?"

"Perhaps you would have more to do in this place if you took the time to consider the individual needs of your patients."

"No one has ever turned down the treatment."

"I find that unfathomable. Who want that stuff in them?"

"Sure, people show some discomfort. But with the threat of death—"

"What? They compromise they integrity?"

"*Integrity?* What you talking about?" There she was. The island girl no amount of schooling could get rid of. Dr. Caldwell's eyebrows arched obscenely, her grotesque red lips hanging open in realization of something. "Is this a religious thing?"

Henrietta turned away from the woman. "Thanks for your time. I will take the stairs back down to the main floor."

"Well, if you change your mind—"

Henrietta closed the door on Dr. Caldwell's words. She made her way to the stairwell and walked down. As she descended, the pain in her lower belly erupted again. It felt as if it had its own heartbeat that matched hers. What an obscene thing it was to have her life controlled by this evil mass, sent by God knew what demons to test her. She would not give it the satisfaction. It had already taken her good health. It would not take her soul, too.

• • •

When Henrietta was thirteen, her mother went to an obeah woman.

Her mother worked at the post office on Main Street until five. This meant Henrietta had to stay at All Saints Cathedral School until her mother got off.

Henrietta usually passed the time reading from her little blue Bible or doing her homework. On this day, she sat on the shaded steps in front of the cathedral. She was reading Revelation. She loved that book in particular because it had the best stories.

This time, she read Revelation 12:

And another sign appeared in heaven: behold, a great, fiery red dragon having seven heads and ten horns…His tail drew a third of the stars of heaven and threw them to the earth. And the dragon stood before the woman who was ready to give birth, to devour her Child as soon as it was born.

Three other students were waiting for their parents as well. It was 1963, so most parents didn't have their own cars. Many of the students caught the school bus, and the older kids walked up or down Garden Street with their friends to get to their homes in the area. Not Henrietta. She wasn't allowed to leave school until her mother came for her. Her mother didn't want her getting into trouble with any of the other kids. Her mother never specified what kind of trouble that might be.

The teachers stuck around until all the students left or got picked up. By five, only four kids remained at the small private school. Two younger girls ran around in the courtyard. They always stuck around after school, annoying Henrietta with their yelling and laughter.

And then there was Jared from her class, sitting across the courtyard, near the school gates, doodling in his notebook. Jared usually saw Henrietta's mother first and would yell across the courtyard to inform Henrietta of her mother's arrival.

"Your mom here!" he yelled as usual, and Henrietta looked up to see her mother standing at the gate in her brown postal uniform.

Henrietta got up and stuffed her Bible in her school bag. She ran across the courtyard. Jared watched her stupidly the entire time.

"Bye, Henri," he said with a chuckle.

"Bye," Henrietta said, not really paying him any mind.

"I don't like that boy," her mother said once she was outside the gate.

"He just childish," said Henrietta.

Her mother didn't respond to that. "What did I tell you about running like that in your uniform? You are wearing a skirt. It is unbecoming."

"Sorry, Mom," Henrietta said with a nervous smile.

"Stop smiling at me."

Henrietta stopped, lowering her head to stare at her worn brown oxfords.

She didn't look much like her mother. She took more after her father. She was lanky and a little bowlegged, five inches taller than her mother and taller than all the other girls her age. She was filling out, too. She had to be more aggressive than she would like with boys so that they wouldn't take liberties.

"Sorry, Mom," she said again, careful not to smile.

Her mother reached into her bag and pulled out a Long John. "Here," she said, handing Henrietta the coconut taffy candy. "I got two more in my bag. I'll give them to you later."

"Okay," Henrietta said between chews. She loved the sweet caramel-coconut taste of Long Johns. It was her favorite candy, and her mother knew it. Henrietta eyed her mother suspiciously. She could sometimes sense her mother's moods, and right now her senses told her to be on the alert.

"I need you to come with me on an errand," her mother said.

"Okay."

"It might make you feel a little uncomfortable, but I need you to be a witness to something."

"Okay." Henrietta tried to read her mother's face. As usual, it was unreadable.

She reached out and held her mother's hand. "Let's go."

Her mother responded to her forthrightness with more malleability than usual. She started walking without a word.

Henrietta lived on Rosen Gade. They had to walk down Garden Street, turn down Back Street, and walk for fifteen minutes before reaching Ninety-Nine Steps. Then they had to climb to the very top and trek up the thin winding street to their house. By then, the sun would be near setting and the journey wouldn't be so unbearable.

They didn't do any of that this time. Instead, they walked up Garden Street. It was steep but wider than the streets near her house. Two massive tamarind trees lined one side of the street, and Henrietta could see an iguana perched lazily on one of the big branches as she passed. When they neared the top, they turned into a narrow alleyway. It smelled wet, and Henrietta could hear crickets and bird calls as she walked with her mother. Big trees towered overhead, making the area several degrees cooler. It was darker than out on the street, and something about it pulled at Henrietta's nerves. She held her mom's hand tighter.

The alleyway was cramped by unwieldy bush on one side and two-story houses on the other, with nothing more than a thin winding dirt path between the starkly different worlds. Henrietta and her mother made their way to the very end of the alley, to a two-story house with red gating and a white exterior. It was wider than the other houses and well kept. The trees parted there, allowing the house to catch more sunlight than anywhere else. Henrietta relaxed.

Her mother knocked on the door, and after about a minute, a young woman answered. She had darker skin than Henrietta and her mother but had piercing light brown eyes that caught the sun. Henrietta was taken aback by such beauty. The woman's hair fell to her shoulders in tidy dreadlocks. Henrietta usually disapproved of the hairstyle, but on this woman it looked lovely.

Her mother didn't look so impressed by the woman's appearance.

"I'm here for the treatment," her mother said plainly.

Henrietta wanted to say something then but knew that her mother would hush her before she could get the full question out. She wanted to know what was wrong, wanted to know the purpose of the treatment. But her mother was secretive. She wouldn't talk about it so openly here—possibly at all. Henrietta would likely have to figure it out on her own.

"Octavia," said the woman. "Yes, my friend told me you

would be coming. I'm Maria. Please come in." The woman spoke formally, but there was a hint of an accent that Henrietta couldn't place. It sounded old-fashioned, somehow.

Maria led Henrietta and her mother to her living room. It was beautifully decorated. Covering most of the floor was a large blue, red, and green woven rug. Mahogany statue heads sat on a large dark wood table at the center of the room, surrounded by four varnished handcrafted straw chairs. They all sat around the table. Henrietta looked around. On the walls, wooden African masks stared back at her from hollow eyes.

"What are those?" Henrietta asked, pointing at the masks.

"Don't bother the woman with questions," said her mother.

"No, it's fine," Maria said. "I don't mind."

Maria went over to the wall and lifted a mask down from its place. She walked back over and sat down.

"This one is Olorun, a sky orisha." Maria smiled at Henrietta's confused expression. "A sky god. He is the ruler of endless space, and creator of the other orishas you see here," she said, waving her hand over the other masks to illustrate. "People are very careful when they worship Olorun. They call on him only in the gravest circumstances."

Maria handed the mask to Henrietta. She stared at it in bewilderment. She had no idea what the woman was talking about.

Her mother grabbed the mask from Henrietta and placed it on the table in front of her. "So how much will the treatment cost?"

"Do not worry. No payment is necessary." Maria smiled.

Henrietta took in a quick breath. Something about the smile gave her a chill.

Maria seemed to notice this. She adjusted herself in her chair, looking more relaxed, more casual. "We can start right away if you like."

"Yes, please," her mother said. "My husband will be expecting us home very soon."

"Yes, of course."

Maria got up and went to a black chest in the corner of the living room, directly under the wall of masks. She pulled out a long thin box and returned to her chair, setting the box on the table before opening it. In the box were a small vial, a metal syringe, and a small, gleaming metal ball. Maria took out the vial first. She opened it and poured two small black capsules into her hand.

"Take this, Octavia," Maria said, handing her the capsules. "You should be able to swallow it just fine without water."

Her mother nodded. Henrietta could see the small ovate capsules in her mother's hand. They seemed so inconsequential. What could something so small possibly do? Her mother stared for a long time at the little things.

"Don't worry," Maria said. "It is perfectly safe."

Her mother didn't seem calmed by the suggestion. She watched the capsules carefully as if she were waiting for some revelation. When she finally brought them to her mouth, it was slow and careful. Henrietta watched her mother intently as she did this. All the while, her mother's eyes were on Maria, looking for some sign of danger. Maria just smiled and waited, her hands resting on her lap. Henrietta felt another chill as she watched the woman. She was too still, not seeming to breathe at all.

After swallowing the capsules, her mother placed her hands on the table, resting one on top of the other. She looked stiff, uneasy. Henrietta had never seen her mother act this way.

"Tell me about the ailment."

Her mother's eyes darted across the table to Henrietta before returning to Maria. "I've been feeling sick to my stomach and very weak. My left breast is swollen. And there's bleeding."

"From the breast?" Maria asked.

Her mother nodded. "It is very painful."

Henrietta was not aware of any of this. She had noticed her mother going to bed early more often but didn't think much of it. Now she was here, in a stranger's house, learning that her mother was sick and that it had something to do with her breasts. Henrietta looked down at her own breasts. She wondered what could cause your own body to betray you.

"Take off your shirt," Maria said.

Her mother stared, taken aback by this. She opened her mouth to say something and then closed it again.

"I need to get the cancer out," Maria added.

Cancer? Henrietta snapped her head toward her mother. She wasn't looking at Henrietta, didn't seem to be aware that she was even in the room anymore. Henrietta looked down at her green pleated skirt, part of her white-and-green school uniform. She played with the creases, running her fingers down the length of them. She felt her eyes burning. She felt her cheeks grow hot.

Her mother took off her shirt and bra quickly, wincing as she removed the bra. A white cloth lay nestled inside it, stained dark brown. Tears collected in her mother's eyes. Was it the pain, or something else? Henrietta couldn't tell.

She could see it now: her mother's swollen left breast. Hard with large pores, it looked like the skin of a grapefruit. The nipple dripped blood.

Maria held the metal ball between her thumb and forefinger

and brought it close to her mother's breast. Her mother made a soft whimper when the cold metal touched her plump flesh. Tears rolled down her cheeks. She bit her lip in an effort to suppress her pain.

Her mother had been having trouble getting food out of cabinets, Henrietta remembered then. This must have been the reason. But this was the first time she had seen her mother in visible pain. It seemed unnatural, frightening. Henrietta wanted to reach out and comfort her mother, but she knew this was not something her mother would allow.

When Maria moved the ball away from her mother's breast, a large red spot glowed where the ball had been. The breast was still swollen, but the pores and skin had softened. Except for the area of red flesh, the rest of the breast returned to the light-brown color of her mother's skin. The purple bruising disappeared. The red spot had an otherworldly glow to it, the radiance changing intensity at regular intervals, growing and shrinking, brightening and fading. It looked as if it were breathing.

Maria then gently picked up the large metal syringe.

"This will hurt just a little," she said before sinking the needle into her mother's left breast, right at the center of the glowing area. She pulled back on the plunger, and Henrietta could see a bright red fluid fill the barrel of the syringe. Once the barrel filled, Maria removed the needle. Her mother winced as this happened, and then the muscles in her face relaxed. She looked completely at ease for just a moment. Then her eyes widened in astonishment.

Her mother touched her left breast, and Henrietta could see the joy on her face. She was not in pain. The breast looked healthy. No bruising. No glowing red blotch. Her mother was cured.

Henrietta watched as Maria returned the syringe to the box,

the glowing liquid still inside. She put back the ball and the vial.

Her mother put her bra back on and buttoned her uniform shirt. "Are you sure there isn't anything I can give?" she asked.

"No," Maria said. "I just wanted to help."

Henrietta watched the woman carefully. Maria smiled, but there were moments when Henrietta could see the facade slide away to reveal something disturbing underneath. The woman was beautiful, but there was something manufactured about it, another version of Maria buried deep beneath this one.

Her mother didn't seem to notice. She thanked the woman over and over. Again tears welled in her eyes, but this time she smiled wider than Henrietta had ever seen.

Henrietta looked out the window. It was getting dark. They would have to leave soon or arouse too much suspicion from her father. He worked as a manager at a small shoe store on Main Street and would be home a little after six. Her mother followed her eyes to the window before reaching the same conclusion.

"We have to go," she said. "But I must repay you for this."

"Oh, no," said Maria. "I can't—"

"I insist," her mother said, handing the woman all the money in her purse. It amounted to nine dollars. Maria smiled graciously.

On the way out, her mother thanked Maria another six times, each time emphatically. Maria smiled and received the praise.

Once outside, they walked quickly down the alley. It was now much darker than before, and the cricket chorus filled Henrietta's ears. They speed-walked down Garden Street and up Back Street. On Ninety-Nine Steps, Henrietta asked her mother if she noticed something wrong about Maria.

"What you mean?"

"Don't know. Something bad inside her."

"No," her mother said. "Maria is a good woman. She helped me."

"Yes, but—"

"But what?"

"I think she's a demon."

Her mother laughed. "Don't be silly, girl. She just got special gifts."

"Didn't God say to be mindful of witches?" Henrietta asked earnestly.

"Stop that, Henrietta."

Henrietta stared, confused, but she didn't say anything. Her mother was the most religious person she knew. That devoutness had rubbed off on Henrietta, had molded her sense of the world. She deeply feared the Lord and trusted in his word. Her mother was behaving strangely. Any other day, she would be quoting passages from the Bible or thanking God for her good health. This version of her mother did not do these things. Perhaps, Maria had changed her somehow. On the inside.

"You should have prayed to God to get better," Henrietta said.

Her mother snatched her by the arm. Henrietta could hear a dog barking a way off, and the sound of laughter from one of the houses bordering the steps. She looked away from her mother's now angry face to the cobbled steps, still wet from the afternoon's rain.

"Listen," her mother said. "Sometimes, you got to do for yourself. God doesn't always answer prayers."

Henrietta didn't like the look in her mother's eyes. She tried to pull away, but her mother held tighter.

"Don't waste your time waiting for help that won't come. God gives you the strength to help yourself."

Henrietta tried again and failed.

"Do you understand me?" her mother yelled, maintaining her gaze. "Do you understand me, girl?" The laughter in the nearby house died down. The dogs, too, fell silent. A man came out to see the source of the commotion. Henrietta saw only his silhouette, a shadow peering down at them.

Her mother grabbed her by the face so that she would look her in the eye. "Do you understand?" she asked a third time.

"Yes," Henrietta said. "I understand."

• • •

When Henrietta got home from the hospital, she went to sit on the couch. She turned on the television to her favorite soap: *All My Children.* She had long stopped paying attention to the convoluted plot. Now she just watched the scenes, trying to piece together enough of the story to amuse herself.

After she had sat there for a few minutes, her granddaughter walked out of the bathroom.

"Hey, Grandma," Lee said, sitting next to her on the couch. "How the checkup went?"

"How you get home?" Henrietta asked.

"Jessica."

Henrietta nodded, relieved it was one of her girlfriends and not some stupid boy. "It went fine. Fix me some bush tea, no?"

Lee sighed and got up. She would have to go out into the backyard to get lemongrass to make the tea. Henrietta knew that Lee hated picking lemongrass—she sometimes came back with little stinging cuts from sticking her hand in kasha—but the tea was the only thing that helped Henrietta feel better and got her to sleep.

She tried watching her soaps for a few minutes before Lee returned with lemongrass in hand, and a fresh cut from the jagged spikes of the kasha vine that threatened to choke her backyard garden. Lee chupsed her teeth in aggravation as she bent the stems of lemongrass into the pot and began boiling the water.

"So did they find something wrong?" Lee asked. She was fishing. Henrietta ignored the question.

The credits for *All My Children* rolled, and after a few commercials, the news at seven came on. On the news, Mera issued a statement about a recent riot against the Ynaa.

"Again?" said Lee from the kitchen.

On the screen, Mera apologized for the altercation and asked humans to use restraint when meeting any Ynaa in public. She expressed concern that her people wouldn't be as diplomatic as she. This was code for *if you aggravate any Ynaa, they will kill you.*

The Ynaa. That was what they called themselves. When they first arrived, Henrietta was in the middle of an early-afternoon nap. Her granddaughter had shaken her awake and brought her out onto the porch to see the spinning blue-white seashell hovering out in Charlotte Amalie Harbor. The hum was so loud, Henrietta was amazed she hadn't woken up on her own.

The first images of them were of Mera, the Ynaa ambassador. Those piercing eyes. Those tidy dreadlocks. That false smile. Henrietta knew immediately who she was. Mera had not arrived with the other Ynaa.

Henrietta had quoted Revelation when she saw Mera's face.

"So the great dragon was cast out of heaven, that serpent of old, called the Devil and Satan, who deceives the whole world; he was cast to the earth, and his angels were cast out with him."

The Ynaa came promising medicine and technology in

exchange for cohabitation. And for *research*. They had outgrown their world, they said. But Henrietta knew better, though she kept how she knew to herself. Let God deal with the devil.

"It's a little hot," Lee said, setting the cup of bush tea on the living room table in front of Henrietta. She dropped down beside Henrietta on the couch, holding a glass of milk in one hand and cookies in the other.

Henrietta picked up her tea and blew over it.

"Be careful, Grandma," Lee said.

"Don't worry yourself, child. I've drank a lifetime of hot bush tea. I'm not decrepit."

Henrietta could feel the throbbing pain of the cancer in her cervix. Now she knew for certain what it meant for her future. She adjusted herself on the couch and took a sip. She groaned through the throbbing and focused on the soothing hot tea coating her throat.

Her mother had died in her sleep at the age of ninety. She was never as devout as she had been before meeting with Maria. Henrietta's father died of a stroke, both her husband and her son of complications from diabetes. In the last weeks of her husband's life, he had cried all the time. Both his legs were cut off above the knee to stave off infection. He was a hollowed-out man. He whispered to himself. He called out in a wailing voice she had never heard from him before. He had always been a quiet man, not prone to such strong emotion. When her son slipped off into a diabetic coma without a word, she saw the silver lining. At least he hadn't had to suffer like that. He just lost consciousness and never woke up again.

Henrietta had outlived them all.

When she did die, she hoped to go just as quietly as her son.

Not wailing. Not pleading for more life. Her granddaughter was a
year away from eighteen and college. She hoped to last until then,
see her graduate from high school.

Then she could let the thing take her. She wouldn't mind one
bit. She would go off to where she belonged, where she had always
longed to be. She would be welcomed in because she hadn't com-
promised herself. She was faithful. She had trusted in God.

FOR TONY

When they were younger, Shawn and Anthony got into a whole mess of trouble all the time. Kid shit. Roughhousing, they would break a plate or a glass or a piece of their mother's "special" china. She'd be spitting mad for a day or two, then replace it with some crystal dolphin or other breakable thing. They would also stay out too late in the neighborhood and get caught throwing rocks at a neighbor's window or beating up neighborhood kids.

"How did I get such terrible children?" their mom would say.

Shawn would feel a momentary pang of guilt, but Anthony would always say something smart or hurtful like, "Because you're a terrible mother."

Mom would get really quiet and disappear to her room, and the next day she would be back to yelling at them for something new that they had done.

Shawn was the big brother by three years, but he spent a lot of time with his little brother. Anthony often seemed older than Shawn, braver and more defiant. Shawn remembered that he himself was usually the one being led into trouble, and also the one who had to clean things up.

Despite how old and cocksure Anthony seemed, he was a kid. When Shawn started his senior year, Anthony had just started ninth grade. He wasn't a big kid. Shawn had expected him to grow tall and menacing, but he was still short, with a big mouth and a hot temper.

When Shawn turned eighteen, Uncle Bennett approached him.

"You a man now," he said. "You'll need money."

This was not a question, but Shawn nodded anyway.

"Don't tell your mother," he said, and handed him a big bag of stinking weed. Shawn's uncle did not have a license, but that didn't matter. Soon enough, his uncle was handing him harder drugs, ones that had not been legalized.

Shawn became the guy people called when they needed some molly dropped off or they wanted to pick up a little ganja for their party. Anthony, being the quick kid he was, would ask, "Unc need another weed guy?"

"No," Shawn said. "And mind your damn business."

Shawn knew that Anthony wouldn't listen to him. He expected him to graduate and have the same talk with Uncle Bennett and get himself shot up somewhere for having a smart mouth and a quick temper. Shawn was preparing himself for that day, the day he would have to tell Anthony that he had to go to college and that Shawn would beat his ass himself if he tried otherwise. A fight would ensue, which Shawn would win, and then Anthony would go quietly off to the University of the Virgin Islands so he could stay on island and live with Mom. Shawn would talk to his uncle, explain it simply to him that Anthony would get himself killed if he got into this sort of work. Uncle Bennett would agree. Shawn had it all figured.

What he didn't expect was that Anthony would attack one of those fucking aliens with a stick and get his neck snapped.

Immediately after it happened, the ambassador of the aliens, whatever the hell her name was, issued another of those fake-ass apologies.

"We are so sorry for this tragedy," she said. "We are still adjusting to life here. We come from a planet where we learned wrath as a defensive mechanism against hostile threats."

"Bullshit!" Shawn yelled at the television screen. His very skin burned with rage. Something about how she said the words, as though their lives mattered more than his brother's death. Murder was merely adjustment issues? "Fuck this bitch!"

His mother sat on the couch near the door, the one Anthony liked to kick up on when he came home from school. It was an indication of her emotional anguish that she didn't tell Shawn to watch his mouth. She just sat there shaking, as if there were ice in her bones she couldn't get out. Fire and ice—that was what home felt like for months after the funeral: Shawn in a rage, his mother shivering in corners.

Shawn didn't like staying up in that house. And he didn't have to, once people got wind of Anthony's death. St. Thomas was in an uproar. When people gathered and marched the streets, Shawn was at the head, screaming chants until his throat ached. The people wanted the aliens to leave or be subject to human laws. Shawn wanted both. He wanted Old Testament justice—a neck for a neck.

What happened was the opposite of all he desired. The alien who killed Anthony never even made a personal apology. Cops came to stifle the protests, as if the protesters had done something wrong. Shawn couldn't believe that shit. And within a week, people went back to work. A few weeks after, they stopped showing up as much at sunset marches. Eventually, it was just a sad story people told. "These damn aliens," they'd say, and then get back to whatever else they were doing.

Shawn learned something from it all. Protests were useless. It was patting yourself on the back, bullshitting around on a sidewalk with a sign in your hand until you were tired and ready to go home. Anger was exhausting. Better to let it go. Move on. What else could you do?

Shawn spent a long time thinking about that very question. What could be done? Maybe before, people could yell and scream at their problems and something would change. But not now, not with them. People couldn't yell at a wall and expect it to fall.

It took a year before the answer came to him, before he knew what he must do.

● ● ●

It all started when his mother planned a one-year remembrance ceremony at Anthony's graveside a year after he was killed. For the community.

Shawn didn't want to go. The fucking community could all suck salt and die. He said as much to his mother, but she wasn't hearing it. She literally pushed him out the door.

"Don't disrespect your brother because you angry."

"Impossible to disrespect someone if they dead," he mut-

tered under his breath. If she had heard him, she pretended
not to.

A lot of people showed up at the cemetery. Maybe over a
hundred. His mother took her place at the front with Uncle Bennett and his cousin Zeke. Shawn stood behind them, watching
the crowd. Faces of family and friends. People who never did a
damn thing when Anthony got murdered, standing there as if
it were nothing. There should be riots in the streets. He would
have done it all by his damn self if he could. VI people didn't
know how to fight for anything. He could feel the sting of tears
in his eyes.

The church pastor led everyone in song. Shawn couldn't
remember the last time he had gone to church. When he was
still a kid, his mother had made him go, but now she didn't even
bother trying. She would get dressed and walk right out the door
without him. He welcomed that freedom of choice. As far as he
could tell, going or not going didn't change the state of affairs in
his life.

He wondered whether there was a verse somewhere in the
good book about invasion by aliens. It was all a fucking charade,
if you asked him. A big lie. Shawn pretended to mouth the words
as he stared blankly at the hymn sheet.

In the middle of Aunt Gena singing "Amazing Grace,"
someone tapped him on the back.

"Hey, man, you won't believe this shit," the someone said,
lowering his voice at the end.

It was Ricardo, one of his boys from high school. Shawn
hadn't hung out with him for a good while, but these things were
a damn magnet for out-of-touch acquaintances.

"What?" Shawn asked.

"What's that little punk's name? Derrick? Well, that pahnah is parked right over there, sitting in his car."

"So?"

"*So?* Well, guess who's with him."

Shawn didn't need to guess. And in the blinding-hot rage that followed, he took off running in Derrick's direction, screaming expletives at the top of his lungs.

Behind him, he could hear Ricardo shouting something, and by the time he reached the line of cars parked between graveyards A and B, he had a certified mob of angry people behind him, yelling words of encouragement.

"Get 'em!" someone yelled.

"How dare she!" said another.

Mingled in with the voices, he could hear his mother yelling something, but he was too enraged to care.

Derrick's car was parked under a lamppost. The sun had nearly set, and the light shone right into his car. Derrick sat in the driver's seat, the ambassador in the passenger seat.

Shawn picked up a rock. He rushed toward the car, and by the time they noticed him—the ambassador turning first and saying something in a panic—he had already hurled the big stone through the windshield. There was a crash, audible above all the screaming.

Shawn searched the ground in front of him for another stone. He found one near an old tree that had grown out of the road. In a flash, Mera was out of the car. Before he could throw another rock, she had him by the hand.

This would have scared a man with any sense, but it only made Shawn angrier. Under the streetlights, a crowd shouting behind him, he lost all grip on himself. He struggled against her with no success.

The expression on the ambassador's face wasn't human; he could see the creature she really was. Her fingers stabbed into him like blunt metal rods. The ambassador watched him, unblinking, and with a swift, effortless motion, she threw him. He felt his feet leave the ground, held up by some inhuman power, and then he was flying. He soared through the air backward, toward the crowd. He crashed into them and sent several people tumbling like bowling pins. Shawn was swimming in legs, arms, heads, and torsos, voices clamoring all around him, people yelling and screaming. He was completely disoriented, trying to find his place again in the world.

"Get back!" said a voice far away. The ambassador's, perhaps; he wasn't sure. He crawled on the ground and felt the softness of flesh under his left foot as a woman screamed out. He stumbled sideways. And then he could see again. She hadn't moved from where she was standing, but it was farther than he had thought. She had thrown him a full twenty feet.

"Fuck you!" he yelled at her. He searched for another rock. He would bash her head in. He would not let her leave this place alive. Not finding any rocks, he tried to get up. He would use his fists, then.

Arms wrapped around him.

"Let go, dehman," Shawn said.

"She'll kill you," said Uncle Bennett.

"Not if I kill her first," he said.

"You stupid, or what?" Bennett said. He pulled Shawn down to the ground and gripped him tightly. "This is not your day to die."

• • •

Shawn was fourteen, on the steps outside his apartment building in Hidden Valley, when the aliens landed. This was 2019, and he had just gotten with this Trini in his class, to the horror of her conservative parents. He was sitting there on the phone with her, telling her sweet and terrible things—things he knew about only from X-rated movies he had stolen from Uncle Bennett's house—when the spaceship appeared in the sky with a loud boom and a hum that made his teeth clatter.

After the bone-rattling fear subsided (calmed mostly because the aliens promptly got themselves on TV and proclaimed their peaceful intentions), Shawn thought the idea of aliens was actually pretty cool. He felt as though he was in the greatest moment in history! They would make movies about this for years to come. They would have to make a whole new genre.

His youthful enthusiasm swelled as he listened to the first broadcasts, played in a loop for twenty-four hours on CNN. The aliens stood stone-faced next to the president as one among them spoke into the microphone. Shawn and Anthony could see the film of sweat on the president's forehead. Anthony laughed and called him a pussy.

The aliens' message was as short as it was prompt. They would stay. They would offer technology in exchange for staying. There was *something* they were looking for, and they needed some time to research on a living planet with lots of diverse life. In a few short years, they would leave the planet as they had found it.

The entire message was cryptic, lacking any valuable information, but what did Shawn care about stuff like that? This was *aliens*!

Next, the alien ambassador Mera came to the stage. She greeted everyone in perfect, fluid English, and she even smiled. "We mean no harm," she said. "We hope that our peoples can live together peacefully."

The aliens weren't tentacled or slimy. They weren't green. They didn't have extra eyes shaped like long black ovals, like what Shawn had seen on *UFO Files*. They looked human. Perfectly human, in fact. But there was something off in how they stood and how they moved. Their movements were wooden, like still images spliced together, and at other times, smooth and light-ning quick, as if they were barely solid at all. Totally cool to an eighth-grader looking at something new and exciting on a television screen.

They settled next to Water Island. They liked the tropical cli-mate and the water, they said. They got comfortable, living mostly in their ship, but also in a few places on the island. They offered humans tech that cured diseases they had been seeking to cure for decades. They provided new ways for humans to power their cars and their cities.

And when they were offended or felt threatened, they ripped you to pieces.

It became immediately clear that the Ynaa were terrible at cohabitation. Shawn's attitude toward them soured.

Every once in a while, someone would make the paper. Torn in half. Head removed from body. Guy takes a drunken swing at alien in bar and gets his heart ripped from his chest. No one arrested. This was always the story. The Ynaa were outside human justice.

"They can't really be doing this," said Anthony. "Why aren't we killing them?"

Shawn didn't really have an answer. When Anthony got his neck broken, Shawn felt relief mixed in with all his anger and sadness. At least, their mother would get to bury him whole.

• • •

A week after the whole mess at the graveyard, Shawn's uncle texted him a name and an address. *He will get you what you need*, he wrote.

It turned out that this he, whoever he was, lived in Dry Yard. Shawn had a difficult time finding the house, because the roads looped in on themselves and led off onto dirt paths packed tight with small houses and old cars. The area had a large Rastafarian population. Shawn had to ask a guy sitting on a wall overlooking a gutter where he could find the house.

"Up that way," he said. He pointed up a short dirt road. Cars lined the left side of it. "That lil' green house there."

Shawn thanked him.

"Jah bless," the man said.

Shawn walked up the path and knocked a few times on the door until a slender Rasta man opened it and greeted him.

"Bennett sent me," Shawn said.

The Rasta looked him over quick and then whisked him inside. "Speak fast. What you want?"

"A high-caliber sniper rifle."

"You ever use one?"

"No."

The man laughed. "People call me Boonie. I like it enough. Call me Boonie."

Shawn gave his name.

"Yes, nephew. My condolences for the young one."

"You got a rifle?"

"Not here. Have to send for it." He told Shawn to have a seat on the couch, then made his way to the kitchen. Same room. The couch smelled like sweat and damp cloth, but the house was clean. "Hard to get guns these days," he started again. "Babylon don't pay no mind when you shooting up your own, but when you point your gun at them, that's when they stop smiling with you." The Rasta stopped and turned to him. "If this is a vengeance killing, be sure to get away fast. Them aliens are highly protective of their own."

"So am I," Shawn said.

"The last guy to shoot at one of them aliens got both his hands ripped right off his arms."

"That's why I want a rifle."

"They're unkillable. Whole body's like a bulletproof vest."

"Not their eyes."

Boonie came to the couch with a plate of bread and fried tofu with green peppers and onions. He handed it to Shawn and stared at him.

The tofu was cooked in soy sauce and vegetable oil—a little greasy, but good. Shawn ate the tofu and the bread separately.

"I'll need a little time," Boonie said. "Come back in a week."

"Okay."

"You sure about this?"

"I will come by late afternoon," Shawn said.

Boonie nodded, but his eyes stayed fixed on Shawn. "See you in a week. Bring two thousand dollars with you."

• • •

When Shawn came back the following week, Boonie rushed him in and sat him on the same ratty couch. He turned on the lights inside since his apartment caught very little natural light. Then he set a large duffel bag down in front of Shawn.

"Open it," Boonie said.

Inside, Shawn found a gleaming black rifle.

"The money?" Boonie asked.

Shawn tossed him the paper bag full of cash he had gotten from his uncle.

"Okay, so check this," Boonie said. And for the next few minutes, he walked Shawn through disassembling and reassembling the rifle's component parts, loading it, and mounting it on its two legs. "You'll need a good spot, high up, but here's the best feature. This computer ..." he pulled a small black tablet the size of a cell phone from the duffel bag and attached it to the left side of the receiver, "... can tell the gun what part of the body you want to hit."

As Shawn watched, Boonie programmed the rifle. He set it for the eyes. "It pretty easy to use, so you shouldn't have trouble reprogramming it yourself if a better idea hits you in the next couple days. That's it."

"That's it?" Shawn started disassembling the weapon, wrapping the parts in some old towels that Boonie provided, and placing them back in the bag.

"Is your car nearby?"

Shawn nodded.

"Get going."

Shawn slung the duffel over his shoulder. It was lighter than he expected.

"Good luck, hot-stepper," Boonie said as he left.

Shawn wouldn't go after Mera. She was too sharp and too cautious. He would wait for that one. Another time, another opportunity. But he would get the one who killed Anthony. That was easy enough since she still walked the path from her house, up on the hill behind the hospital, down to Back Street. She had a thing for roti, and a small restaurant on Back Street served the best. She walked there every weekday, undeterred by sun or distance. She took her time, too. About an hour of walking.

He tailed her, studied the path, and found the right spot. There was an abandoned jewelry store on Main Street, still unrepaired since Hurricane Irma, that she passed every day. It would have to be on Tuesday because the street's jewelry and accessory shops were crowded with tourists on all the other days. He spent two weeks tailing and planning. Before he knew it, all that was left was the doing. He had to climb and find an entrance to the second floor. He jimmied the old lock, slipped inside, and shut the door tight behind him. He pried the wood loose from the corner of a boarded-up window overlooking the street, making a big enough gap for him to see when the time came.

On the day, Shawn climbed to his spot early and waited. He checked the tablet over and over to make sure it was programmed right. The abandoned building was hot, his sweat making his clothes stick to him.

He didn't have to wait long. There she was, walking past one of the tall utility poles that lined the sidewalk. She moved in that same slow way, taking her time. The rifle was already trained in her direction.

Main Street was crowded with people entering and leaving the jewelry and souvenir shops. A man dressed in a carnival outfit of red feathers greeted tourists outside Diamonds International. An older white couple stood outside Cardow Jewelers, studying an open map. The female Ynaa strode past them all. A red Jeep honked as two boys in Charlotte Amalie High School uniforms ran across the street. They spun out of the way when they saw the Ynaa.

On the tablet, he could see video of the street. The shot vector danced from one person to the next. He directed the vector to the Ynaa and confirmed her as the target. The gun locked in on her eyes. All he had to do was press the button on the touch screen. Not even a trigger to squeeze. So easy.

Shawn's hand hovered above the glowing green circle at the corner of the touch screen.

The Ynaa was tall and brown, with very short hair. Almost bald. She wore hoop earrings as part of her facade. She looked human enough, even attractive, but her wooden steps gave her away. He recognized the expression on her face—the same one Mera had worn on that day at the cemetery. Tranquility. Not a care in the world. The Ynaa was certain that nothing could touch her. How wonderful it must be to float through the world with all that certainty, knowing that you could do anything and it wouldn't come back to you. How wonderful it must be to feel safe.

Shawn pressed the button.

There was a sharp zipping sound as the high-velocity bullet left the chamber and cut through the air. Then a wet, sucking sound, loud enough to hear over the crowd, as it entered her eyeball. The Ynaa wailed. The unnatural sound reached him and throbbed in his ears. Then she collapsed on the street and curled into a ball, shaking, before going completely still. A moment passed before the passersby, registering what had happened, erupted all at once in a frenzy of screaming.

• • •

Shawn went to his brother's grave. He rested his hand on the grass and told his brother that he had gotten the Ynaa and that it was all over. He had done what no one else was willing to do. Shawn's eyes burned, and he allowed himself to cry. He stayed there for an hour and told his brother the whole thing. How he had done it. How it felt. He allowed himself a joyous laugh of triumph.

Then he drove home feeling as though he had earned his place on the earth, feeling that he had gotten his soul back, his pride. He felt no remorse and marveled at the lack of it. He knew then that he could do this again. He could do it a thousand times more.

When he got home, he met his mother sitting on the couch with the TV on. The news cycle had already picked up the killing. The governor talked somberly to the camera, the words "Ynaa Assassinated" in bold letters at the bottom of the screen.

Shawn sat in Anthony's chair. He stared quietly at the screen and allowed a flicker of a smile to show on his face. He didn't look at his mother—didn't notice her eyes on him, or the sudden recognition coming to her face.

"What did you do?" she asked him. She tried to ask again, but the last of it caught in her throat.

"I did something," he said, and he told her not to worry. The aliens were afraid now. They could be touched. They could be killed. No longer could they hide behind the idea of their own safety. Things would be different now, he promised. Things would be better.

THE LESSON

At the base of Ship Tower, a slender blue-white column like a stalk of sugarcane ascended to the ship proper. Mera stepped onto the platform that fanned out from the thin stalk at its base, the reefs immediately coming alive and speaking to her in Ynaa. She commanded them to take her to the top level. The reefs curved around her like a curtain of water.

Once she stepped inside the column, the reefs shot her up to the top level of the ship. As she stepped out, they made space for her again, gently brushing against the outline of her body. Mera thanked them and walked along the silky white corridors to Ohoim's domicile. She passed no other Ynaa in the hall.

At Ohoim's door, she whispered to his reefs, "Tell him we need to talk."

A few minutes passed before the door unfolded for her.

Inside, Ohoim sat at a table, eating a plate of rice and peas with johnnycake and fried kingfish.

Ohoim looked up as Mera entered. "Do you want any?" he asked in his slow, deliberate way. Even among Ynaa, Ohoim sounded too slow, too deliberate. He had slowed down over his long life, which was several thousand years to Mera's few hundred. One of the oldest Ynaa still alive.

She shook her head at his offer with the same deliberateness. Apparently, they were going to talk around the issue. Mera had to push down her frustration. She had become unpracticed with the Ynaa.

"The food here …" A long pause. "… is delicious, isn't it?" Mera nodded.

"The raw materials themselves aren't so good. But put together like this"—he looked down at his plate—"it creates something better than its parts." Ohoim was not in his human skin. As he spoke, the tentacles on his head squirmed and he revealed the tiniest slivers of knife-edged teeth. A traditional long black cloak covered the rest of his body.

"We can leave," Mera said.

Ohoim stood. The movement was so fluid, she lost track of him for the briefest moment as he blurred and then resolidified. Ohoim's gills expanded with a slow breath. The dark orbs of his eyes shimmered. "You're finished with your work, then?"

"Yes," Mera said, taking from her purse a blue pearl the size of a golf ball. It was the culmination of hundreds of years of research, and the answer to all the Ynaa's hopes and dreams. Mera hoped it would be enough. "Everything is there. We can set off for Sa right away."

The streaks of orange on Ohoim's cheeks brightened as he took the pearl. "Such good timing."

Mera ignored the way Ohoim's tentacles flexed, the accusation in them. She had finished her work a week ago, but she wanted to be thorough, to make sure. She didn't want the Ynaa to leave only to come back and reignite fear in the humans. Waiting had seemed smart, prudent. Now it seemed a terrible mistake on her part.

"We know who did it," Ohoim said.

"Will action be taken against him?"

"Yes." Ohoim's orange streaks flared like fire.

"And no one else?"

Ohoim moved again, first slowly, then fast, to the far side of the room, where a human bed stood against the wall. Next to it stood the tall cylindrical chamber, filled with oxygen-rich saline liquid, where Ynaa traditionally slept. Image windows of different sizes occupied all the space around and above the two beds.

Images of the Ynaa home world cycled through the windows, one after another. Ynaa Sky and Ynaa Water. Snowcapped hills. An endless ocean, a massive moon hanging over dark water, backdropped by a star-filled sky. The pictures were methodical but stylized, indicating an equal partnership between the Ynaa imagination and the reefs' painstaking attention to detail. Using this method, one could do a thousand paintings in a day—paint every frame of their entire lifetime, if they chose. Ohoim had ripped these images from the memories of a world he left a long time ago.

"I like to look at these when I am homesick," Ohoim said.

The last word was an older form of the Ynaa word for homesick: *dursazen*. The Ynaa who had never seen Sa never used that word. They would say they were *durzen*, which meant they simply missed the familiarity of space once they had been land bound for a while. *Dursazen* was reserved for the Sa-born, the ones who had left Sa behind for the black.

"Sometimes, I wonder if I will ever go back to that place. Sometimes, I wonder why I didn't stay behind. We're so far from that world now. So far." He took a breath so deep, Mera could feel it vibrating in her own chest. "This cruel universe—it takes everything." He turned to look at her. His eyes glistened like obsidian. "We will teach the lesson that all creatures must learn: that we will survive this black prison even if we have to stand on the bones of every dead thing in existence."

Mera took a few steps back, toward the entrance. "Who will you kill?"

"The men on the island," Ohoim said with the casualness that only Ynaa could use in speaking of mass murder.

Only the men, Mera sent to Derrick over the reef link between them.

Okay, he sent back. His response had a touch of terror in it, suppressed but noticeable.

"When?" Mera asked Ohoim.

He watched her, his tentacles flexing. Then he revealed a mouth full of sharp teeth. They crowded his smile like a nest of needles.

Mera's breath caught. *Get moving*, she sent to Derrick. *Now.*

• • •

Jackson was already heading to Aubrey's when he got the call from Derrick. An hour ago, the governor had issued a curfew, ordering everyone into their homes. Jackson had no intention of following that order. When Derrick told him to come to the house, he knew he had been right.

Jackson arrived at the house at sunset. He had to block what looked like a government-issued SUV. Derrick immediately got out of the SUV and ran over, motioning for him to roll down his window. Jackson obliged.

"Hey," he said, his face covered in sweat. "You need to go down to Hull Bay."

"What about my family?"

"Don't worry about them. The Ynaa only coming after the men."

Jackson's stomach sank.

Derrick handed him a cup through the window. "Drink this." He slammed the top of Jackson's car very hard with the flat of his hand and said, "Get going."

Jackson inspected the cup. It looked like water with some mucous floating in it. "Is this spit?" he asked with narrowed eyes, but Derrick had already walked away from the car.

Derrick jumped into the SUV and started it. The SUV was all black with a government license plate. Through the tinted windshield, Jackson could see Derrick talking to someone over the phone.

His own phone rang. He put down the cup and answered.

"Dad?" Patrice's voice quivered on the line. A few seconds of silence passed, filled with her panicked breaths and loud, frantic footsteps.

"Don't worry," Jackson said. "It's going to be all right."

"I coming out!"

"Stay inside."

The door creaked open, and Patrice flew out of the house, her maternity dress flowing behind her. His ex-wife's maternity dress that she had worn when she was pregnant with Patrice.

"Stay inside!" Derrick yelled from the SUV.

Ignoring him, Patrice rushed toward the car. In seconds, she was at Jackson's window, reaching in to touch him. Jackson leaned up toward her, pulling her into an embrace. Her tears wet the side of his face.

"I love you, lil' miss," he said. "Keep your mother safe." Try as he might to see his daughter as a grown woman, right then all he could see was his little girl, her eyes rimmed with tears. He wanted to keep her safe, and right now safety meant distance. He had to get as far away from them as possible. "I gotta go, Pat."

Patrice pulled back to look at him, her hands in the scruff of his unkempt beard. "Don't get killed," she ordered.

"I won't," he promised.

Derrick honked his horn. Patrice chupsed her teeth but stepped back from the car.

Jackson stole one more look at his daughter. In the child's place stood the woman once again. She smiled and nodded him on, one hand cradling her belly.

Jackson felt the sting of the possibility that he would never meet his grandchild. He hesitated once more before his right mind asserted itself. Then he reversed and peeled out of the parking lot so fast, he spilled the contents of the cup, resting precariously in a cup holder too large for it, all over his jeans. He swore but didn't stop, speeding up the hill from the house he and Aubrey had built together.

The streetlights around him went out all at once, and the rock in his throat finally gave way to the cold terror of self-preservation.

• • •

Uncle Bennett came over at his sister's request. Shawn sat silent as they talked, the two of them not seeming to notice him.

"What foolishness is this?" his mother asked. It wasn't really a question. "I already lost Tony to these damn aliens. What they gon' do when they find out about this? Oh, Lord …" His mother sat back in her chair. She had worn herself out yelling.

Uncle Bennett kept his head down. "Don't worry, sister. It'll be just fine."

"You don't know that!" Shawn's mother pressed at her temples, tears staining her cheeks. "Oh, Lord in heaven …"

"They don't know it was him, sis." Uncle Bennett reached out to touch her with one hand. The hand, resting on her shoulder, rose and fell with each heave as she tried and failed to settle herself.

"My only remaining child," she said. "Please, please, Lord. Save us!"

"They don't know," Uncle Bennett repeated. "They don't know."

His mother looked up at Uncle Bennett then. Her face went blank, unreadable. "Where would he get the money for a gun like that, anyway?"

Shawn glanced over at his uncle.

Uncle Bennett took his hand from her shoulder. "There are a lot of people on this island sympathetic to what happened to our family," he said coolly.

"But not everyone has access to a gun like that."

"Uncle Ben had nothing to do with it," Shawn said.

"Shut up, boy," said his uncle, keeping his eyes on Shawn's mother.

"No, let him speak," she said. "Let him do his own lying."

Uncle Bennett said nothing, but his face turned to stone.

Shawn's mother leaned in, her voice low. "You think I stupid, eh? You think I don't know the kind of man you are, the kind of things you do?"

Uncle Bennett leaned in, too, their faces nearly touching. "I know you know. I let you pretend you don't, because I don't need you nagging me when I have to get shit done for this family."

"I shoulda drown your little mother skunt in the tub when you was a baby," his mother whispered, rage trembling at the edge of each word. "If anything happen to my son, I *will* kill you."

Shawn sank deeper into his chair. His mother looked to him like a shark's fin breaking the surface of the water, the thing to be feared lying underneath.

Uncle Bennett's expression still didn't change. "All that God talk before, and now you want to murder your own brother for getting vengeance on the thing that took your youngest?"

"*You* didn't take vengeance on anything."

Uncle Bennett's composure finally broke, his nose flaring, the vein in his neck looking like a fat earthworm.

Shawn saw his mother smell the blood. "You put my son on the line because you couldn't do it yourself," she said. "Because you a coward."

The house lights went out.

For a moment, no one spoke. A few years back, a power outage wouldn't have been alarming. Everyone knew that the VI Water and Power Authority was shit. But that was before the Ynaa arrived.

"You got flashlights?" Uncle Bennett asked, breaking the silence. He sounded normal, though Shawn knew better.

Shawn couldn't see anyone, not even a silhouette. He blinked, trying to peer into the darkness.

"Shawn, go get a flashlight." his mother said, fear creeping back into her voice.

"Where?" he asked.

"Try under the sink."

He got up and felt his way to the kitchen. Bumping his side against the edge of the kitchen counter, he swore quietly and moved his hand along the counter's seam to avoid any further collisions. Once he felt the cool metal of the sink, he stooped down and opened the cabinet. He felt his way to the back, where he found a big industrial lantern they used during WAPA's once-frequent blackouts and brownouts. Shawn pulled it out, found the big rubber-shrouded switch, and pressed it. Fortunately, the light came on.

"Bring it here," his mother said. She turned on the light on her phone, providing a second source of illumination.

Shawn rubbed his side bitterly as he made his way back to the living room. "You couldn't have turned that on a few minutes ago?"

His mother ignored him. "I got no service."

"Maybe we should make our way to one of the bedrooms," Uncle Bennett said.

"Mine," Shawn said.

"I think my room is better," his mother said.

"But …" Shawn started, not knowing how to say that he had the gun in his room. It was in a duffel bag under his bed. He looked to Uncle Bennett, communicating all he could.

Uncle Bennett nodded slightly. "We should go to the boy's room."

His mother squinted at them but didn't say anything. She got up and began walking to the room. Shawn followed, lantern in hand.

Shawn made his way across the living room before noticing that Uncle Bennett had not gotten up. Then he heard soft choking sounds coming from behind him. Turning to look, he saw Uncle Bennett still sitting on the couch, his hands trembling.

Shawn pointed the lantern at his uncle's face and stifled a scream. He felt the hairs rise on his neck as a wave of cold ran down his spine.

"What's wrong?" his mother asked from behind him. He listened to her footsteps come near but still jumped when he felt her hand on his shoulder.

Now she could see what he saw. And she did scream.

Uncle Bennett's eyes had rolled up into the back of his head, and blood oozed from his eye sockets, his nose, his mouth. He still trembled, though the motions had become spaced out, erratic. Shawn could hear him softly choking.

"Get in the room, Mom," he said, walking over to his uncle.

"Should we get a neighbor? Is it a stroke?"

"No," Shawn said to both questions. As he stepped closer, he could feel the ice creeping through him, the slow crawl of fear along his skin. His mother hadn't moved. He heard no footsteps behind him, only heavy breathing.

Shawn reached out and touched his uncle, and for a moment his uncle seemed to gain some awareness. He tried to speak but couldn't. He screeched out something, but the paralysis was so severe, he couldn't move his lips to articulate it. He continued choking softly. Without knowing how, Shawn was certain now. This was not a stroke.

Uncle Bennett croaked out another syllable, and Shawn could guess what it was. He was telling them to run.

The door to the house flew open.

His mother squealed in a vocal expression of both surprise and terror.

Shawn didn't have time to see what was there. He turned to his mother, pulling her back from the living room, retreating to his bedroom. He pushed her in and followed, closing and locking the door. His mother kept screaming.

"Shut up!" he said more sternly than he had ever talked to his mother in his entire life.

She accepted the order, shrinking back from the door, cowering behind the bed, near the window, as far from the thing outside as she could get.

Shawn rested the lantern on the dresser by the door. He pulled the duffel bag from under the bed and sat down on the mattress, unpacking the rifle and clicking the barrel, stock, and receiver together. It swayed awkwardly on the mattress as he tried to position himself.

When he was ready, he turned on the viewfinder on the tablet, setting it to heat-seeking mode. As he did all this, he tried to keep his nerves in check. Why hadn't they barged into the room? How many were there? He looked through the viewfinder and could see his uncle through the walls, his body cooling on the couch. The weapon detected no other heat signatures.

His mother cowered quietly, her breath fast and heavy. When he turned to look at her, she was looking at him—for how long, he couldn't say. He put his finger to his lips and tried to project calm self-possession.

Someone knocked at the door. Shawn snapped his head

toward the sound. For a moment, there was no other indication that something was happening. The stress of the situation made him question whether he had even heard the knock. He looked to his mother for confirmation. She wasn't looking at him anymore, just staring wide-eyed at the door.

"I don't want to hurt your mother," said a voice, the words low and thin, spaced farther apart than normal speech. "But mothers are protective. They end up getting hurt." Another pause, this time longer. "Come outside." The voice had an indefinable quality to it. Even after it stopped, it whistled in the air.

"Why?" Shawn asked.

No answer for a moment. His heartbeat ramped up, thumping time.

"I want to snap your neck," the voice said.

Shawn fired three bullets at the door.

The door splintered, the first bullet hitting something solid with an unmistakable pop. The other two bullets punched through the door and sang in the air. They passed through the open doorway to his mother's room, on the opposite side of the hall, before shattering the window on the far wall of the house.

His mother hadn't made a sound. He glanced in her direction and saw her bunched up in the corner, staring terrified at the splintered door.

Shawn wiped sweat from his forehead. He felt the sweat from his armpits trickle down his sides. There were no sounds in the house, but he could hear the wind slipping through the broken window, carrying with it the faint screams of neighbors across the way.

"They killing people!" his mother confirmed, her voice trembling so much, Shawn could hardly decipher the words. "Oh, my God, they killing people!"

My fault. The thought had come up through the horror and panic of the moment. He had avenged his brother thinking it would change things. It had made them unimaginably worse. They were killing people. And they would get away with it, just as they had before.

Shawn heard something thrashing in the hall, and he fired six more shots, screaming as he did so. They rippled through the air, tearing fresh holes in the door. He didn't hear where they ended up. A couple of minutes passed, with more screams carried on the wind. Shawn felt as though he was going to throw up.

Then he heard it: soft choking coming from behind him once again. *Oh, no.* He slowly turned to look at his mother. Her mouth hung open, her body strangely stiff and contorted. Her wide eyes were on him. She tried to choke out words, but nothing came. Jagged coughs sputtered from her mouth with a sound like skipping stones.

"For her own protection," said the voice.

Shawn let one more shot out before his hands tightened up and his whole body seized.

"If you believe you have any control here," said the voice—slow, soft, and hissing—"then let me educate you."

Shawn tried to scream but couldn't. His whole body felt like one giant muscle cramp, on fire with pain. He couldn't move anything. And now he could hear himself choking, trying desperately to breathe and failing. The sound of it terrified him.

The door creaked open, and out of the dark he saw a creature come inside. He forgot about his struggle for breath, or the hot pain throughout his body, as the creature came slowly toward him. Shawn's mind screamed at him to flee. The thing was not encumbered by human skin.

The creature eased forward, painfully slowly, the streaks on its cheeks glowing hot. The light from the lantern revealed dark pools for eyes, and five large tentacles on its head, slowly writhing. These, too, were streaked with orange, and they flared up like a fire as the thing drew near. Its body was large with slick, muscled gray-black skin. Shawn couldn't tell the gender of the thing.

"She was my sister," said the thing, its voice now so low, so harsh, that Shawn could feel the words resonate in the bones of his spine.

A flash of color streaked across his sight, and he felt coarse hands on his neck, the pain of it adding to the throbbing agony everywhere else.

"I had plans to do this slowly," said the thing, its layers of sound forming a dark chorus. "But I won't do that to your mother. I'm not a monster."

The thing squeezed. Shawn felt the pressure, and then he felt his neck snap. After that, there was nothing.

• • •

Twenty-five thousand. As Derrick waited for Louie to come out of his house, he tried to understand the number, feel it in his bones. It was too big to feel real. He couldn't quite bring it down to human terms. But the number was human. Twenty-five thousand men and boys on the island. And babies. He had made Patrice drink just in case the Ynaa would snatch the life right out of women's wombs. Twenty-five thousand dead people. *His* people. And what had he done to stop any of it? All his lofty hopes and dreams, his naive plans, stacked atop twenty-five thousand men and boys.

Mera was trying to help him save family and friends. There were others, too, who would be saved. She had managed some small alliances among the Ynaa. But what did that mean against a number so large? He tried to feel what it would be like to mourn each of those souls, but his mind rebelled. It couldn't grasp the number. What would it mean after? How would they grieve something so vast? Enough blood to drown all reason, all understanding.

What could he have done differently? What *had* he done? Nothing. Nothing at all.

Derrick listened to the quiet outside the SUV. Savan had not been hit yet. He tried to imagine all those people waiting in their homes, not knowing what would come. Just waiting to die. To lose the ones they loved. To stand helpless over seizing, shuddering bodies.

He had taken the back roads so he could get to Savan, had passed over a dozen stalled cars. Many of them had men at the wheel, had little boys in back seats, not understanding what was happening, not knowing enough to understand, not capable of counting that high.

Derrick had passed them all. Driven right past. To get to Louie, he told himself. To save his best friend who he had hung out with only once in the past three months. He knew it for the lie it was. He had passed those people because he couldn't tell which among them he could trust not to kill him. His forehead throbbed with psychosomatic intensity as he passed each car. The Ynaa hadn't tried to kill him. His own people had. And they would likely try again.

Sitting in the SUV, he couldn't blame them. Even now he couldn't get out to knock on Louie's door, afraid he would be spotted, recognized. Dread filled him up, made his limbs feel like lead. He couldn't stop shaking.

The truth was, all that he had done had been for himself. Because he liked feeling important. Because he wanted to touch the stars. He didn't consider that they would touch back, that so many wouldn't survive the price. He had chosen a stranger over his own people. He had loved her, and now he had lost everything. They would never understand. He would never have a place there ever again.

He tried again to open the car door, but his head hurt. He was crying and noticed only now that it was difficult to see.

Why hadn't Louie come out yet? He needed to go get him. He needed to do this one little thing. The neighborhood hadn't been attacked, but that wouldn't last. He needed to do something. Why wasn't he doing something?

Derrick always had trouble with things right in front of him. They never seemed big enough, grand enough. It was strange coming to terms with that, staring at oneself and seeing the ugly truth stare back. Not being able to flinch away from it, to hide. He still wanted to save the world. And still feared being hated for not doing so. He couldn't get out of his own way.

He had to let go of that, make tonight about something else. Someone else.

Derrick wiped away his tears. He took several long, deep breaths. Then he grabbed the coffee cup resting in the cup holder and opened the door. It was hard at first. His head itched. But then he stepped out of the SUV, the night heat hitting him. A dog barked in the distance. Somewhere far away, he heard gunshots. No more time to wait. Time to go. He willed his feet forward.

He pounded up the steps to Louie's house and knocked hard on the door.

Louie opened. "What you doing?" he whispered.

"We have to go," Derrick said.

Louie sighed. "Just come inside."

"Why?" Derrick asked as he entered. "What going on?"

Louie shut the door but kept his voice low. "My mother is scared. She doesn't want me to leave."

"Okay, let me talk to her."

"And," Louie added.

"What? What is it?"

"Can Omari come with us?"

Derrick didn't know Louie was seeing Omari. But Derrick had abandoned everything because of his fixation on Mera. Of course he didn't know. "What happened to Sandra?" he asked.

"Dude, we broke up so long," Louie said.

Derrick nodded. "Is Omari here?"

"Yeah, in the back with Mom."

Louie led Derrick through the cramped dark hallway of his house to a back room that smelled faintly of mothballs. A few candles lit the small bedroom. Omari sat next to Louie's mother on the bed. Both of them met Derrick's eyes as soon as he entered.

"Hey, Mom," Derrick said.

"Child, me'n see you in so long. What you been up to?" Debra got up and gave Derrick a hug. She smelled like sweat and perfume.

"I just been busy with work," Derrick said, the words sounding slimy as he spoke them.

Debra's expression grew dark. The candlelight illuminated the lines of her face. "They killing people, you know. Your boss orders?" The question came out matter-of-fact, but Derrick could see the seriousness in her eyes.

"No," he said. "She's trying to help."

Debra nodded, apparently satisfied. He couldn't believe it.

"Then keep these boys safe," she said. "Don't want nothing happening to them, okay?"

"Yes, Mom." He tried a smile, but it didn't feel right. His facial muscles spasmed minutely.

"Should we go now?" Omari asked, piping up for the first time. Derrick knew Omari from his high school days. He'd been a few years ahead of Louie and Derrick, a senior when they were just freshmen. Popular. Not that it mattered now.

Derrick handed Louie the coffee cup in his hand. "You two need to drink this."

Louie drank right away, then said, "Why you giving me hot sweet tea to drink?"

"It was cold when I left the house," Derrick said, handing the cup over to Omari.

He just stared at the cup. "You'n answer his question," he noted, the candlelight flashing on his scowling face.

Derrick glanced at Debra. She was paying attention to the entire exchange but had no words of her own. Then he returned to Omari. "I gon' tell you on the drive, but we need to hurry."

Derrick caught Debra reading him and saw the moment when she decided it didn't matter what he was trying to hide. "A'you just hurry up and get to safety, hear me? I'n about to lose any of my boys tonight."

Omari drank from the cup and passed it back to Derrick.

As they left, Debra gave Derrick a kiss and reiterated that they be careful. "Get where you going fast. The roads must be a menace."

Derrick nodded in confirmation but shared no stories.

The three poured out of the house. Debra stood watching them descend the stairs and then closed the door behind them.

"Where we going?" Omari asked too loudly for Derrick's liking.

"I gon' tell you when we get in the car," he whispered.

"Aye," said someone. Not any of Derrick's little group.

Derrick, Louie, and Omari didn't move. They stood near the SUV, Derrick's hand inches from the door.

"You'n hear me talking to you?" said the voice. Just then three men materialized from the shadow of an alley across the street. "Come here," said the one at the front.

The street was dark, making it hard to see any faces. Derrick hoped this would be a blessing for their group as well. If he couldn't see them, they couldn't see him. And the last thing he wanted was to be recognized.

"We 'bout to leave," Omari said.

"How?" asked the one at the front. "That vehicle working?"

"On foot," Derrick said.

"Where?" The three inched forward. Derrick's group didn't budge.

Omari whispered something to Louie that Derrick couldn't make out. Something about a gun.

One of the men, not the ringleader but the one to his left, lifted his hand. Derrick flinched instinctively.

A stream of hard light revealed Derrick's group but kept the men in shadow. Light lined the ringleader's left side like a sinister halo.

"I thought I recognize that car," said the man to the ringleader's left. "Thought the ambassador would be behind the wheel. What a surprise to find you."

"We don't want trouble," Derrick said.

"Neither do we," said the ringleader.

The third man, to the ringleader's right, had been quiet the entire time. The light in Derrick's face made it difficult, but he still strained to see what the man was doing with his hands. By the looks of it, they were tucked into his hoodie.

"If I use it now, we got the advantage," Omari whispered to Louie.

Somewhere, a dog started barking, starting up a chorus of other dogs in the neighborhood.

"We just want to get into the car," Derrick said.

"So it works," said the ringleader. "Maybe a'you could give us a ride, too."

Derrick watched the silhouette of the three men. He was sure now that at least one of them had a gun. His forehead itched again, the animal fear intensifying. He thought of all the people he had passed on the way. He did the math again.

"So you gon' let us come, or what?" said the ringleader.

A few years ago, before the Ynaa, Savan had been a dangerous neighborhood. It still was, though the danger had lessened over the years since the Ynaa arrived. Derrick still didn't like driving through Savan. Safer generally didn't mean safer for *him*. It was part of the reason he hadn't seen Louie in so long. He had feared for his own life.

Derrick adjusted his math, subtracting five from twenty-five thousand. "Okay," he said. "You got any little nephews or brothers you want to bring along?"

"Are you fucking crazy?" Omari said under his breath.

"Yeah," said the one with the flashlight. "I got some cousins nearby."

"Let's go get them," Derrick said. "You three will have to drink from this cup. I'll explain later."

"Fuck this, I'm doing it," Omari whispered.

"No," Derrick whispered back.

"What going on out here?" yelled Debra from the doorway.

Derrick turned. "Shit. Go back inside, Mom!"

And then a few things happened at once.

The man with the flashlight turned his stream of light on Debra. Omari moved so quickly, Derrick couldn't get a word out in protest, and then three shots whizzed past Derrick's ears. Two somehow hit their impossible marks in the darkness. The ringleader screamed, and the man with the flashlight fell dead. And the third man, the one who had been quiet the whole time, fired his weapon.

Derrick had enough time to hear the sound of the first shot, and then just enough time to feel that last bit of hope he was holding on to disappear. The bullet stole the rest.

• • •

Hull Bay doubled as a beach and a docking area for small boats. The beach also had a bar, Hull Bay Hideaway, the name suggesting how difficult it was to find the damn place. Designed like a giant open shed, the bar had a high roof supported by thick wooden poles, some painted yellow and green. Around the property was a wooden fence, with vintage surfboards in various stages of ruin providing decoration near the entrance.

North-side Frenchies and expats made up most of the bar's patrons. Jackson hadn't been to Hull Bay in years, but now he found himself wishing he had. The bar lay quiet inside its fence, all the action happening on the beach.

Jackson could hear the excited chatter of a small crowd as he approached. He parked between two trucks that made his electric mini look like a child's toy, and got out. He wouldn't have noticed it if he hadn't stopped to take one last look at his car. A small fighting-conch shell was stuck like some barnacle to the front of his hood. Little threads of light fanned out from the shell. He remembered when Derrick tapped the top of his hood with something hard. This must have been it.

Jackson marveled at the thing, realizing how little he knew about the Ynaa even after all this time—how little any of them knew. He hoped Derrick had made his way back to the ambassador. He didn't expect him to be at the beach and had no way of contacting him, so he used hope instead. It didn't seem an especially useful instrument, doing nothing to ease his mind.

You're not safe yet, either, he reminded himself. The thought got him back on mission. He headed to the beach.

Jackson met a couple dozen people as he walked onto the concrete docking ramp that also served as the main entrance to the beach. The wide ramp descended into calm but surprisingly deep water at high tide. People were idling inches from the incoming surf. A few weren't on the ramp, choosing instead to stand on the beach.

Jackson watched people's faces, the half-moon and stars overhead providing some visibility. Everyone looked uneasy or upset. Some stood in stunned silence. A woman sat in the sand sobbing openly, comforted by the hand of an older man. Jackson assumed that she had already lost people, that many of the people around him had, too. There would be a lot more of that tonight.

"What's going on?" Jackson asked a man standing next to him, a younger guy with short hair and a patchy beard. "Will there be rescue?"

"Boats coming in," the man said. "Several are ferrying people off island."

When Jackson asked how the boats were still operating, the man shrugged. "Don't know. Just happy to get out of here."

On the water, Jackson could see a small light blinking. Too far out to make out what it was yet, but he guessed it was one of the boats the man had just mentioned. Other boats of various sizes idled a few yards out from shore. Not as many as he remembered seeing the last time he was out here at night. Which meant some people had already used their boats to flee the island. Smart decision. Good on them.

Next to Jackson, a woman flashed her phone light at the water, to reveal dozens of long, thin fish idling below the surface, near the dock, their eyes reflecting the woman's light.

"Oh shit," said the woman. "But what the rass is that?"

"Sharks," said a teenage boy.

"They better come right up to the dock with those boats," said the woman, "because me'n going in no water with no damn sharks."

Jackson smiled just a little. More likely, the fish were barracudas. "Have they called for help?" he asked the man with the patchy beard.

"They're being blocked," a different woman said. "We don't know how they doing it. Besides, America ain't gon' help us no way."

"All right," said an older Frenchie standing ankle-deep in the surf. "Men and boys, step forward." He spoke loud enough to be heard over the chatter while not bothering to glance back at the crowd.

The crowd quieted. Men and boys, Jackson included, stepped forward.

"The boat should be here in a minute or so," the Frenchie continued. "It seats about ten people, so I want a'you to form a line on the incline. When it comes, get in as fast as possible."

Jackson and the rest of the men and boys followed the man's orders. Jackson got the fifth spot in line, standing behind the man with the patchy beard.

"What about women?" asked the woman still flashing her phone.

A few people made noises of annoyance.

A man sighed. "They only killing the men. What you worried 'bout?"

"I want to stay with my family," she said.

More groans from the crowd.

"Hush your mouth, lady," said the man at the front of the line. "People trying to live and you over there making noise."

"Don't talk to me like that!" she yelled. "Arnold, you gon' let him talk to me like that?"

One of the men in front of Jackson looked back at her sheepishly. "Please calm down, baby," he said. "We have to save our son. Don't antagonize these people."

The woman chupsed her teeth but didn't say anything after that.

Jackson could see the boat slicing through the water now. So close, he dared hope. He imagined himself on the other shore, safe and waiting. He imagined himself holding his grandchild in his arms in some future when the Ynaa threat no longer loomed over them all. The VI people would get back their island and pick up the pieces of their shattered lives.

Because they had to. Because that was what they always did.

We tough people, the young folks liked to say. *Island strong.*

The ringing sounded far away at first. Then it was closer, like a train coming in at great speed. Jackson looked around. Several of the other men glanced around as well, confused and frightened.

Jackson felt his entire body tighten, pain pushing optimism out of reach.

"What—" he started to say. The rest of the sentence lodged in his throat. He collapsed on his side, his body trembling from wave after wave of some unseen force. Many of the other men collapsed, too. In the distance, he heard women scream.

From his vantage point on the incline, Jackson could see some new arrivals writhing in the sand, and women trying to drag some of them toward the water.

He became aware that the boat had arrived. When did it get there? Time seemed to be moving both fast and slow at the same time. His mind struggled. He started choking on his own tongue. He felt someone's hands on him, the sensation far away from the loud pain throbbing through him. He could just barely make out that gentle touch as his body shifted under the pressure of the stranger's hands. The hands rolled him over onto his back, and he could see delicate clouds and flickering stars and a man's face hovering over him. The man's fingers pushed between Jackson's lips, exposing his clenched teeth. Had his jaw been clenched this entire time? His body sprinted away from him and then back again, like a wave breaking and pulling back out to sea. He was beneath himself now, trapped in the pain. He could do nothing to help the man with his objective or even to fight back.

The man's fingers slipped along the soft flesh inside Jackson's mouth. Then he leaned in and made a hawking sound, drawing something forth from the back of his throat and spitting it between Jackson's parted lips. The slick mucous slid along Jackson's clenched teeth, seeping little by little between the gaps. Even in the throes of pain, the experience almost made him gag.

The pain retreated, slow at first and then faster. Then Jackson regained control of his limbs. The noise of the world around him came back, and the canvas of stars above him warped back into focus.

"Can you move?" the man asked.

Jackson nodded, squinting away the tears in his eyes. He had not realized he'd been crying.

The man nodded back and got up, leaving him to his own devices. Jackson turned his head and watched the man go down the line of men, spitting in their mouths. The repeated action seemed fast and brusque compared to Jackson's own experience with the man. He observed as some of the men regained their ability to move.

Jackson got to his feet and looked down the beach. People ran along the sand. Women, shoulder-deep in the water, lugged paralyzed men on their backs, trying their best to keep the shuddering, contorted faces above the surface. The boat bobbed in the disturbed water. Three men had already been hurled into the boat. The female boat pilot leaned over each man and spat into his mouth.

"Hey!" someone yelled. Jackson turned and saw the spitting man from earlier still working his way down the line. "Help me get some of these guys into the boat!" the man yelled.

Jackson sprang up. Picking up the boy behind him in the line, he carried him to the edge of the incline, passed him to two men in the boat who had regained their strength. Then he hauled a man to his feet. The man moaned, his mouth slack. Jackson repeated the pass and then turned to the next man in the line only to find him dead, leaking blood from his mouth and nose.

The man who had saved Jackson came toward him, with a man's arm draped over each shoulder. The two limped toward the boat, propped up by the man in the middle.

"The rest?" Jackson asked.

The spitter shook his head. Jackson helped him get the two men into the boat. Then he and the spitter followed, finding their place among the passengers. The boat, a twenty-six-foot pleasure craft, was stuffed with eight men and six boys—well over capacity, but that didn't matter now. The boat would not return.

Every so often, Jackson heard a voice on shore go quiet in midscream. The trees surrounding the beach bustled as shadowed figures ran under their outstretched limbs. Several bodies lay motionless on the beach—effects with no visible cause. Jackson's fellow passengers stared uncomprehendingly at the shore.

The boat pilot started the motor. Jackson watched as the women in the water waded back to shore. One lingered to give her son a kiss on the forehead.

"Be safe," she said, and the boy nodded. Jackson couldn't see her tears, but he could hear the quiver in her voice. The woman pushed off from the boat and swam back to shore.

The men were all quiet as the boat turned in the water. Some looked around, others sat hunched over, staring at their knees. Jackson kept his eyes on the shore. The women sitting and standing on the beach watched them leave.

"Look!" said the boy beside him.

At first, Jackson didn't know what he was looking at. Beyond the women, flickering lights grew brighter and bigger in the brush surrounding the beach. And then, all at once, the lights crossed the threshold from the shadowed tree line onto the sand, and Jackson knew exactly what he was looking at.

Glowing flesh.

One of the women turned and screamed so loud Jackson had no problem hearing it from the boat. After that, the women scattered in all directions along the beach. The creatures didn't pursue them. Instead, they walked to the water's edge and stood, nine of them in a line.

No one on the boat made a sound.

Jackson had learned enough about the Ynaa through his conversations with Derrick to know that they were excellent swimmers. He was sure they could catch up with the boat if they wanted to. But the creatures didn't budge from their position on the beach. They simply watched the overloaded craft as it pushed through the water. Why not pursue?

A possible answer occurred to Jackson. The order was to kill all the men on the island. Had the Ynaa decided to take this instruction literally? *Mercy*, Jackson thought, watching the Ynaa on the shoreline shrink to the size of action-figure dolls. They were showing mercy.

Jackson clasped his shaking hands together as the boat slapped over weak waves, and the dark mass of St. Thomas receded from view. Not so far off, the British island of Tortola lay in front of them, its interspersed lights glowing with the promise of power and safety. They would be standing on its shore before long.

"How are you feeling?" asked the man sitting next to him—the same man who had saved his life, who had saved so many of the lives on the boat.

"I'm fine," Jackson said. "Better than most."

"We lost a lot of people on that beach," the man said.

"Lost a lot of people on the island," Jackson added.

The man nodded. He didn't say anything else. In the silence, Jackson listened to the whispers of other people in the boat. Some of the men who were hit hardest by the seizures—that was what Jackson had decided they were—had regained some presence of mind.

"You know what happened, don't you?" Jackson asked the man next to him. "The seizures."

"I do," he said.

"You spit in my mouth."

"To give you reefs," he said, answering the nonquestion. "Reefs to kill the reefs already inside you. Inside everyone."

Jackson recognized the term the Ynaa used for their smart cells. "Yeah, but *spit*?" he asked, making a face.

"Only way. Can't command the reefs like the Ynaa can."

"Where'd you get the reefs?"

"From a friend." The man offered no further elaboration.

In that final answer, however, Jackson managed to pick up a well of anger and bitterness, concrete and deeply personal. "Well," he said, "thank you for saving my life."

"You welcome," the man said.

"What's your name?" Jackson asked.

"Jason," he answered. "But my friends call me Jammie."

• • •

Mera went to the last spot Derrick had been. She already knew what she would find. The reefs had told her the moment it happened, but she wanted to see it with her own eyes. On the dark street lay five dead bodies. A woman knelt over the sixth, who was near death. The reefs Mera sensed in his system had already failed to save him. The woman didn't look up when Mera made herself known, so Mera went cautiously to the one person she knew.

Derrick had a bullet hole in his head, and she could see flecks of blood and brain spread on the road behind him. She took in the carnage, her strong emotions wrapped snug in the center of herself. The woman moved a little but still didn't look up.

"I'm sorry," Mera said to the woman, to Derrick, to herself.

"I told you to be careful with that boy," said a voice.

Mera didn't acknowledge Okaios with words. She just turned slightly in his direction.

"Some of your pets got away in Hull Bay," he said, walking out from a dark alley across the street. He shrugged. "Small victories."

Unlike the other Ynaa, Okaios still wore his human skin, the one from the last time Mera had seen him in her office.

"Did Ohoim send you?" Mera asked.

"No," he said. "Father O didn't send me."

"Then why are you here?"

"Because of that one."

Mera looked back at the man bleeding out in the street, and the woman leaning over him. Yes. It made sense that the not-dead man would interest Okaios. The reefs were ordered to kill all the men in this area.

The older woman still had not moved. Mera tracked the man's vitals through her reefs. His breath was even shallower, his heartbeat faint and rapid. Just a few more minutes of life left in him.

"The kill reefs are meant to be frightening," Okaios said. "And painful." He paused, getting closer. "I didn't want that for him. I wanted it to be quick. Peaceful."

Mera turned completely toward Okaios, giving him her full attention. She revised her earlier conclusion.

"He ended things a while ago," he continued. "He said I was too violent. Too dangerous."

The woman began to sob.

"It is done, then," Okaios said. "I supposed this was better than the alternative."

The sadness in his voice reminded Mera of an owner who has lost his prize pet. "No," she said. "A better alternative would have been no one dying."

"Then how would they learn?" Okaios asked.

The sobbing stopped, and she heard the woman scream in rage. Mera turned to look at her. Too late already. Always too late.

The woman was on her feet in an instant, a gun in her right hand. She didn't hesitate before firing. The first bullet hit Mera, bouncing off her flesh, the reefs acting quickly to protect her. She dodged the other two shots, but the woman continued firing two more at Okaios. He easily dodged the bullets and flew at the woman, picking her up by the throat in one hand.

"Put her down," Mera pleaded.

Okaios didn't respond to Mera, but he didn't kill the woman, either. She dangled in his grasp, her feet swaying, trying to find the ground beneath her. She was suffocating slowly, trying to suck air through her nose.

"She is his mother," Mera said. "She wasn't in her right mind."

"Not my problem."

"Don't do this," Mera said, inching closer. The streets were quiet, but she could hear crying from many of the surrounding houses. She was sure Okaios heard them, too. "Please. There's been enough death today."

Okaios responded with an old Ynaa proverb. "And what is another body to a mountain of dead? What is a drop of water in an endless sea?" With a regretful frown, he returned to his work.

He realized his mistake only when Mera darted toward him. Reflexively he dropped the woman and pivoted to face Mera, putting up his hands in defense. Another bad decision that he didn't know he was making. Mera touched him on the forearm—a simple, gentle tap of her first two fingers, and then leaped back, watching him.

"What are you doing?" Okaios asked.

Mera didn't answer. He would know soon enough.

The telomerase enzyme Mera had redesigned from human to Ynaa physiology could elongate chromosomal telomeres indefinitely, but the reefs still had to manage cell growth, speeding it up or slowing it down when necessary, retiring cells that might produce cancers. The system had to be in balance for the two parts not to overwhelm each other. Mera had painstakingly achieved that balance during testing. It was also during testing that she stumbled across a use for intentional imbalance.

Okaios barely had time to turn back to the woman before he felt the heat rising under his skin as his insides began to cook. He stumbled back, wearing an expression she had never seen on an Ynaa before.

In his body, her reefs were fast at work, duplicating themselves, prodding his cells to replicate abnormally, relentlessly, thanks to the enzyme. His reefs were trying to fix the problem, exerting themselves to slow the growth of the perceived tumors spreading through his vital organs. The reefs' efforts caused a massive uptick in the internal temperature of his body. A trillion tiny suns going nova at once. What was that emotion on his face? Fear? No. More than that.

"You ..." he managed to say. He was sweating, his mouth open, eyes oceans of white against dark irises.

Mera came close.

If she could guess, Okaios was experiencing what she had felt so long ago, when she was falling from that cliff, outstretching her hand to a man she could not reach and could not save. She realized then that she had made a terrible miscalculation about the universe and herself. There was no safety; everyone was always at risk.

Okaios screamed in unbearable pain.

There was another thing Mera had experienced, too—something he couldn't feel just yet. To feel it, he would need time. It had taken her centuries to find that feeling and learn what it was. It was a lesson deeper than that of the Ynaa. Truer.

The universe is bigger than you know. You are bigger than you know. There is no armor big enough to save you. Nowhere. Ever.

She would spare him that one.

Mera's reefs worked on all his organs—except for one. His reefs wouldn't know to guard that organ, thinking that the threat was everywhere else. The last mistake.

Mera punched Okaios in his face, tearing the human flesh, crushing the Ynaa bone, cutting his brain with shards of his own skull. The impact did the rest, turning his brain to mush. He made a sound so soft, it hurt Mera to hear it, and then he collapsed under his own weight, no brain function remaining to keep him upright.

When it was done, Mera stood over the body. She told her

reefs to die, and they obeyed. His reefs would continue for some time, trying to repair what could not be repaired. Then they, too, would die, having nothing to feed on but death.

She had not told Ohoim that her research could be used this way, but he would know soon enough, when he learned that his son was dead. And he would know who had done it. She was now the Ynaa's greatest enemy in the known universe.

Mera went over to Derrick's body. There was no hiding it now. The tight knot inside her had unwound, tears falling hot on her cheeks.

She leaned down to pick up the body.

The woman watched her do this. And just as before, without warning, she lunged at Mera.

"You won't take my boys!" she said. "You devil! You demon!"

She was hitting Mera over and over with her fists. They weren't weak blows; they would have hurt a normal person. But they had no effect on Mera. She ignored the woman and remained leaning, touching Derrick's stiff body. Even with all her defenses, he had gotten in, changed her. And she had destroyed him.

The woman wrapped her hands around Mera's neck. Mera turned to her. They both had tears in their eyes.

Mera sent her reefs from her neck through the woman's hands and straight to the woman's brain. "Sleep," Mera ordered. The woman stumbled back as if drunk. She crumpled to her knees and fell over to one side. She tried to speak, but sleep took her quickly.

Mera moved the woman to her stoop and then returned to Derrick. She carried him to the SUV and sat him in the passenger seat, bending his limbs and leaning his head against the window. She had to hurry now and get to her ship.

The last time they were together, she had kissed Derrick—a

soft, lingering touch of lips. She caressed his face. She'd had a bad feeling at the time but wasn't close enough to herself to know it.

As she drove to the docks, she kept glancing over at him. He looked as if he were sleeping. She half expected him to yawn and stretch and ask her how long it would take to get there.

"Just a little longer," she would say. She would call her ship from the ocean floor, and then it wouldn't take long to reach orbit, and then they would go to Ganymede as she promised.

"And then what?" he would ask.

She hadn't gotten that far. Other solar systems? Other galaxies? They would have all the time in the universe … if he had survived.

A thought occurred to her then.

Over her long life, Mera had learned that although the universe fought against the divulging of its secrets, it didn't stop one from using them once they were known. Cleverness was rewarded. Knowledge, once found, could be implemented.

In the corner of her eye, Derrick turned to her. But when she glanced his way, she saw that his head had simply shifted. His head wound was dark and gaping.

"If I could do it, would you want me to?" she asked the corpse.

She imagined him saying yes.

YN ALTAA

Aubrey sat on the porch in the morning cool, the sun just rising on the horizon. Sometimes when she couldn't sleep, she would come out in the morning like this, watching the dark sky bleed into orange and blue. She didn't have to be at work until nine, so she had the mornings mostly to herself.

She heard Alice in the kitchen, probably making breakfast. She listened as the cabinets opened and closed, and then it was quiet for a long time until the kettle screamed and Alice tramped to the kitchen, her footsteps echoing like some giant's.

Aubrey listened absently to the whole drama. Eventually, Alice would come out and sit on her lap, kiss her, and coax her back into the house. But for now, she wanted to be outside, letting her thoughts roam while she listened to the birds wake and the crickets rub the teeth of their wings together.

Something rustled in the bush, drawing Aubrey's attention. She looked down from their porch on the second floor to see a black cat come out from the hibiscus into the backyard. She knew the cat well, had even named her. It was Aubrey's job to take in strays at the shelter, but the shelter was always full and she didn't want to risk having to put the cat down if they didn't have space. Besides, this one would be hard to catch. Jezza was suspicious by nature and stealthy, revealing herself only for brief moments.

Jezza mewed and waited in the yard. Two other cats came out of the bush. One was black with white paws, the other a spiral of black and brown. Both were smaller than Jezza—kittens fast approaching their "teens." Aubrey watched them convene in the yard as if they were holding some secret conclave.

A rooster appeared on the other side of the yard, its feathers a vibrant blend of red and green against dark brown. Aubrey didn't have much time to marvel at the feline communion in her back-yard before the rooster caught Jezza's attention and she gave chase. The magnificent bird screeched, spreading its wings. It leaped into the air, landing on a branch of a nearby tree. Jezza circled the tree. A few minutes later, she gave up, returning to her kittens, who had seemed uninterested in the bird. All three sauntered back into the bush. The rooster belted out its morning declaration before exiting the stage the way he had come on.

All this happened in a matter of moments, as if Aubrey weren't even there to witness it. A small world separate from hers, with its own concerns. For a time, she considered what giants inhabited the reaches above, staring down at her. A chill swept through her at the thought of another alien ship from some other distant world breaking through the clouds overhead. Her ears buzzed with the drone of spectral engines, and she had to search the sky to make sure nothing was there. The hues of night had pulled back, orange and blue now dominating the morning. The harbor glittered like shards of sapphire. She calmed at the sight.

As expected, Alice stepped out onto the porch and sat on Aubrey's lap. "Morning, love," Alice said, kissing her on the lips. "Want to come inside?"

"Not just yet." Aubrey played in Alice's frizzy hair. She liked getting her fingers stuck in that nest of lovely curls. Alice smiled appreciatively.

"Lee will be up soon," Alice said. "I'm going to make her breakfast."

"Let her eat cereal."

"No." Wrapped up in the tacit rebuke was a longer answer. Lee appreciated the breakfasts; she talked more when she had eggs and butter bread in her mouth than when there was only a box of Cheerios waiting for her. Today was going to be tough. She would need the breakfast.

"You right," Aubrey said. She had forgotten herself again. She felt awful about the little bit of resentment she felt toward the girl. Before Patrice came back home, she had gotten used to having the house, and Alice, all to herself. Now she had to share her life again. This wasn't a bad thing. More good than bad came out of it. Still, she had enjoyed her space.

Alice kissed her again, this time on the forehead. She got off her lap, which Aubrey's knees appreciated. They both were small women, but Alice was a little bigger and Aubrey was getting older.

"See you in a bit," Alice said, stomping back into the house.

When the sun finally climbed all the way out from behind the hills, and the morning cool gave way to heat, Aubrey decided to go inside.

Lee sat at the table in her school uniform, her short cotton tie hanging loose from her neck like two navy-blue tongues. She was eating eggs. A half-eaten piece of buttered bread rested on her plate. She looked up as Aubrey walked in, acknowledged her presence, and returned to her food.

"You gon' be here when I come home?" Aubrey asked, sitting beside Lee. "I'm making barbecue chicken and baked macaroni and cheese."

Lee smiled. "Maybe a little later. Me and Jess are going to do a thing."

Aubrey nodded. "A'you have fun."

"Yeah," Lee said, biting into her bread.

Alice glided over and set a plate in front of Aubrey. She glanced at Alice and caught an expression on her face. Alice tilted her head toward Lee, coaxing Aubrey to say what needed to be said.

Aubrey gave a quick flick of her head. Also a message: *I'll do it, but stop hovering.* Alice received the message and went back to the kitchen.

"You know—" Aubrey started.

"Actually I might stay over at Jess'," Lee said. "Since it's Friday. That cool?"

Aubrey took a breath and then nodded. "Sure, sweetie. No problem with that. You coming back Saturday or Sunday night?"

"Sunday."

To tell the truth, Aubrey loved the idea of having Alice to herself for the weekend. "Okay," she said. "Be good."

"I will."

Alice sat down at the table with her plate. She kept her eyes on Aubrey as she brought a forkful of scrambled eggs to her mouth. Aubrey just shook her head. Alice scowled but let the silence continue.

When Lee was done, she took her plate and mug to the kitchen and washed them. The girl was wonderful that way, leaving few remnants of her presence behind.

"You need me to drop you to school?" Alice offered.

Lee pulled out her phone and began texting. "Nah, Jess gon' swing by for me." Then she went back to her room to finish getting ready.

"You have to push," Alice said after Lee was out of earshot.

"The girl fine. You got to let her deal with things her own way."

"Sometimes, you have to intervene."

Aubrey sighed. She picked up the remaining dishes and went to the kitchen. She cleaned the plates and poured herself another cup of tea.

"I'm going to shower," Alice said. She was being short.

"I love you." Aubrey smiled and gave her an air kiss.

Alice glared at her, but her mouth was twitching into a smile. "Take care of the frying pan for me?"

"Of course," Aubrey said, though she really didn't want to. But what could she do? The amends had begun. "I'll try again after the weekend," she added.

"Yeah," Alice said. "I'll believe it when I see it." She disappeared down the hall.

Aubrey nursed her cup of tea and then started to work on the frying pan.

The past several months had been easier on her than on most. Her father had died years ago. Her younger brother had been living in Atlanta for several years. She had an uncle who was killed, but he was elderly and she didn't have a deep relationship with him. Alice was an expat, so she had no family on island.

But Aubrey had not gone untouched by the disaster. She had friends who had died—people she knew from back in high school. Her three other coworkers besides Alice had been men. It all felt unreal, as if they all had gone on a trip somewhere and never returned. And then there was her cousin, Mike. He had called her a few days before to tell her how much he disapproved of her and Alice's relationship.

"What's this I been hearing about you butching out?" he had asked.

Aubrey hung up the phone on him and ignored his calls. And then he died. They had been close once. She quietly mourned his death along with the others.

And then there was the boy from downstairs. She had watched him grow up, cooked him dinner more times than she could count. She had smiled approvingly when her daughter finally decided to give him a chance, comforted him when her daughter then decided to go stateside and not return his calls. This had been a significant loss. She felt it deep in the pit of her being. How much more of a loss had it been for Lee? For Patrice? Neither would talk about it, and she didn't want to raise the dead if they were content in burying him.

But nothing ever stayed buried. It came out in strange and dangerous ways. Alice was right, but what could she do?

Aubrey put the dishes in the drainer and sat back down at the dining table. She listened for the bathroom door to open so she could jump into the shower. As she waited, Lee rushed past her.

"See you, Aubrey," she said as she went. She was at the door before Aubrey even responded. She managed to say goodbye just before the door slammed. She heard the muffled sound of a car revving up and climbing the hill outside their house. Alfie's barks continued long after the car was gone.

Alice came out of the bathroom, so Aubrey went to take her shower. She let the water run over her for ten minutes before she even picked up the soap.

It would be a long day at work. The population of strays had gone up since it happened. They had to put down so many animals. It wasn't as bad as in the beginning, though. Many of the animals now were sick, emaciated, almost at the end of their rope. Right after it happened, she had to put down a lot of perfectly healthy dogs and cats. There simply wasn't enough room, and with their owners dead or having left the island, there was nothing else to do with them.

So many people had left, and not just the men. The trauma of the whole event had caused a mass exodus. The entire island was straining under the absence of so many essential people, which meant a lot of the responsibility to keep things going fell on those who remained.

On the way out of the house, Aubrey filled Alfie's bowl. She had adopted the dog the same day he arrived at the shelter, a few weeks after the massacre. Both she and Alice felt an immediate connection. At night, Aubrey would take him for a walk and then let him inside until they were ready for bed, but he spent most of his time in the yard.

"I'm worried about her," Alice said on their way to work. "Especially with the trouble at school."

Alice was not going to let this go. Aubrey kept her eyes on the road but moved one hand to stroke Alice's knee, feeling the coarse denim against her palm and fingers. Another thing that had changed since it happened: a lot less traffic. The car eased from stoplight to stoplight without the slow crawl typical for this hour a year ago.

"I'm serious," Alice said. "It's about time."

"I know." They had gone this long without pressing the issue, content just to offer a shoulder when Lee couldn't stop the tears.

But what Aubrey was thinking about now was her own daughter. She didn't mention it, but Lee reminded her very much of Patrice: that same stubbornness, that guarded way they both approached the world, as if they would break should they let their armor down for even a moment. Aubrey understood this from Lee, but who had Patrice learned it from?

"Are you okay?" Alice asked.

Aubrey nodded. "You want to catch a movie this weekend?"

"No," Alice said. "All the movies are depressing these days."

"Okay."

"I want to go on a trip. Get away from all this bullshit."

"To St. John."

"Sure, that's far enough."

Aubrey gave Alice's knee one last caress. She turned on the radio, and when the news came on, she switched to music from her phone. An instrumental throbbed in her ears: contemporary classic. Music these days also had a quality Alice didn't like. The Ynaa had changed everything. References to them, to the tragedy, could not be avoided. The world could not stop talking about the massacre. Aubrey resented it. The tragedy had happened to them, no one else. It wasn't as if the world cared about them before.

On the other hand, now that the Ynaa were gone, Alice liked the idea of returning to the way things were. Aubrey wasn't so sure about that, either. It seemed as though the Ynaa, despite the terror they left in their wake, had shifted humanity. People would never be so self-involved as they once were, never so fixated on their own greatness. The Ynaa had taught them humility. How long that lasted, and what good it could do, depended on how long their impact lasted on the collective psyche. And also on how humans decided to respond to that impact. So far, not terribly. Aubrey hoped for that continued grace.

"Let's get married," she said to Alice. She took her eyes off the road long enough to see Alice's face. The smile she found there was so bright, it lit up her face, too.

"Sounds good."

• • •

Lee's day started out quietly. She went to school and sat under the big tree by the high school's auditorium, talking to Jess until the bell rang. Then she went to English class and pretended to listen to Ms. Kerry go on about *When the Night Falls*, a novella about the Massacre of Men.

It was after class when things turned. On her way down the stairs from Building B to Building A, a boy from Croix pushed her. He was big for his age, but he wasn't a senior; no tie hung from his neck.

"They should have killed him twice," the boy said.

Lee rounded on him, punching him in the nose. Blood poured from the boy's nostrils all over his hands and shirt.

"You fucking—"

Lee didn't let him finish. She kicked him where the sun don't shine, and that sent him to his knees. He groaned. He looked up to say something else—his teeth now red with blood from his nose—but he caught himself when he saw Lee winding up to kick him in the face. Her leg was cocked, foot in the air. Seeing that, he curled up into a ball.

Lee walked away. When she caught up with Jess, she told her what happened.

"Shit," Jess said. "If Dian was here ..." She stopped talking. Dian was dead. Milton was dead. All their male friends were dead. Angela's ex-boyfriend, Woody, was dead, too, which was the one silver lining. The boys now at the school were all from other places, some from the VI but many from farther off—complete strangers to the Massacre of Men.

"Let's go," Lee said.

"I thought we were going to wait until after school," Jess said.

Lee just watched her, hoping Jess would finish the rest of the conversation in her own head instead of bothering her with it.

Jess rolled her eyes. "Okay. Let's go."

In the old days, Lee and Jess had to sneak out of school through the special-education building in the back of campus and then walk fast through the field next to Lockhart Elementary. The two schools were separated only by a badly maintained fence, and you could slip from one to the other through an opening.

If it was lunchtime, you could slip out the front gate and go to Barbel Plaza, across the street, for food. If you wanted to skip the rest of the day, all you had to do was not come back.

But now you didn't need to do any of that. Leaving school had become as easy as walking out the front gate anytime you liked. The school's security was understaffed, and because only eleven months had passed since the Massacre of Men, the unofficial policy was to let students leave if they wanted, and let them face the repercussions later. The repercussions amounted to a stern warning. Lee had several of those already.

No one was there when they drove out the front gate. They drove over to Barbel Plaza and each had a paté: saltfish for Jess, chicken for Lee. Once they were finished they went to the graveyard.

It was the old big graveyard, not the new one that was made after the Massacre of Men. Lee and Jess made their way to Angela's grave. They put down the flowers they had brought and shared a few memories of Angela. The time they had gone to Jost Van Dyke over the weekend, and Jess and Angela had very brief romances with two local boys. And that time they all went to Fat Turtle and got drunk off drinks her shitty boyfriend Woody had gotten for them. At the end of the night, Angela was throwing up in one of the potted plants.

"You got vomit all over your clothes, too," Jess said to Angela's gravestone. "So nasty."

Lee laughed. She allowed herself to feel what she had felt then, rubbing Angela's head as she puked, laughing mercilessly.

"Stop laughing at me," Angela had said between bouts of throwing up. At school, they'd all had a good laugh. They harped on it for weeks, until Angela got mad and yelled at them never to bring it up again. They obeyed—mostly. Milton just couldn't let it go.

Lee didn't notice the precise moment when her laughter turned to crying. And not just tears, either. She was bawling, her body shaking with wave after wave of grief. Through a tear-smeared world, she could see Jess staring, her face stuck in a frown. She gently stroked Lee's shoulder, not saying a word.

It would be easy to assume that Lee had started crying because of Angela, but no one made assumptions about these things anymore. Not now. Tears for one friend could lead you down a bitter road, stopping at each house to mourn one life after another. There was no way to parse something so compounded, so endless. It just swelled and swelled.

Before long, Lee had stopped at her grandmother's house. She had died just a few months after everything happened. Grams had stopped sleeping in her own room. She spent most of her time on the couch, watching soaps and sitcoms. She would laugh herself into coughing fits. Lee would hear her in the middle of the night, whimpering. "Stupid boy!" she would hear Grams yell at odd hours. When Lee went out, she would see Grams shaking her head in her sleep. Lee assumed it was just grief. One morning, Lee woke up and Grams had simply slipped away. No amount of yelling or tears would rouse her. Later, she found out she had cancer and hadn't told a soul.

Jess had her share of things to mourn. She had lost her father and brother in the massacre. It had taken quite a toll on her, made her stony where she was once soft. "It could have been worse," Jess had said several times afterward. Her father and brother died quickly: paralysis, choking, then death. Other people weren't as lucky. Those who had encounters with the Ynaa and watched them murder their loved ones were suffering from severe PTSD. There had been an uptick in suicides. Women would disappear for days, until a friend or neighbor came over and caught the whiff of death.

Jess was there to pull the knife from her mother's hand—a bit of good fortune that proved itself when her mother didn't try again. Yet.

"Look who's here," Jess said.

Lee sniffled, wiped her eyes, and followed Jess' gaze. Her eyes lit on a frail woman standing over another grave. It was Tony's mother. Shawn's mother, too, Lee had to remind herself. She had lost both sons, a little over a year apart. Lee took off walking toward the woman.

Jessica's voice followed behind Lee. "Stop!" she said a few times. "Slow down." Lee didn't slow down. Not then. The woman looked up and caught sight of Lee. She tensed, her face changing from sorrow to straight-up terror.

Lee finally slowed when the woman did this, though she was only a few steps from being right in her face. Jess caught up but stayed behind Lee.

The woman stepped back and put her hands up, palms out as if to ward off blows. "What?" she asked. "Leave me alone!"

Lee stepped back in response. "Don't mean to scare you," she said. "Just wanted to talk."

The woman wrinkled her eyebrows, looking genuinely puzzled. She didn't put down her hands. "About what?"

Lee hadn't thought of this, either, but now she could guess. She had been detached from any real interpretation of her internal emotions lately. But seeing the woman lift her hands in defense, she understood. She had been attacked by people on the street before, by those who recognized her connection to her son, the man who unleashed Ynaa wrath on the men of St. Thomas. In this, Lee felt some kinship with the woman—the burden of blame for loving foolish men who had played with fire and burned everyone.

Lee spoke slowly. She gave her name and asked for the woman's.

"Mary," the woman answered.

"You're Tony's mom," Lee said, not really a question. "I used to go to school with him. He was a grade under me."

Mary just watched Lee, waiting for a shoe to drop that never did.

"We're sorry for your losses," Jess chimed in, seeing that the conversation had lapsed into awkward silence.

"Yes," Lee said. "We're so sorry."

"Sorry for your losses," Mary said. The words applied to every local. She looked away from them for a moment, quick like a frightened mouse.

"Derrick Reed was my brother," Lee said.

Anger and defensiveness flared in Mary's face, but it subsided almost as fast, replaced by a guilty look. "I'm sorry."

"It's okay," Lee said.

"How you been?" Jess asked. The question was innocent enough, but Lee could guess at a possible subtext. *How you been?* meaning *Have you had dangerous thoughts?*

"Been okay," Mary said. "Can't complain."

The answer you gave when you really were okay. And also the one you gave when you wanted to keep bad feelings private. Lee didn't have to guess which.

"Take care of yourself," Lee said, and then thought to walk away. Something stopped her. All at once, she became aware of how strange this whole interaction was. But even weirder was the fact that she didn't want it to end.

"You, too," Mary said. "Crazy world out there."

Not here, though, Lee thought. Most of the people in these graves died oblivious to the world she now lived in. They were invaded, tormented, massacred, and abandoned. But the dead slept, unaware. It was the living who suffered.

"Didn't really know your sons," Lee said. "Not like that." She placed her hand on Mary's shoulder, steeling herself to look into the woman's eyes without flinching. "But I want to tell you that it's not their fault. Not nobody fault. We all were helpless against them."

Mary nodded, though Lee could see in her eyes that the gesture was too much. Mary wanted to deny the reassurance but couldn't, since she recognized it as a gift. She settled on a meek thank-you.

When Lee looked to Jess, she was staring back at her, but Jess didn't give her away. Jess knew Lee better than this, knew that what she had said was a lie. Lee blamed a lot of people, not just the Ynaa. But she didn't blame Tony, and that was the grave they were standing at. And even if she did, Jess would honor the lie.

"Can we stand with you?" Jess asked. "Pay respects."

"Yes," Mary said with a smile that warmed only the bottom of her face, leaving the rest mournful.

For a long time, no more words were said. Everyone stood staring down at the grave. After several minutes, Lee started swaying on her legs, and then stopped when she came back from her own thoughts, realizing that Mary and Jess had not moved for some time. She continued in silence. She would let this go on for as long as Mary needed. An act of kindness for a stranger in this now-strange world.

• • •

"Don't worry," Jackson said. "People have been very forth-coming. Mostly."

Mostly. Patrice gave her best patronizing smile to the webcam. "Okay," she said. He was trying to reassure her, but she still felt uneasy about her father going around asking people about the most traumatic moment of their lives, especially since one of those people had nearly killed him.

"Come on, Pat," Jackson said, reading her face. "It was a minor hospital visit."

"Three days in the hospital is not a 'minor visit.'"

Jackson gave an exasperated huff. "When did you become the parent?"

"From long," Patrice said, chupsing her teeth. "Someone has to protect you from yourself."

Jackson had abandoned his previous project. He didn't tell Patrice why, only that it would fuel dangerous paranoia. "The world doesn't need that story," he had said. "Not now."

His new book was about the Massacre of Men, which had afforded him enough stories to fill a hundred books. But it also meant he had to ask people about the most painful moments of their lives.

The woman who had caused her father's "minor" hospital visit was a distraught survivor of three boys and a husband. She had ignored his calls and messages, sending only a text with a single question: *How did you get my number?* Her father told the woman that he had gotten her number through one of her friends; he didn't say which. The larger question of how he got in contact with the friend was left unanswered. Everyone on island knew somebody who knew somebody who knew somebody. You could find anyone within two or three degrees of separation.

The woman didn't respond to her father's reply. Still, her father was eager to get the woman's story. On the night of the massacre, an Ynaa had showed up at the woman's house to kill her husband—one of the random acts of extreme violence the Ynaa doled out on top of the widespread seizures. Jackson needed more descriptions of the Ynaa. He neglected to note what the larger trauma of losing three young children and watching her husband's murder would do to the woman's psyche.

When he showed up at her house, the woman hit him several

times with a frying pan. Neighbors had to drag her off him.

"I won't go to people's houses unannounced," Jackson reassured Patrice. "And I've been taking Jammie around with me."

"Ah. The infamous Jammie." Patrice would have to do it. She knew it now. Against his will, if she had to.

Someone was coming down the stairs. She waited to hear the keys jingle and then brought her attention back to her father.

"When will you be back over?" she asked. She would try talking to him about it first.

"In a few days. But I'll be there for a week. I'll need to stay with you."

Lee bounced in. She threw her bag on the couch and went to the kitchen.

"Nicole ain't frustrated with all the time you spending away from her?" Patrice asked.

"She understands."

The fridge opened, and Patrice could hear Lee pouring something into a glass.

"She should come over with you sometime," Patrice suggested. "I want to meet her—in person, not over a screen."

"She works a lot. But I might convince her to come over on the weekend this time. Keep you posted?"

"Sure." Patrice watched Lee come back into the living room. She sat on the couch, sipping water from her glass. She watched Patrice, too, but stayed where she was. Patrice told her father she had to go.

"Okay," he said. "Talk soon, love."

"Yeah." She smiled and waved him off. "Love you."

"I love you, too."

Patrice hung up. "How long you staying over?" she asked Lee.

"The weekend," Lee answered.

Patrice just smiled.

"They on me again," Lee said. "All that mothering is suffocating."

"Sounds like them." Patrice gave another nonintrusive smile. This worked better than pressing. Perhaps that was all of it. Patrice had a feeling, though, that something else had happened.

Lee finished her cup and went back into the kitchen. Patrice followed.

"Someone started some shit at school today," Lee volunteered.

"Oh?"

"He was saying things about Derrick." She stood frozen in front of the fridge, grasping the handle.

"What happened?" Patrice asked. She wasn't pressing. Lee wanted to talk about this.

"I punched him in the face," she said, punctuating the statement by opening the fridge. She pulled out a gallon of water. "You want some?"

"Yes, thank you." Lee almost always told her about these altercations. This was probably because Patrice never condemned her acts of violence.

"It's hard," Lee said, taking a glass from the cupboard.

Patrice wasn't sure what, exactly, Lee was referring to, but she said, "I know."

"I want vengeance," Lee said.

Patrice didn't have to guess what she meant there. That statement was quite common. She looked at Lee sadly. "No, you don't. You want your brother and grandmother back."

Right at that moment, the glass slipped from Lee's hand. From Patrice's perspective, it fell in slow motion to the countertop.

Patrice's body tensed. Lee tried to correct the mistake, but it was too late. The glass shattered, sending bits across the countertop and the floor.

"Fuck!" Lee said.

Patrice put her finger to her lips and made a shushing sound. "You gon' wake him up."

"Sorry," Lee said.

"Don't worry about it."

Lee was breathing hard, her hands up as if surrendering to some unseen threat. She looked at all the scattered glass and was overwhelmed, not budging from her place. She just stood there, glancing around herself.

Patrice got the broom from the hall closet. She put on her house slippers and began sweeping the glass into a pile.

"I miss him, too," Patrice said as she swept the shards into the dustpan.

Lee glared at her, still standing in the same position.

Patrice didn't say anything at first. This was what it was like, talking to Lee: invisible land mines. Then Patrice decided to push, for both their sakes.

"We both lost Derrick," Patrice said, sharpening her voice and readying herself for what would come.

"You lost an ex-boyfriend. I lost a brother."

"We were more than exes. We grew up together."

"And then you left!"

Patrice leaned the broom against the wall, listening for her son's cry. She was relieved when she didn't hear it. "I couldn't stay," she said. She stumbled through her mind to offer an explanation. She wanted to finally give voice to all the feelings she'd had. Again she failed. "It was too much," she said.

Lee was breathing even harder now. "I didn't have that luxury to run away. And even if I did, I wouldn't. I'm not a coward."

"I came back."

"Too late!" Lee said. She was panting, her hand clawing at her shirt. "Too late," she repeated, the words softer and breathier.

Patrice went over to Lee and wrapped her arms around her. The girl fought her at first, trying to wrest herself free from the embrace, but eventually she gave in to Patrice's persistence.

It took Lee some time to settle. Her breaths were fast and jagged. A few times, she tried to speak, but her body would seize up. Half-muted syllables would escape from her lips—stray consonants and vowels devolving into gasps. Patrice felt her own pain in Lee's attempts to find footing. Tears came to her eyes, too, but she made no sounds.

Again she felt the weight of the Ynaa on her, as she had when they first arrived, as she always had, even when she ran away. They were somewhere up there, self-satisfied with the destruction they had left. Patrice hated them with all her heart.

Lee found herself again. Her body stopped shaking, and her breaths grew even again. Patrice's tears, however, continued to fall, waterfalls on soft stone. Lee pulled away just enough to look at her. She saw her tears. Her own face was slick with grief. She reached out and touched Patrice's face, wiping away some of the water and salt.

"You look terrible," Lee said.

Patrice smiled. "You, too."

"Need me to check on Lil' Derrick?" Lee asked. Her eyes were red, the lids puffy.

"No, it's okay," Patrice said. Sometimes, the boy would wake up if you even stepped in the room, as if he had radar constantly probing for human bodies. Normal perceptibility, Patrice hoped, and not a sign of something else.

Quietly they both continued cleaning up the rest of the glass. A few times, Lee would look at Patrice, a subtle smile on her face. A gift of a smile.

When they were done, Lee went to the couch to watch TV, and Patrice went to her room, careful to speed silently past her son's room.

Patrice had moved into Grandma Reed's old room. At first, she had felt uneasy about sleeping in it, the room belonging to a dead woman, and all. But this was a house of dead people.

As she lay in bed, Patrice went over the argument. She could understand Lee's resentment. Lee had to stick around, deal with all the conflict that Derrick's decisions brought on the family. She had been stuck with most of the caretaking of her grandmother, who was quite frail in those last months. And before that, she had lost her mother and her father. She was now the only living member of her immediate family, orphaned twice over. And then there was her best friend, dead now for how long? Two years? It was a miracle the girl held it together at all.

What happened in the kitchen could be the beginning of a dark descent or the beginning of healing. Patrice hoped for the latter but figured Lee would most likely remain as she was, the dam breaking only on occasions when she didn't have the strength to hold it in.

Patrice could relate only so much.

Lying in bed, she caught a whiff of Grandma Reed in the air. Sometimes, she could smell her in the room, her familiar human scent lingering in a place that had grown used to a certain person's presence and now had to make room for another. The woman had lived a long life in this room. It would be a long time before the room forgot her.

Patrice closed her eyes, letting herself exist in that blur of time between sleepiness and sleep. Eventually, she slipped off into dreams.

• • •

They had learned about Derrick from Louie's mother, Debra. If not for her, no one would have known what happened to him. All the other witnesses were dead.

"The ambassador took him," Debra had said, the words bitter on her lips.

Patrice saw Derrick in her dreams often. He was in a room amorphous and white, like the inside of a lightbulb. She could feel the vacuum outside the room; her dream ears popped continually, as if she were in an airplane. Occasionally, her feet would float up from the floor. Derrick lay in some pod. The light from the room made his skin look a sickly grayish-brown. His eyes were always closed. In some dreams, she would just stay there, watching him, until she floated up from the floor and rose so far that all she could see was a distant dot where he should be.

In another variation of the dream, she could feel someone's presence in the room with her. As she watched Derrick, tentacles would creep into her vision. They would wrap around her and squeeze, and she would wake up before her body burst.

In this version of the dream, Patrice spent a long time staring down at Derrick's corpse. As always, he didn't open his eyes. She screamed at him, her tears wetting the glass that separated them.

"He's sleeping," said a voice behind her. "Do you want me to wake him up?"

The voice had a hiss to it, but other than that, she couldn't tell who it belonged to. She tried to turn around and couldn't.

"No," she answered.

Something screamed. When she looked at Derrick's mouth, she could see that it was open wide, the sound flowing out of it.

"I can wake him up," the voice said again.

"They'll kill him," she said, her voice swallowed up by the scream.

The scream changed. At first, it sounded like a cat's cry, then like a steaming teakettle, but now it sounded like a baby's wail.

Patrice clawed her way out of the dream. She launched up from her bed and went to Lil' Derrick's room.

She confirmed that her son had been crying, the wails reaching all the way into her dream. When she picked him up, he quieted immediately from the full-throated screech to a soft babbling. Patrice pressed him gently to her chest and walked around the room.

The room had been cleared out a long time ago, but sometimes she could still see how it once was. She could remember the shelves of books, that old stupid computer with its heavy breathing. She remembered the bed where they would sometimes lie. She remembered Derrick's breath, slow and steady, the pulse of his heart.

Some of his books were still in the closet. The best ones were under her bed. She had read a few, now that he was gone. Through them, she understood some of his wonder at the unknown. She recognized why the arrival of the Ynaa had sent him running to meet them. The stupid boy and his books. She simultaneously loved and hated them: for bringing her closer to him in death, for keeping them apart in life. She could never fill that desire Derrick had taught himself to have, that those books had infected him with. Beyond reason. Beyond good sense. How could he be so stupid? How could she have let him be so stupid?

Her son had settled in her arms. He lay quiet now, fidgeting only a little, letting out a few fussy murmurs. Patrice heard Lee's soft footsteps before she appeared at the doorway.

"Need me to fix him a bottle?" Lee asked.

Patrice shook her head. "No, he gon' be fine."

Lee lingered at the doorway. "I'm restless," she said. "Can I stay?"

Patrice nodded. She watched Lee creep into the room and stand against the far wall, away from the crib, most of her body hidden in shadow.

Her son made a little noise but soon settled again.

"Poor Lil' Derrick," Lee cooed. "So fussy."

Derrick was her son's middle name. It felt wrong giving it to him, but Patrice decided that a middle name would be sufficient to remember her fallen friend by. It didn't matter, though; Lee called him Lil' Derrick from the beginning. Patrice tried to call him by his first name, Jason, after her long-dead grandfather on her father's side—and, incidentally, the man who had saved her father's life—but this did nothing to stop "Lil' Derrick" from catching on. Even her father called him this, despite the many connections the name Jason had for him personally. Patrice had made her bed, though, had invited the comparison. She had her regrets now, but there was no turning back. The damage was done.

"How's work?" Lee asked.

"What?" Patrice shifted Derrick to her other shoulder and bounced him gently a few times.

"How is work going?" Lee asked again.

The room was dark, so Patrice couldn't see Lee's face. One of her legs caught the moonlight coming in from the window. "You looking for a job?"

"No. Just curious."

"So you into politics now?" Lil' Derrick was silent and still, breathing softly. Patrice kept him in her arms.

"Yes," Lee said with no hint of sarcasm in her voice.

Patrice smiled at Lee and then wondered whether she could even see the smile from her position in the dark corner. "Work is work," Patrice answered. "All the interesting political stuff is happening out there, in the streets."

"Oh," Lee said, sounding deflated.

"Look," Patrice said, "those white folks ain't gon' save us. That's something we gotta do ourselves."

Lee said nothing.

"And with elections coming up …" Patrice said, trying to fill the silence, but she had nothing really to add. Elections were still a year and a half away. Who knew what sorts of people would come out of the woodwork to grab at a slice of power.

Since the Massacre of Men, the US government had sent in all these appointed officials to keep the island afloat. Most of the senators had been men. The governor and the lieutenant governor had been men. All but one local male senator had died—he was off island during the massacre. The appointed officials were a short-term fix to a long-term problem.

Patrice worked in the office of Dorothy Simmons, a former congresswoman and a military veteran, brought out of retirement to stand in as a senator. She was white. Many of the appointees were white statesiders who had never set foot in the Virgin Islands before the Ynaa decided to kill half the population of St. Thomas. But Dorothy was nice enough, considering. Patrice worked as a glorified secretary, but the woman had never made her feel small, and that was more than she could ask for.

"You should run," Lee said.

"*What?*" She said it louder than she had intended, and it woke Lil' Derrick from his sleep. He cried out, and she had to rock him back and forth again to settle him. When he was quiet, she repeated the question softly.

"You should run. With elections coming up, we need people with some sense running."

Did Patrice consider herself someone with sense? Surely she had more sense than half the asshats who had occupied government positions before the massacre, but that wasn't saying much. She had imagined someone older, with more years in politics. And someone local. But few fell inside that Venn diagram after the severe culling at the hands of the Ynaa.

"You don't think you would be good for it?" Lee asked. "You getting a degree in political science."

"Don't have it yet. Going to school part time means I won't have a degree for another year at least." Patrice listened to her son's easy breathing. His eyes were closed again. A gentle island breeze whipped the trees outside, their shadowed limbs dancing on the wind.

"Don't matter," Lee said. "Most of them dead politicians had no political science degree. I've been thinking about this. I think you'd do a good job."

And here Patrice had thought this conversation was spontaneous. Now she knew it for the ambush it was. "I'm too young."

"Derrick wanted to run for senate," Lee said. "Eventually."

It would have been too abrupt a shift if anyone else had said it. But Patrice understood where it came from, what it meant.

"He thought he could help humans and Ynaa reach a better peace," Lee said. "Now that they gone, we are the only ones left to fix things."

Lee moved out of the corner. The light from outside wrapped around her frame. She was so tall. Patrice remembered that little girl she knew from so long ago. Not a little girl anymore.

"Think about it," Lee said.

"I will," Patrice said, and looked down to find intelligent eyes looking back up at her. Her son smiled and waited for her to answer with one of her own. Satisfied, he closed his eyes again, and any signs of wakefulness melted off his face.

"Your kid creeps me out," Lee said. "The way he stares at me sometimes—"

"Your birthday is coming up, right?" Patrice noted that her mother's birthday was coming up, too, in another month.

Lee didn't answer right away. Then she said, "Next week. Why?"

"We should go out. Have some fun."

"And who gon' watch Lil' Derrick?" Lee asked with interest.

"Our mothers."

"Okay," Lee said, laughing. "You better get me a nice present, too, since you in such a giving mood."

"Oh, I will," Patrice said, smiling. "The greatest gift in the universe."

"I'm holding you to that." Lee yawned and stretched, then gave Patrice a lazy salute—her way of saying good night. Patrice nodded back. Lee walked away, her footsteps retreating to the living room. The television flicked on, the volume set to a whisper. A sitcom laugh track came through faintly. Lee had trouble sleeping sometimes. The TV helped.

Patrice carried her son back to the crib. She laid him down and gave him a light kiss on the forehead. He felt it, his tiny nose wrinkling and smoothing out again. Patrice looked down at her son. "Don't wake up until morning," she whispered, staring at that small face, those tiny limbs. He would likely sleep through the night, now that she had commanded it. Soon, he would be talking and walking, screaming down the house, going off on his little adventures.

There were no abnormalities so far. She had been worried about that, and she likely would for a very long time, as all parents did. She didn't think she was that different. Not really. Just an extra bit of worry to keep the monsters away, and an extra bit of time to do it.

• • •

Patrice found the box on the foot of her bed when she woke up one morning, weeks after the massacre. She had no idea how it got there. The nightmares had been bad then, and she had hardly ever slept through the night. This time, she did, the morning light greeting her when she opened her eyes.

She saw the box when she sat up, and felt mostly confusion. No panic yet. That would come later. She picked it up, feeling its weight. Something shifted inside it. The wooden box was simple. No aesthetic markings. No symbols. No lock.

Patrice opened the box. Inside, she found a glass case with a dozen thin capsules inside, the kind you would take if you had a headache, except that they didn't have any markings, either. Underneath the glass case was an envelope. Beside it was what looked like a large blue pearl.

She moved the case and picked up the envelope. It had her name on it. Now she began to worry. But she also was curious. She sat there for several minutes before the stronger of the feelings won out.

The small piece of paper inside the envelope was folded in half. Patrice unfolded it to find a short letter. The words were slanted and cursive. Attractive and methodical. Old-fashioned.

You asked me once what we were doing on your planet, the letter read. *I didn't answer then. I regret not answering. I'll do so now.*

There it was. The panic.

"Yn" means life. *"Ynaa":* the living. *Yn Altaa is the one true thing that all living beings desire, or so I once believed. If there is a god to my people, it is this one true thing. It has motivated us for a very long time. Above all else, including our souls.*

Yn Altaa: life everlasting.

There was a space between those words and what followed—a pause that must have been meaningful. Patrice felt a chill creep up her back, an impulse to flee.

She read on.

Enclosed is that singular obsession. I'm leaving it with you in hopes that you will use it wisely. This is not an apology. I could give nothing that would equal the losses you and your people have endured. It is an offering. Do with it as you will.

The message ended with a P.S.: *When the reefs start to speak, listen. They'll tell you all you need to know.*

For a month, Patrice just read and reread the letter, staring at the capsules, considering the proposition. She hadn't been sure she could trust it, especially after the massacre. But despite her hatred of the Ynaa and of Mera specifically, she trusted her. Mera had killed one of her own to protect Louie's mother. Debra had grudgingly said so herself. She had never hurt any human, that Patrice knew of. She had tried to protect Derrick. On the other hand, she was also the one who got him in trouble. And ultimately, she had failed to save him.

Patrice considered throwing the whole thing away, and she almost did. Or maybe that was just what she told herself. *Almost* didn't count with something so big. *Almost* was an excuse.

When she was certain Grandma Reed was dying, Patrice showed her the letter and offered her one of the capsules. "I'm worried about what it will do. But maybe you might want to take the risk." As she said the words, Patrice questioned them, unsure of her true motives.

Grandma Reed turned cold. "Life ain't up to us," she said, her voice trembling. "It is up to God!" She said other things, too, such as "get rid of them!" and "they're evil!"

Patrice promised she would get rid of the box. Instead, she hid it. In the end, she made her decision based on what she wanted, not what she knew for sure. By that time, Grandma Reed had already died and Patrice's son had been born.

The wooden box was now under her bed, under a stack of books in Derrick's old crate. On the top of the stack was *Oriental Mythology*, the book she had borrowed from Derrick when they were teenagers. *The Masks of God*. Patrice still read it from time to time.

Still standing over her son's crib, she considered going back to sleep. But fearful of bad dreams, she decided against it. Instead, she leaned over his sleeping body and gave him another kiss. He didn't wake, only whimpered softly. She listened to the soft noises from the living room for a while until the television flicked off. The couch creaked a few times, and then nothing. The house was quiet except for the hum of the fridge.

She didn't know when it happened exactly, when she finally lost her faith. She guessed it happened in stages. She had punctured it somewhere a long time ago, and eventually all her belief in high powers and miracles had seeped out through the hole. And at some point, without being fully aware, Patrice had filled those places inside herself with something more substantial, something more real. Her *own* desires. Her *own* truth. An existential distrust of all powers besides her own.

And now she had another to look after, another life to preserve.

Looking down at her son, she promised him again what she had promised every night before. She would watch over them both. Keep them safe. She would do so because no one else really could. Because the universe was a dangerous place.

Saying it, she knew that it wasn't enough, wasn't true. She couldn't promise danger away. But perhaps the promise would be enough for now. Perhaps it was a lie she could make true with time.

ACKNOWLEDGMENTS

I got a big list.

Anju Manandhar, my wife and love. For listening to all my ideas, reading my stories and giving me honest responses, encouraging me when I was doubting myself, and challenging me when I needed the hard truth. I don't know how I got so lucky.

My mother, Sharon; my sister, Shawell; my brother, Kareem; and all the extended family that smiled approvingly when I said I wanted to be a writer. I was a strange kid with a lot of ideas. I'm grateful that they believed in me. I'm especially grateful to my mom, for just being who she is. Her strength makes me want to be strong.

My grandmothers. They've found their way into everything I do.

My father, Big Will. My grandfather, Pops. Wish they were here for this. Hope I've made them proud.

Michael Carr, my editor and worker of miracles. He made this book what it needed to be. And Courtney Vatis, my copy editor, for catching what Carr and I missed. Every writer needs great editors and I got the best.

Martha Millard, Nell Pierce, and the people at Sterling Lord Literistic. For believing in *The Lesson*. A special thanks to Martha for choosing to represent me when I had only a couple stories and a half-completed manuscript to my name. And for finding the right publisher for this book. I couldn't have had anyone better in my corner.

Haila Williams, Jeff Yamaguchi, Lauren Maturo, and the whole Blackstone family. For putting so much love and effort behind this novel. I didn't deserve a publicist as dedicated as Lauren, but I got her anyway.

My MFA instructors: Wilton Barnhardt, Belle Boggs, and John Kessel. For telling me this was a novel even when I didn't believe it myself. For pushing me and for all the help along the way. Wilton convinced me that NC State was where I needed to be. I'm glad I had the good sense to agree.

My MFA peers. For all their comments in workshop, great and small. I wasn't very good starting out. I'm a little better now thanks to them.

My people at Clarion West. Team Tuesday and Team Arsenic. My instructors, the directors and the whole staff. I'm so grateful for having such a large and supportive community. Finding all of them changed my life.

Jess and Larry. My home away from home. For all those talks in their dining room about books and life and making a difference. And for letting me play with their dogs.

All the friends I've met in Raleigh, Pittsburgh, Greater Boston, and around the world. For all sorts of reasons, too numerous to name. Mostly for just putting up with me.

My readers. Thank you for taking this journey with me. I hope I got most of this right. I apologize for where I've fallen short. If you stuck around anyway, I'm grateful beyond words.